THE DAMNED
& OTHER
WEIRD TALES

TALES OF
HORROR
BY
ALGERNON BLACKWOOD
EDITED
BY
ZACHARY VON HOUSER

OFF SOUTH PRESS
PHILA. PA

OFF SOUTH PRESS
PHILA. PA

ACKNOWLEDGEMENTS

For Cacey, an indefatigable source of encouragement and announcements as to whether I'm being an asshole at the moment.

I suppose I should also thank Algernon himself, because without his efforts, the name Lovecraft would have surely vanished into obscurity.

CONTENTS

The Damned..1

Ancient Lights..85

TheWillows...92

The Kit-Bag...144

The Occupant of the Room...................................156

The Glamour of the Snow.....................................166

The Man Who Found Out.....................................187

THE DAMNED

I

"I'm over forty, Frances, and rather set in my ways," I said good-naturedly, ready to yield if she insisted that our going together on the visit involved her happiness. "My work is rather heavy just now too, as you know. The question is, could I work there--with a lot of unassorted people in the house?"

"Mabel doesn't mention any other people, Bill," was my sister's rejoinder. "I gather she's alone--as well as lonely."

By the way she looked sideways out of the window at nothing, it was obvious she was disappointed, but to my surprise she did not urge the point; and as I glanced at Mrs. Franklyn's invitation lying upon her sloping lap, the neat, childish handwriting conjured up a mental picture of the banker's widow, with her timid, insignificant personality, her pale grey eyes and her expression as of a backward child. I thought, too, of the roomy country mansion her late husband had altered to suit his particular needs, and of my visit to it a few years ago when its barren spaciousness suggested a wing of Kensington Museum fitted up temporarily as a place to eat and sleep in. Comparing it mentally with the poky Chelsea flat where I and my sister kept impecunious house, I realized other points as well. Unworthy details flashed across me to entice: the fine library, the organ, the quiet work-room I should have, perfect service, the delicious cup of early tea, and hot baths at any moment of the day--without a geyser!

"It's a longish visit, a month--isn't it?" I hedged, smiling at the details that seduced me, and ashamed of my man's selfishness, yet knowing that Frances expected it of me. "There are points about it, I admit. If you're set on my going with you, I could manage it all right."

I spoke at length in this way because my sister made no answer. I saw her tired eyes gazing into the dreariness of Oakley Street and felt a pang strike through me. After a pause, in which again she said no word, I added: "So, when you write the letter, you might hint, perhaps, that I usually work all the morning, and--er--am not a very lively visitor! Then she'll understand, you see." And I half-rose to return to my diminutive study, where I was slaving, just then, at an absorbing article on Comparative Aesthetic Values in the Blind and Deaf.

But Frances did not move. She kept her grey eyes upon Oakley Street where the evening mist from the river drew mournful perspectives into view. It was late October. We heard the omnibuses thundering across the bridge. The monotony of that broad, characterless street seemed more than usually depressing. Even in June sunshine it was dead, but with autumn its melancholy soaked into every house between King's Road and the Embankment. It washed thought into the past, instead of inviting it hopefully towards the future. For me, its easy width was an avenue through which nameless slums across the river sent creeping messages of depression, and I always regarded it as Winter's main entrance into London--fog, slush, gloom trooped down it every November, waving their forbidding banners till March came to rout them.

Its one claim upon my love was that the south wind swept sometimes unobstructed up it, soft with suggestions of the sea. These lugubrious thoughts I naturally kept to myself, though I never ceased to regret the little flat whose cheapness had seduced us. Now, as I watched my sister's impassive face, I realized that perhaps she, too, felt as I felt, yet, brave woman, without betraying it.

"And, look here, Fanny," I said, putting a hand upon her shoulder as I crossed the room, "it would be the very thing for you. You're worn out with catering and housekeeping. Mabel is your oldest friend, besides, and you've hardly seen her since he died--"

"She's been abroad for a year, Bill, and only just came back," my sister interposed. "She came back rather unexpectedly, though I never thought she would go there to live--" She stopped abruptly. Clearly, she was only speaking half her mind. "Probably," she went on, "Mabel wants to pick up old links again."

"Naturally," I put in, "yourself chief among them." The veiled reference to the house I let pass.

It involved discussing the dead man for one thing.

"I feel I ought to go anyhow," she resumed, "and of course it would be jollier if you came too. You'd get in such a muddle here by yourself, and eat wrong things, and forget to air the rooms, and--oh, everything!" She looked up laughing. "Only," she added, "there's the British Museum--?"

"But there's a big library there," I answered, "and all the books of reference I could possibly want. It was of you I was thinking. You could take up your painting again; you always sell half of what you paint. It would be a splendid rest too, and Sussex is a jolly country to walk in. By all means, Fanny, I advise--"

Our eyes met, as I stammered in my attempts to avoid expressing the thought that hid in both our minds. My sister had a weakness for dabbling in the various "new" theories of the day, and Mabel, who before her marriage had belonged to foolish societies for investigating the future life to the neglect of the present one, had fostered this undesirable tendency. Her amiable, impressionable temperament was open to every psychic wind that blew. I deplored, detested the whole business. But even more than this I abhorred the later influence that Mr. Franklyn had steeped his wife in, capturing her body and soul in his somber doctrines. I had dreaded lest my sister also might be caught.

"Now that she is alone again--"

I stopped short. Our eyes now made pretence impossible, for the truth had slipped out inevitably, stupidly, although unexpressed in definite language. We laughed, turning our faces a moment to look at other things in the room. Frances picked up a book and examined its cover as though she had made an important discovery, while I took my case out and lit a cigarette I did not want to smoke. We left the matter there. I went out of the room before further explanation could cause tension. Disagreements grow into discord from such tiny things--wrong adjectives, or a chance inflection of the voice. Frances had a right to her views of life as much as I had. At least, I reflected comfortably, we had separated upon an agreement this time, recognized mutually, though not actually stated.

And this point of meeting was, oddly enough, our way of regarding some one who was dead.

For we had both disliked the husband with a great dislike, and during his three years' married life had only been to the house once--for a weekend visit; arriving late on Saturday, we had left after an early breakfast on Monday morning. Ascribing my sister's dislike to a natural jealousy at losing her old friend, I said merely that he displeased me. Yet we both knew that the real emotion lay much deeper. Frances, loyal, honorable creature, had kept silence; and beyond saying that house and grounds--he altered one and laid out the other--distressed her as an expression of his personality somehow ('distressed' was the word she used), no further explanation had passed her lips.

Our dislike of his personality was easily accounted for--up to a point, since both of us shared the artist's point of view that a creed, cut to measure and carefully dried, was an ugly thing, and that a dogma to which believers must subscribe or perish everlastingly was a barbarism resting upon cruelty. But while my own dislike was purely due to an abstract worship of Beauty, my sister's had another twist in it, for with her "new" tendencies, she believed that all religions were an aspect of truth and that no one, even the lowest wretch, could escape "heaven" in the long run.

Samuel Franklyn, the rich banker, was a man universally respected and admired, and the marriage, though Mabel was fifteen years his junior, won general applause; his bride was an heiress in her own right-- breweries--and the story of her conversion at a revivalist meeting where Samuel Franklyn had spoken fervidly of heaven, and terrifyingly of sin, hell and damnation, even contained a touch of genuine romance. She was a brand snatched from the burning; his detailed eloquence had frightened her into heaven; salvation

came in the nick of time; his words had plucked her from the edge of that lake of fire and brimstone where their worm dieth not and the fire is not quenched. She regarded him as a hero, sighed her relief upon his saintly shoulder, and accepted the peace he offered her with a grateful resignation.

For her husband was a "religious man" who successfully combined great riches with the glamour of winning souls. He was a portly figure, though tall, with masterful, big hands, his fingers rather thick and red; and his dignity, that just escaped being pompous, held in it something that was implacable. A convinced assurance, almost remorseless, gleamed in his eyes when he preached especially, and his threats of hell fire must have scared souls stronger than the timid, receptive Mabel whom he married. He clad himself in long frock-coats hat buttoned unevenly, big square boots, and trousers that invariably bagged at the knee and were a little short; he wore low collars, spats occasionally, and a tall black hat that was not of silk. His voice was alternately hard and unctuous; and he regarded theaters, ballrooms, and racecourses as the vestibule of that brimstone lake of whose geography he was as positive as of his great banking offices in the City. A philanthropist up to the hilt, however, no one ever doubted his complete sincerity; his convictions were ingrained, his faith borne out by his life--as witness his name upon so many admirable Societies, as treasurer, patron, or heading the donation list. He bulked large in the world of doing good, a broad and stately stone in the rampart against evil. And his heart was genuinely kind and soft for others--who believed as he did.

Yet, in spite of this true sympathy with suffering and his desire to help, he was narrow as a telegraph wire and unbending as a church pillar; he was intensely selfish; intolerant as an officer of the Inquisition, his bourgeois soul constructed a revolting scheme of heaven that was reproduced in miniature in all he did and planned. Faith was the sine qua non of salvation, and by "faith" he meant belief in his own particular view of things--"which faith, except every one do keep whole and undefiled, without doubt he shall perish everlastingly." All the world but his own small, exclusive sect must be damned eternally--a pity, but alas, inevitable. He was right.

Yet he prayed without ceasing, and gave heavily to the poor--the only thing he could not give being big ideas to his provincial and suburban deity. Pettier than an insect, and more obstinate than a mule, he had also the superior, sleek humility of a "chosen one." He was churchwarden too. He read the lesson in a "place of worship," either chilly or overheated, where neither organ, vestments, nor lighted candles were permitted, but where the odor of hair-wash on the boys' heads in the back rows pervaded the entire building.

This portrait of the banker, who accumulated riches both on earth and in heaven, may possibly be overdrawn, however, because Frances and I were "artistic temperaments" that viewed the type with a dislike and distrust amounting to contempt. The majority considered Samuel Franklyn a worthy man and a good citizen. The majority, doubtless, held the saner view. A few years more, and he certainly would have been made a baronet. He relieved much suffering in the world, as assuredly as he caused many souls the agonies of torturing fear by his emphasis upon damnation.

Had there been one point of beauty in him, we might have been more lenient; only we found it not, and, I admit, took little pains to search. I shall never forget the look of dour forgiveness with which he heard our excuses for missing Morning Prayers that Sunday morning of our single visit to The Towers. My sister learned that a change was made soon afterwards, prayers being "conducted" after breakfast instead of before.

The Towers stood solemnly upon a Sussex hill amid parklike modern grounds, but the house cannot better be described--it would be so wearisome for one thing--than by saying that it was a cross between an overgrown, pretentious Norwood villa and one of those saturnine Institutes for cripples the train passes as it slinks ashamed through South London into Surrey. It was "wealthily" furnished and at first sight imposing, but on closer acquaintance revealed a meager personality, barren and austere. One looked for Rules and Regulations on the walls, all signed By Order. The place

was a prison that shut out "the world." There was, of course, no billiard-room, no smoking-room, no room for play of any kind, and the great hall at the back, once a chapel, which might have been used for dancing, theatricals, or other innocent amusements, was consecrated in his day to meetings of various kinds, chiefly brigades, temperance or missionary societies. There was a harmonium at one end--on the level floor--a raised dais or platform at the other, and a gallery above for the servants, gardeners, and coachmen. It was heated with hot-water pipes, and hung with Doré's pictures, though these latter were soon removed and stored out of sight in the attics as being too unspiritual. In polished, shiny wood, it was a representation in miniature of that poky exclusive Heaven he took about with him, externalizing it in all he did and planned, even in the grounds about the house.

Changes in The Towers, Frances told me, had been made during Mabel's year of widowhood abroad--an organ put into the big hall, the library made livable and re-catalogued--when it was permissible to suppose she had found her soul again and returned to her normal, healthy views of life, which included enjoyment and play, literature, music and the arts, without, however, a touch of that trivial thoughtlessness usually termed worldliness. Mrs. Franklyn, as I remembered her, was a quiet little woman, shallow, perhaps, and easily influenced, but sincere as a dog and thorough in her faithful Friendship. Her tastes at heart were catholic, and that heart was simple and unimaginative. That she took up with the various movements of the day was sign merely that she was searching in her limited way for a belief that should bring her peace. She was, in fact, a very ordinary woman, her caliber a little less than that of Frances. I knew they used to discuss all kinds of theories together, but as these discussions never resulted in action, I had come to regard her as harmless. Still, I was not sorry when she married, and I did not welcome now a renewal of the former intimacy. The philanthropist she had given no children, or she would have made a good and sensible mother. No doubt she would marry again.

"Mabel mentions that she's been alone at The Towers since

the end of August," Frances told me at teatime; "and I'm sure she feels out of it and lonely. It would be a kindness to go. Besides, I always liked her."

I agreed. I had recovered from my attack of selfishness. I expressed my pleasure.

"You've written to accept," I said, half statement and half question.

Frances nodded. "I thanked for you," she added quietly, "explaining that you were not free at the moment, but that later, if not inconvenient, you might come down for a bit and join me."

I stared. Frances sometimes had this independent way of deciding things. I was convicted, and punished into the bargain.

Of course there followed argument and explanation, as between brother and sister who were affectionate, but the recording of our talk could be of little interest. It was arranged thus, Frances and I both satisfied. Two days later she departed for The Towers, leaving me alone in the flat with everything planned for my comfort and good behavior--she was rather a tyrant in her quiet way--and her last words as I saw her off from Charing Cross rang in my head for a long time after she was gone:

"I'll write and let you know, Bill. Eat properly, mind, and let me know if anything goes wrong."

She waved her small gloved hand, nodded her head till the feather brushed the window, and was gone.

II

After the note announcing her safe arrival a week of silence passed, and then a letter came; there were various suggestions for my welfare, and the rest was the usual rambling information and description Frances loved, generously italicized.

" ...and we are quite alone," she went on in her enormous handwriting that seemed such a waste of space and labor, "though some others are coming presently, I believe. You could work here to your heart's content. Mabel quite understands, and says she would love to have you when you feel

free to come. She has changed a bit--back to her old natural self: she never mentions him. The place has changed too in certain ways: it has more cheerfulness, I think. She has put it in, this cheerfulness, spaded it in, if you know what I mean; but it lies about uneasily and is not natural--quite. The organ is a beauty. She must be very rich now, but she's as gentle and sweet as ever. Do you know, Bill, I think he must have frightened her into marrying him. I get the impression she was afraid of him." This last sentence was inked out, I but I read it through the scratching; the letters being too big to hide. "He had an inflexible will beneath all that oily kindness which passed for spiritual. He was a real personality, I mean. I'm sure he'd have sent you and me cheerfully to the stake in another century--for our own good. Isn't it odd she never speaks of him, even to me?" This, again, was stroked through, though without the intention to obliterate--merely because it was repetition, probably. "The only reminder of him in the house now is a big copy of the presentation portrait that stands on the stairs of the Multitechnic Institute at Peckham--you know--that life-size one with his fat hand sprinkled with rings resting on a thick Bible and the other slipped between the buttons of a tight frock-coat. It hangs in the dining room and rather dominates our meals. I wish Mabel would take it down. I think she'd like to, if she dared. There's not a single photograph of him anywhere, even in her own room. Mrs. Marsh is here--you remember her, his housekeeper, the wife of the man who got penal servitude for killing a baby or something--you said she robbed him and justified her stealing because the story of the unjust steward was in the Bible! How we laughed over that! She's just the same too, gliding about all over the house and turning up when least expected."

Other reminiscences filled the next two sides of the letter, and ran, without a trace of punctuation, into instructions about a Salamander stove for heating my work-room in the flat; these were followed by things I was to tell the cook, and by requests for several articles she had forgotten and would like sent after her, two of them blouses, with descriptions so lengthy and contradictory that I sighed as I read them--

"unless you come down soon, in which case perhaps you wouldn't mind bringing them; not the mauve one I wear in the evening sometimes, but the pale blue one with lace round the collar and the crinkly front. They're in the cupboard--or the drawer, I'm not sure which--of my bedroom. Ask Annie if you're in doubt. Thanks most awfully. Send a telegram, remember, and we'll meet you in the motor any time. I don't quite know if I shall stay the whole month--alone. It all depends...." And she closed the letter, the italicized words increasing recklessly towards the end, with a repetition that Mabel would love to have me "for myself," as also to have a "man in the house," and that I only had to telegraph the day and the train.... This letter, coming by the second post, interrupted me in a moment of absorbing work, and, having read it through to make sure there was nothing requiring instant attention, I threw it aside and went on with my notes and reading. Within five minutes, however, it was back at me again. That restless thing called "between the lines" fluttered about my mind. My interest in the Balkan States--political article that had been "ordered"--faded. Somewhere, somehow I felt disquieted, disturbed. At first I persisted in my work, forcing myself to concentrate, but soon found that a layer of new impressions floated between the article and my attention. It was like a shadow, though a shadow that dissolved upon inspection. Once or twice I glanced up, expecting to find some one in the room, that the door had opened unobserved and Annie was waiting for instructions. I heard the buses thundering across the bridge. I was aware of Oakley Street.

Montenegro and the blue Adriatic melted into the October haze along that depressing Embankment that aped a riverbank, and sentences from the letter flashed before my eyes and stung me. Picking it up and reading it through more carefully, I rang the bell and told Annie to find the blouses and pack them for the post, showing her finally the written description, and resenting the superior smile with which she at once interrupted. "I know them, sir," and disappeared.

But it was not the blouses: it was that exasperating thing "between the lines" that put an end to my work with its elu-

sive teasing nuisance. The first sharp impression is alone of value in such a case, for once analysis begins the imagination constructs all kinds of false interpretation. The more I thought, the more I grew fuddled. The letter, it seemed to me, wanted to say another thing; instead the eight sheets conveyed it merely. It came to the edge of disclosure, then halted.

There was something on the writer's mind, and I felt uneasy. Studying the sentences brought, however, no revelation, but increased confusion only; for while the uneasiness remained, the first clear hint had vanished. In the end I closed my books and went out to look up another matter at the British Museum library. Perhaps I should discover it that way--by turning the mind in a totally new direction. I lunched at the Express Dairy in Oxford Street close by, and telephoned to Annie that I would be home to tea at five.

And at tea, tired physically and mentally after breathing the exhausted air of the Rotunda for five hours, my mind suddenly delivered up its original impression, vivid and clear-cut; no proof accompanied the revelation; it was mere presentiment, but convincing. Frances was disturbed in her mind, her orderly, sensible, housekeeping mind; she was uneasy, even perhaps afraid; something in the house distressed her, and she had need of me. Unless I went down, her time of rest and change, her quite necessary holiday, in fact, would be spoilt. She was too unselfish to say this, but it ran everywhere between the lines. I saw it clearly now. Mrs. Franklyn, moreover--and that meant Frances too--would like a "man in the house." It was a disagreeable phrase, a suggestive way of hinting something she dared not state definitely. The two women in that great, lonely barrack of a house were afraid.

My sense of duty, affection, unselfishness, whatever the composite emotion may be termed, was stirred; also my vanity. I acted quickly, lest reflection should warp clear, decent judgment.

"Annie," I said, when she answered the bell, "you need not send those blouses by the post. I'll take them down tomorrow when I go. I shall be away a week or two, possibly longer." And, having looked up a train, I hastened out to tele-

graph before I could change my fickle mind.

But no desire came that night to change my mind. I was doing the right, the necessary thing. I was even in something of a hurry to get down to The Towers as soon as possible. I chose an early afternoon train.

III

A telegram had told me to come to a town ten miles from the house, so I was saved the crawling train to the local station, and traveled down by an express. As soon as we left London the fog cleared off, and an autumn sun, though without heat in it, painted the landscape with golden browns and yellows. My spirits rose as I lay back in the luxurious motor and sped between the woods and hedges. Oddly enough, my anxiety of overnight had disappeared. It was due, no doubt, to that exaggeration of detail which reflection in loneliness brings. Frances and I had not been separated for over a year, and her letters from The Towers told so little. It had seemed unnatural to be deprived of those intimate particulars of mood and feeling I was accustomed to. We had such confidence in one another, and our affection was so deep. Though she was but five years younger than myself, I regarded her as a child. My attitude was fatherly.

In return, she certainly mothered me with a solicitude that never cloyed. I felt no desire to marry while she was still alive. She painted in watercolors with a reasonable success, and kept house for me; I wrote, reviewed books and lectured on aesthetics; we were a humdrum couple of quasi-artists, well satisfied with life, and all I feared for her was that she might become a suffragette or be taken captive by one of these wild theories that caught her imagination sometimes, and that Mabel, for one, had fostered. As for myself, no doubt she deemed me a trifle solid or stolid--I forget which word she preferred--but on the whole there was just suffi-cient difference of opinion to make intercourse suggestive without monotony, and certainly without quarrelling.

Drawing in deep draughts of the stinging autumn air, I felt happy and exhilarated. It was like going for a holiday, with comfort at the end of the journey instead of bargaining for

centimes.

But my heart sank noticeably the moment the house came into view. The long drive, lined with hostile monkey trees and formal wellingtonias that were solemn and sedate, was mere extension of the miniature approach to a thousand semidetached suburban "residences"; and the appearance of The Towers, as we turned the corner with a rush, suggested a commonplace climax to a story that had begun interestingly, almost thrillingly. A villa had escaped from the shadow of the Crystal Palace, thumped its way down by night, grown suddenly monstrous in a shower of rich rain, and settled itself insolently to stay. Ivy climbed about the opulent red-brick walls, but climbed neatly and with disfiguring effect, sham as on a prison or--the simile made me smile--an orphan asylum. There was no hint of the comely roughness of untidy ivy on a ruin. Clipped, trained, and precise it was, as on a brand-new protestant church. I swear there was not a bird's nest nor a single earwig in it anywhere. About the porch it was particularly thick, smothering a seventeenth-century lamp with a contrast that was quite horrible. Extensive glass-houses spread away on the farther side of the house; the numerous towers to which the building owed its name seemed made to hold school bells; and the windowsills, thick with potted flowers, made me think of the desolate suburbs of Brighton or Bexhill. In a commanding position upon the crest of a hill, it overlooked miles of undulating, wooded country southwards to the Downs, but behind it, to the north, thick banks of ilex, holly, and privet protected it from the cleaner and more stimulating winds. Hence, though highly placed, it was shut in. Three years had passed since I last set eyes upon, it, but the unsightly memory I had retained was justified by the reality. The place was deplorable.

It is my habit to express my opinions audibly sometimes, when impressions are strong enough to warrant it; but now I only sighed "Oh, dear," as I extricated my legs from many rugs and went into the house. A tall parlor-maid, with the bearing of a grenadier, received me, and standing behind her was Mrs. Marsh, the housekeeper, whom I remembered

because her untidy back hair had suggested to me that it had been burnt. I went at once to my room, my hostess already dressing for dinner, but Frances came in to see me just as I was struggling with my black tie that had got tangled like a bootlace. She fastened it for me in a neat, effective bow, and while I held my chin up for the operation, staring blankly at the ceiling, the impression came--I wondered, was it her touch that caused it?--that something in her trembled. Shrinking perhaps is the truer word. Nothing in her face or manner betrayed it, nor in her pleasant, easy talk while she tidied my things and scolded my slovenly packing, as her habit was, questioning me about the servants at the flat. The blouses, though right, were crumpled, and my scolding was deserved. There was no impatience even. Yet somehow or other the suggestion of a shrinking reserve and holding back reached my mind. She had been lonely, of course, but it was more than that; she was glad that I had come, yet for some reason unstated she could have wished that I had stayed away. We discussed the news that had accumulated during our brief separation, and in doing so the impression, at best exceedingly slight, was forgotten. My chamber was large and beautifully furnished; the hall and dining room of our flat would have gone into it with a good remainder; yet it was not a place I could settle down in for work. It conveyed the idea of impermanence, making me feel transient as in a hotel bedroom. This, of course, was the fact. But some rooms convey a settled, lasting hospitality even in a hotel; this one did not; and as I was accustomed to work in the room I slept in, at least when visiting, a slight frown must have crept between my eyes.

"Mabel has fitted a work-room for you just out of the library," said the clairvoyant Frances.

"No one will disturb you there, and you'll have fifteen thousand books all catalogued within easy reach. There's a private staircase too. You can breakfast in your room and slip down in your dressing gown if you want to." She laughed. My spirits took a turn upwards as absurdly as they had gone down.

"And how are you?" I asked, giving her a belated kiss. "It's jolly to be together again. I did feel rather lost without you, I'll admit."

"That's natural," she laughed. "I'm so glad."

She looked well and had country color in her cheeks. She informed me that she was eating and sleeping well, going out for little walks with Mabel, painting bits of scenery again, and enjoying a complete change and rest; and yet, for all her brave description, the word somehow did not quite ring true. Those last words in particular did not ring true. There lay in her manner, just out of sight, I felt, this suggestion of the exact reverse--of unrest, shrinking, almost of anxiety. Certain small strings in her seemed over-tight. "Keyed-up" was the slang expression that crossed my mind. I looked rather searchingly into her face as she was telling me this.

"Only--the evenings," she added, noticing my query, yet rather avoiding my eyes, "the evenings are--well, rather heavy sometimes, and I find it difficult to keep awake."

"The strong air after London makes you drowsy," I suggested, "and you like to get early to bed."

Frances turned and looked at me for a moment steadily. "On the contrary, Bill, I dislike going to bed--here. And Mabel goes so early." She said it lightly enough, fingering the disorder upon my dressing table in such a stupid way that I saw her mind was working in another direction altogether. She looked up suddenly with a kind of nervousness from the brush and scissors.

"Billy," she said abruptly, lowering her voice, "isn't it odd, but I hate sleeping alone here? I can't make it out quite; I've never felt such a thing before in my life. Do you--think it's all nonsense?"

And she laughed, with her lips but not with her eyes; there was a note of defiance in her I failed to understand.

"Nothing a nature like yours feels strongly is nonsense, Frances," I replied soothingly.

But I, too, answered with my lips only, for another part of my mind was working elsewhere, and among uncomfortable things. A touch of bewilderment passed over me. I was not certain how best to continue. If I laughed she would tell me no more, yet if I took her too seriously the strings would tighten further. Instinctively, then, this flashed rapidly across me: that something of what she felt, I had also felt, though interpreting it differently. Vague it was, as the coming of rain or storm that announce themselves hours in advance with their hint of faint, unsettling excitement in the air. I had been but a short hour in the house--big, comfortable, luxurious house--but had experienced this sense of being unsettled, unfixed, fluctuating--a kind of impermanence that transient lodgers in hotels must feel, but that a guest in a friend's home ought not to feel, be the visit short or long. To Frances, an impressionable woman, the feeling had come in the terms of alarm. She disliked sleeping alone, while yet she longed to sleep. The precise idea in my mind evaded capture, merely brushing through me, three-quarters out of sight; I realized only that we both felt the same thing, and that neither of us could get at it clearly.

Degrees of unrest we felt, but the actual thing did not disclose itself. It did not happen.

I felt strangely at sea for a moment. Frances would interpret hesitation as endorsement, and encouragement might be the last thing that could help her.

"Sleeping in a strange house," I answered at length, "is often difficult at first, and one feels lonely. After fifteen months in our tiny flat one feels lost and uncared-for in a big house. It's an uncomfortable feeling--I know it well. And this is a barrack, isn't it? The masses of furniture only make it worse. One feels in storage somewhere underground--the furniture doesn't furnish. One must never yield to fancies, though--"

Frances looked away towards the windows; she seemed disappointed a little.

"After our thickly-populated Chelsea," I went on quickly, "it seems isolated here."

But she did not turn back, and clearly I was saying the wrong thing. A wave of pity rushed suddenly over me. Was she really frightened, perhaps? She was imaginative, I knew, but never moody; common sense was strong in her, though she had her times of hypersensitiveness. I caught the echo of some unreasoning, big alarm in her. She stood there, gazing across my balcony towards the sea of wooded country that spread dim and vague in the obscurity of the dusk. The deepening shadows entered the room, I fancied, from the grounds below. Following her abstracted gaze a moment, I experienced a curious sharp desire to leave, to escape. Out yonder was wind and space and freedom. This enormous building was oppressive, silent, still.

Great catacombs occurred to me, things beneath the ground, imprisonment and capture. I believe I even shuddered a little.

I touched her shoulder. She turned round slowly, and we looked with a certain deliberation into each other's eyes.

"Fanny," I asked, more gravely than I intended, "you are not frightened, are you? Nothing has happened, has it?"

She replied with emphasis, "Of course not! How could it--I mean, why should I?" She stammered, as though the wrong sentence flustered her a second. "It's simply--that I have this ter--this dislike of sleeping alone."

Naturally, my first thought was how easy it would be to cut our visit short. But I did not say this. Had it been a true solution, Frances would have said it for me long ago.

"Wouldn't Mabel double-up with you?" I said instead, "or give you an adjoining room, so that you could leave the door between you open? There's space enough, heaven knows."

And then, as the gong sounded in the hall below for dinner, she said, as with an effort, this thing:

"Mabel did ask me--on the third night--after I had told her. But I declined."

"You'd rather be alone than with her?" I asked, with a certain relief.

Her reply was so gravely given, a child would have known there was more behind it: "Not that; but that she did not really want it."

I had a moment's intuition and acted on it impulsively. "She feels it too, perhaps, but wishes to face it by herself-- and get over it?"

My sister bowed her head, and the gesture made me realize of a sudden how grave and solemn our talk had grown, as though some portentous thing were under discussion. It had come of itself--indefinite as a gradual change of temperature. Yet neither of us knew its nature, for apparently neither of us could state it plainly. Nothing happened, even in our words.

"That was my impression," she said, "--that if she yields to it she encourages it. And a habit forms so easily. Just think," she added with a faint smile that was the first sign of lightness she had yet betrayed, "what a nuisance it would be--everywhere--if everybody was afraid of being alone--like that."

I snatched readily at the chance. We laughed a little, though it was a quiet kind of laughter that seemed wrong. I took her arm and led her towards the door.

"Disastrous, in fact," I agreed.

She raised her voice to its normal pitch again, as I had done. "No doubt it will pass," she said, "now that you have come. Of course, it's chiefly my imagination." Her tone was lighter, though nothing could convince me that the matter itself was light--just then. "And in any case," tightening her grip on my arm as we passed into the bright enormous corridor and caught sight of Mrs. Franklyn waiting in the cheerless hall below, "I'm very glad you're here, Bill, and Mabel, I know, is too."

"If it doesn't pass," I just had time to whisper with a feeble attempt at jollity, "I'll come at night and snore outside your door. After that you'll be so glad to get rid of me that you won't mind being alone."

"That's a bargain," said Frances.

I shook my hostess by the hand, made a banal remark about the long interval since last we met, and walked behind them into the great dining room, dimly lit by candles, wondering in my heart how long my sister and I should stay, and why in the world we had ever left our cozy little flat to enter this desolation of riches and false luxury at all. The unsightly picture of the late Samuel Franklyn, Esq., stared down upon me from the farther end of the room above the mighty mantelpiece.

He looked, I thought, like some pompous Heavenly Butler who denied to all the world, and to us in particular, the right of entry without presentation cards signed by his hand as proof that we belonged to his own exclusive set. The majority, to his deep grief, and in spite of all his prayers on their behalf, must burn and "perish everlastingly."

IV

With the instinct of the healthy bachelor I always try to make myself a nest in the place I live in, be it for long or short. Whether visiting, in lodging-house, or in hotel, the first essential is this nest--one's own things built into the walls as a bird builds in its feathers. It may look desolate and uncomfortable enough to others, because the central detail is neither bed nor wardrobe, sofa nor armchair, but a good solid writing-table that does not wriggle, and that has wide elbowroom.

And The Towers is vividly described for me by the single fact that I could not "nest" there.

I took several days to discover this, but the first impression of impermanence was truer than I knew. The feathers of the mind refused here to lie one way. They ruffled, pointed, and grew wild.

Luxurious furniture does not mean comfort; I might as well have tried to settle down in the sofa and armchair department of a big shop. My bedroom was easily managed; it was the private workroom, prepared especially for my reception, that made me feel alien and outcast.

Externally, it was all one could desire: an antechamber to the great library, with not one, but two generous oak tables, to say nothing of smaller ones against the walls with capacious drawers.

There were reading desks, mechanical devices for holding books, perfect light, quiet as in a church, and no approach but across the huge adjoining room. Yet it did not invite.

"I hope you'll be able to work here," said my little hostess the next morning, as she took me in--her only visit to it while I stayed in the house--and showed me the ten-volume Catalogue.

"It's absolutely quiet and no one will disturb you."

"If you can't, Bill, you're not much good," laughed Frances, who was on her arm. "Even I could write in a study like this!"

I glanced with pleasure at the ample tables, the sheets of thick blotting paper, the rulers, sealing wax, paper knives, and all the other immaculate paraphernalia. "It's perfect," I answered with a secret thrill, yet feeling a little foolish. This was for Gibbon or Carlyle, rather than for my potboiling insignificancies. "If I can't write masterpieces here, it's certainly not your fault," and I turned with gratitude to Mrs. Franklyn. She was looking straight at me, and there was a question in her small pale eyes I did not understand. Was she noting the effect upon me, I wondered?

"You'll write here--perhaps a story about the house," she said, "Thompson will bring you anything you want; you only have to ring." She pointed to the electric bell on the central table, the wire running neatly down the leg. "No one has ever worked here before, and the library has been hardly used since it was put in. So there's no previous atmosphere to affect your imagination--er--adversely."

We laughed. "Bill isn't that sort," said my sister; while I wished they would go out and leave me to arrange my little nest and set to work.

I thought, of course, it was the huge listening library that made me feel so inconsiderable--the fifteen thousand silent, staring books, the solemn aisles, the deep, eloquent shelves. But when the women had gone and I was alone, the beginning of the truth crept over me, and I felt that first hint of disconsolateness which later became an imperative No. The mind shut down, images ceased to rise and flow. I read, made copious notes, but I wrote no single line at The Towers.

Nothing completed itself there. Nothing happened.

The morning sunshine poured into the library through ten long narrow windows; birds were singing; the autumn air, rich with a faint aroma of November melancholy that stung the imagination pleasantly, filled my antechamber. I looked out upon the undulating wooded landscape, hemmed in by the sweep of distant Downs, and I tasted a whiff of the sea. Rooks cawed as they floated above the elms, and there were lazy cows in the nearer meadows. A dozen times I tried to make my nest and settle down to work, and a dozen times, like a turning fastidious dog upon a hearth rug, I rearranged my chair and books and papers. The temptation of the Catalogue and shelves, of course, was accountable for much, yet not, I felt, for all. That was a manageable seduction. My work, moreover, was not of the creative kind that requires absolute absorption; it was the mere readable presentation of data I had accumulated. My notebooks were charged with facts ready to tabulate--facts, too, that interested me keenly. A mere effort of the will was necessary, and concentration of no difficult kind. Yet, somehow, it seemed beyond me: something forever pushed the facts into disorder ... and in the end I sat in the sunshine, dipping into a dozen books selected from the shelves outside, vexed with myself and only half-enjoying it. I felt restless. I wanted to be elsewhere.

And even while I read, attention wandered. Frances, Mabel, her late husband, the house and grounds, each in turn and sometimes all together, rose uninvited into the stream of thought, hindering any consecutive flow of work. In disconnected fashion came these pictures that interrupted concentration, yet presenting themselves as broken fragments of a bigger thing my mind already groped for unconsciously. They fluttered round this hidden thing of which they were aspects, fugitive interpretations, no one of them bringing complete revelation. There was no adjective, such as pleasant or unpleasant, that I could attach to what I felt, beyond that the result was unsettling. Vague as the atmosphere of a dream, it yet persisted, and I could not dissipate it.

Isolated words or phrases in the lines I read sent questions scouring across my mind, sure sign that the deeper part of me was restless and ill at ease.

Rather trivial questions too--half-foolish interrogations, as of a puzzled or curious child: Why was my sister afraid to sleep alone, and why did her friend feel a similar repugnance, yet seek to conquer it? Why was the solid luxury of the house without comfort, its shelter without the sense of permanence? Why had Mrs. Franklyn asked us to come, artists, unbelieving vagabonds, types at the farthest possible remove from the saved sheep of her husband's household? Had a reaction set in against the hysteria of her conversion? I had seen no signs of religious fervor in her; her atmosphere was that of an ordinary, high-minded woman, yet a woman of the world. Lifeless, though, a little, perhaps, now that I came to think about it: she had made no definite impression upon me of any kind. And my thoughts ran vaguely after this fragile clue.

Closing my book, I let them run. For, with this chance reflection came the discovery that I could not see her clearly--could not feel her soul, her personality. Her face, her small pale eyes, her dress and body and walk, all these stood before me like a photograph; but her Self evaded me. She seemed not there, lifeless, empty, a shadow--nothing. The picture was disagreeable, and I put it by. Instantly she melted out, as though light thought had conjured up a phantom that had no real existence. And at that very moment, singularly enough, my eye caught sight of her moving past the window, going silently along the gravel path. I watched her, a sudden new sensation gripping me. "There goes a prisoner," my thought instantly ran, "one who wishes to escape, but cannot."

What brought the outlandish notion, heaven only knows. The house was of her own choice, she was twice an heiress, and the world lay open at her feet. Yet she stayed--unhappy, frightened, caught. All this flashed over me, and made a sharp impression even before I had time to dismiss it as absurd. But a moment later explanation offered itself, though it seemed as far-fetched as the original impression. My mind, being logical, was obliged to provide something, apparently. For Mrs. Franklyn, while dressed to go out, with thick walking-boots, a pointed stick, and a motor-cap tied on with a veil as for the windy lanes, was obviously content to go no farther than the little garden paths. The costume was a sham and a pretence. It was this, and her lithe, quick movements that suggested a caged creature--a creature tamed by fear and cruelty that cloaked themselves in kindness--pacing up and down, unable to realize why it got no farther, but always met the same bars in exactly the same place. The mind in her was barred.

I watched her go along the paths and down the steps from one terrace to another, until the laurels hid her altogether;

and into this mere imagining of a moment came a hint of something slightly disagreeable, for which my mind, search as it would, found no explanation at all. I remembered then certain other little things. They dropped into the picture of their own accord. In a mind not deliberately hunting for clues, pieces of a puzzle sometimes come together in this way, bringing revelation, so that for a second there flashed across me, vanishing instantly again before I could consider it, a large, distressing thought. I can only describe vaguely as a Shadow.

Dark and ugly, oppressive certainly it might be described, with something torn and dreadful about the edges that suggested pain and strife and terror. The interior of a prison with two rows of occupied condemned cells, seen years ago in New York, sprang to memory after it-- the connection between the two impossible to surmise even. But the "certain other little things" mentioned above were these: that Mrs. Franklyn, in last night's dinner talk, had always referred to "this house," but never called it "home"; and had emphasized unnecessarily, for a well-bred woman, our "great kindness" in coming down to stay so long with her. Another time, in answer to my futile compliment about the "stately rooms," she said quietly, "It is an enormous house for so small a party; but I stay here very little, and only till I get it straight again." The three of us were going up the great staircase to bed as this was said, and, not knowing quite her meaning, I dropped the subject. It edged delicate ground, I felt. Frances added no word of her own. It now occurred to me abruptly that "stay" was the word made use of, when "live" would have been more natural. How insignificant to recall! Yet why did they suggest themselves just at this moment ...?

And, on going to Frances's room to make sure she was not nervous or lonely, I realized abruptly, that Mrs. Franklyn, of course, had talked with her in a confidential sense that I, as a mere visiting brother, could not share. Frances had told me nothing. I might easily have wormed it out of her, had I not felt that for us to discuss further our hostess and her house merely because we were under the roof together, was not quite nice or loyal.

"I'll call you, Bill, if I'm scared," she had laughed as we parted, my room being just across the big corridor from her own. I had fallen asleep, thinking what in the world was meant by "getting it straight again."

And now in my antechamber to the library, on the second morning, sitting among piles of foolscap and sheets of spotless blotting-paper, all useless to me, these slight hints came back and helped to frame the big, vague Shadow I have mentioned. Up to the neck in this Shadow, almost drowned, yet just treading water, stood the figure of my hostess in her walking costume. Frances and I seemed swimming to her aid. The Shadow was large enough to include both house and grounds, but farther than that I could not see.... Dismissing it, I fell to reading my purloined book again. Before I turned another page, however, another startling detail leaped out at me: the figure of Mrs. Franklyn in the Shadow was not living. It floated helplessly, like a doll or puppet that has no life in it. It was both pathetic and dreadful.

Any one who sits in reverie thus, of course, may see similar ridiculous pictures when the will no longer guides construction. The incongruities of dreams are thus explained. I merely record the picture as it came. That it remained by me for several days, just as vivid dreams do, is neither here nor there. I did not allow myself to dwell upon it. The curious thing, perhaps, is that from this moment I date my inclination, though not yet my desire, to leave. I purposely say "to leave."

I cannot quite remember when the word changed to that aggressive, frantic thing which is escape.

V

We were left delightfully to ourselves in this pretentious country mansion with the soul of a villa. Frances took up her painting again, and, the weather being propitious, spent hours out of doors, sketching flowers, trees and nooks of woodland, garden, even the house itself where bits of it peered suggestively across the orchards. Mrs. Franklyn seemed always busy about something or other, and never interfered with us except to propose motoring, tea in anoth-

er part of the lawn, and so forth. She flitted everywhere, pre-occupied, yet apparently doing nothing. The house engulfed her rather. No visitor called. For one thing, she was not supposed to be back from abroad yet; and for another, I think, the neighborhood--her husband's neighborhood--was puzzled by her sudden cessation from good works. Brigades and temperance societies did not ask to hold their meetings in the big hall, and the vicar arranged the school-treats in another's field without explanation. The full-length portrait in the dining room, and the presence of the housekeeper with the "burnt" back hair, indeed, were the only reminders of the man who once had lived here. Mrs. Marsh retained her place in silence, well-paid sinecure as it doubtless was, yet with no hint of that suppressed disapproval one might have expected from her. Indeed there was nothing positive to disapprove, since nothing "worldly" entered grounds or building. In her master's lifetime she had been another "brand snatched from the burning," and it had then been her custom to give vociferous "testimony" at the revival meetings where he adorned the platform and led in streams of prayer. I saw her sometimes on the stairs, hovering, wandering, half-watching and half-listening, and the idea came to me once that this woman somehow formed a link with the departed influence of her bigoted employer. She, alone among us, belonged to the house, and looked at home there. When I saw her talking --oh, with such correct and respectful mien--to Mrs. Franklyn, I had the feeling that for all her unaggressive attitude, she yet exerted some influence that sought to make her mistress stay in the building forever --live there. She would prevent her escape, prevent "getting it straight again," thwart somehow her will to freedom, if she could. The idea in me was of the most fleeting kind. But another time, when I came down late at night to get a book from the library antechamber, and found her sitting in the hall--alone--the impression left upon me was the reverse of fleeting. I can never forget the vivid, disagreeable effect it produced upon me. What was she doing there at half-past eleven at night, all alone in the darkness? She was sitting upright, stiff, in a big chair below the clock. It gave me a turn.

It was so incongruous and odd. She rose quietly as I turned the corner of the stairs, and asked me respectfully, her eyes cast down as usual, whether I had finished with the library, so that she might lock up. There was no more to it than that; but the picture stayed with me--unpleasantly.

These various impressions came to me at odd moments, of course, and not in a single sequence as I now relate them. I was hard at work before three days were past, not writing, as explained, but reading, making notes, and gathering material from the library for future use. It was in chance moments that these curious flashes came, catching me unawares with a touch of surprise that sometimes made me start. For they proved that my under-mind was still conscious of the Shadow, and that far away out of sight lay the cause of it that left me with a vague unrest, unsettled, seeking to "nest" in a place that did not want me. Only when this deeper part knows harmony, perhaps, can good brainwork result, and my inability to write was thus explained.

Certainly, I was always seeking for something here I could not find--an explanation that continually evaded me. Nothing but these trivial hints offered themselves. Lumped together, however, they had the effect of defining the Shadow a little. I became more and more aware of its very real existence. And, if I have made little mention of Frances and my hostess in this connection, it is because they contributed at first little or nothing towards the discovery of what this story tries to tell. Our life was wholly external, normal, quiet, and uneventful; conversation banal--Mrs. Franklyn's conversation in particular. They said nothing that suggested revelation.

Both were in this Shadow, and both knew that they were in it, but neither betrayed by word or act a hint of interpretation. They talked privately, no doubt, but of that I can report no details.

And so it was that, after ten days of a very commonplace visit, I found myself looking straight into the face of a Strangeness that defied capture at close quarters. "There's something here that never happens," were the words that rose in my mind, "and that's why none of us can speak of it."

And as I looked out of the window and watched the vulgar blackbirds, with toes turned in, boring out their worms, I realized sharply that even they, as indeed everything large and small in the house and grounds, shared this strangeness, and were twisted out of normal appearance because of it. Life, as expressed in the entire place, was crumpled, dwarfed, emasculated. God's meanings here were crippled, His love of joy was stunted. Nothing in the garden danced or sang.

There was hate in it. "The Shadow," my thought hurried on to completion, "is a manifestation of hate; and hate is the Devil." And then I sat back frightened in my chair, for I knew that I had partly found the truth.

Leaving my books I went out into the open. The sky was overcast, yet the day by no means gloomy, for a soft, diffused light oozed through the clouds and turned all things warm and almost summery. But I saw the grounds now in their nakedness because I understood. Hate means strife, and the two together weave the robe that terror wears. Having no so-called religious beliefs myself, nor belonging to any set of dogmas called a creed, I could stand outside these feelings and observe. Yet they soaked into me sufficiently for me to grasp sympathetically what others, with more cabined souls (I flattered myself), might feel. That picture in the dining room stalked everywhere, hid behind every tree, peered down upon me from the peaked ugliness of the bourgeois towers, and left the impress of its powerful hand upon every bed of flowers. "You must not do this, you must not do that," went past me through the air. "You must not leave these narrow paths," said the rigid iron railings of black. "You shall not walk here," was written on the lawns. "Keep to the steps," "Don't pick the flowers; make no noise of laughter, singing, dancing," was placarded all over the rose-garden, and "Trespassers will be--not prosecuted but--destroyed" hung from the crest of monkey tree and holly. Guarding the ends of each artificial terrace stood gaunt, implacable policemen, warders, jailers. "Come with us," they chanted, "or be damned eternally."

I remember feeling quite pleased with myself that I had discovered this obvious explanation of the prison feeling the place breathed out. That the posthumous influence of heavy old Samuel Franklyn might be an inadequate solution did not occur to me. By "getting the place straight again," his widow, of course, meant forgetting the glamour of fear and foreboding his depressing creed had temporarily forced upon her; and Frances, delicately minded being, did not speak of it because it was the influence of the man her friend had loved. I felt lighter; a load was lifted from me. "To trace the unfamiliar to the familiar," came back a sentence I had read somewhere, "is to understand." It was a real relief. I could talk with Frances now, even with my hostess, no danger of treading clumsily. For the key was in my hands. I might even help to dissipate the Shadow, "to get it straight again." It seemed, perhaps, our long invitation was explained!

I went into the house laughing--at myself a little. "Perhaps after all the artist's outlook, with no hard and fast dogmas, is as narrow as the others! How small humanity is! And why is there no possible and true combination of all outlooks?"

The feeling of "unsettling" was very strong in me just then, in spite of my big discovery which was to clear everything up. And at the moment I ran into Frances on the stairs, with a portfolio of sketches under her arm.

It came across me then abruptly that, although she had worked a great deal since we came, she had shown me nothing. It struck me suddenly as odd, unnatural. The way she tried to pass me now confirmed my newborn suspicion that--well, that her results were hardly what they ought to be.

"Stand and deliver!" I laughed, stepping in front of her. "I've seen nothing you've done since you've been here, and as a rule you show me all your things. I believe they are atrocious and degrading!" Then my laughter froze.

She made a sly gesture to slip past me, and I almost decided to let her go, for the expression that flashed across her face shocked me. She looked uncomfortable and ashamed; the color came and went a moment in he cheeks, making me think of a child detected in some secret naughtiness. It was almost fear.

"It's because they're not finished then?" I said, dropping

the tone of banter, "or because they're too good for me to understand?" For my criticism of painting, she told me, was crude and ignorant sometimes. "But you'll let me see them later, won't you?"

Frances, however, did not take the way of escape I offered. She changed her mind. She drew the portfolio from beneath her arm instead. "You can see them if you really want to, Bill," she said quietly, and her tone reminded me of a nurse who says to a boy just grown out of childhood, "you are old enough now to look upon horror and ugliness--only I don't advise it."

"I do want to," I said, and made to go downstairs with her. But, instead, she said in the same low voice as before, "Come up to my room, we shall be undisturbed there." So I guessed that she had been on her way to show the paintings to our hostess, but did not care for us all three to see them together. My mind worked furiously.

"Mabel asked me to do them," she explained in a tone of submissive horror, once the door was shut, "in fact, she begged it of me. You know how persistent she is in her quiet way. I--er--had to."

She flushed and opened the portfolio on the little table by the window, standing behind me as I turned the sketches over--sketches of the grounds and trees and garden. In the first moment of inspection, however, I did not take in clearly why my sister's sense of modesty had been offended. For my attention flashed a second elsewhere. Another bit of the puzzle had dropped into place, defining still further the nature of what I called "the Shadow." Mrs. Franklyn, I now remembered, had suggested to me in the library that I might perhaps write something about the place, and I had taken it for one of her banal sentences and paid no further attention. I realized now that it was said in earnest. She wanted our interpretations, as expressed in our respective "talents," painting and writing. Her invitation was explained. She left us to ourselves on purpose.

"I should like to tear them up," Frances was whispering behind me with a shudder, "only I promised--" She hesitated a moment.

"Promised not to?" I asked with a queer feeling of distress, my eyes glued to the papers.

"Promised always to show them to her first," she finished so low I barely caught it.

I have no intuitive, immediate grasp of the value of paintings; results come to me slowly, and though every one believes his own judgment to be good, I dare not claim that mine is worth more than that of any other layman, Frances had too often convicted me of gross ignorance and error. I can only say that I examined these sketches with a feeling of amazement that contained revulsion, if not actually horror and disgust. They were outrageous. I felt hot for my sister, and it was a relief to know she had moved across the room on some pretence or other, and did not examine them with me. Her talent, of course, is mediocre, yet she has her moments of inspiration--moments, that is to say, when a view of Beauty not normally her own flames divinely through her. And these interpretations struck me forcibly as being thus "inspired"--not her own. They were uncommonly well done; they were also atrocious. The meaning in them, however, was never more than hinted. There the unholy skill and power came in: they suggested so abominably, leaving most to the imagination. To find such significance in a bourgeois villa garden, and to interpret it with such delicate yet legible certainty, was a kind of symbolism that was sinister, even diabolical. The delicacy was her own, but the point of view was another's.

And the word that rose in my mind was not the gross description of "impure," but the more fundamental qualification--"un-pure."

In silence I turned the sketches over one by one, as a boy hurries through the pages of an evil book lest he be caught.

"What does Mabel do with them?" I asked presently in a low tone, as I neared the end. "Does she keep them?"

"She makes notes about them in a book and then destroys them," was the reply from the end of the room. I heard a sigh of relief. "I'm glad you've seen them, Bill. I wanted you to-- but was afraid to show them. You understand?"

"I understand," was my reply, though it was not a question

intended to be answered. All I understood really was that Mabel's mind was as sweet and pure as my sister's, and that she had some good reason for what she did. She destroyed the sketches, but first made notes! It was an interpretation of the place she sought. Brother-like, I felt resentment, though, that Frances should waste her time and talent, when she might be doing work that she could sell. Naturally, I felt other things as well....

"Mabel pays me five guineas for each one," I heard. "Absolutely insists."

I stared at her stupidly a moment, bereft of speech or wit. "I must either accept, or go away," she went on calmly, but a little white. "I've tried everything. There was a scene the third day I was here--when I showed her my first result. I wanted to write to you, but hesitated--"

"It's unintentional, then, on your part--forgive my asking it, Frances, dear?" I blundered, hardly knowing what to think or say. "Between the lines" of her letter came back to me. "I mean, you make the sketches in your ordinary way and--the result comes out of itself, so to speak?"

She nodded, throwing her hands out like a Frenchman. "We needn't keep the money for ourselves, Bill. We can give it away, but--I must either accept or leave," and she repeated the shrugging gesture. She sat down on the chair facing me, staring helplessly at the carpet.

"You say there was a scene?" I went on presently, "She insisted?"

"She begged me to continue," my sister replied very quietly. "She thinks--that is, she has an idea or theory that there's something about the place--something she can't get at quite." Frances stammered badly. She knew I did not encourage her wild theories.

"Something she feels--yes," I helped her, more than curious.

"Oh, you know what I mean, Bill," she said desperately. "That the place is saturated with some influence that she is herself too positive or too stupid to interpret. She's trying to make herself negative and receptive, as she calls it, but can't, of course, succeed. Haven't you noticed how dull and imper-

sonal and insipid she seems, as though she had no personality? She thinks impressions will come to her that way. But
they don't--"

"Naturally."

"So she's trying me--us--what she calls the sensitive and
impressionable artistic temperament. She says that until she
is sure exactly what this influence is, she can't fight it, turn it
out, 'get the house straight', as she phrases it."

Remembering my own singular impressions, I felt more
lenient than I might otherwise have done. I tried to keep
impatience out of my voice.

"And this influence, what--whose is it?"

We used the pronoun that followed in the same breath, for
I answered my own question at the same moment as she did:

"His." Our heads nodded involuntarily towards the floor,
the dining room being directly underneath.

And my heart sank, my curiosity died away on the instant; I felt bored. A commonplace haunted house was the
last thing in the world to amuse or interest me. The mere
thought exasperated, with its suggestions of imagination,
overwrought nerves, hysteria, and the rest.

Mingled with my other feelings was certainly disappoint-
ment. To see a figure or feel a "presence," and report from
day to day strange incidents to each other would be a form
of weariness I could never tolerate.

"But really, Frances," I said firmly, after a moment's pause,
"it's too far-fetched, this explanation. A curse, you know, belongs to the ghost stories of early Victorian days." And only
my positive conviction that there was something after all
worth discovering, and that it most certainly was not this,
prevented my suggesting that we terminate our visit forth-
with, or as soon as we decently could. "This is not a haunted
house, whatever it is," I concluded somewhat vehemently,
bringing my hand down upon her odious portfolio.

My sister's reply revived my curiosity sharply.

"I was waiting for you to say that. Mabel says exactly the
same. He is in it--but it's something more than that alone,
something far bigger and more complicated." Her sentence
seemed to indicate the sketches, and though I caught the in-

ference I did not take it up, having no desire to discuss them with her just them indeed, if ever.

I merely stared at her and listened. Questions, I felt sure, would be of little use. It was better she should say her thought in her own way.

"He is one influence, the most recent," she went on slowly, and always very calmly, "but there are others--deeper layers, as it were-- underneath. If his were the only one, something would happen. But nothing ever does happen. The others hinder and prevent--as though each were struggling to predominate."

I had felt it already myself. The idea was rather horrible. I shivered.

"That's what is so ugly about it--that nothing ever happens," she said. "There is this endless anticipation--always on the dry edge of a result that never materializes. It is torture. Mabel is at her wits' end, you see. And when she begged me--what I felt about my sketches--I mean--"

She stammered badly as before.

I stopped her. I had judged too hastily. That queer symbolism in her paintings, pagan and yet not innocent, was, I understood, the result of mixture. I did not pretend to understand, but at least I could be patient. I consequently held my peace. We did talk on a little longer, but it was more general talk that avoided successfully our hostess, the paintings, wild theories, and him--until at length the emotion Frances had hitherto so successfully kept under burst vehemently forth again.

It had hidden between her calm sentences, as it had hidden between the lines of her letter. It swept her now from head to foot, packed tight in the thing she then said.

"Then, Bill, if it is not an ordinary haunted house," she asked, "what is it?"

The words were commonplace enough. The emotion was in the tone of her voice that trembled; in the gesture she made, leaning forward and clasping both hands upon her knees, and in the slight blanching of her cheeks as her brave eyes asked the question and searched my own with anxiety that bordered upon panic. In that moment she put herself under my protection. I winced.

"And why," she added, lowering her voice to a still and furtive whisper, "does nothing ever happen? If only,"--this with great emphasis-- "something would happen--break this awful tension--bring relief. It's the waiting I cannot stand." And she shivered all over as she said it, a touch of wildness in her eyes.

I would have given much to have made a true and satisfactory answer. My mind searched frantically for a moment, but in vain. There lay no sufficient answer in me. I felt what she felt, though with differences. No conclusive explanation lay within reach. Nothing happened. Eager as I was to shoot the entire business into the rubbish heap where ignorance and superstition discharge their poisonous weeds, I could not honestly accomplish this. To treat Frances as a child, and merely "explain away" would be to strain her confidence in my protection, so affectionately claimed. It would further be dishonest to myself--weak, besides--to deny that I had also felt the strain and tension even as she did. While my mind continued searching, I returned her stare in silence; and Frances then, with more honesty and insight than my own, gave suddenly the answer herself--an answer whose truth and adequacy, so far as they went, I could not readily gainsay:

"I think, Bill, because it is too big to happen here--to happen anywhere, indeed, all at once--and too awful!"

To have tossed the sentence aside as nonsense, argued it away, proved that it was really meaningless, would have been easy--at any other time or in any other place; and, had the past week brought me none of the vivid impressions it had brought me, this is doubtless what I should have done. My narrowness again was proved. We understand in others only what we have in ourselves. But her explanation, in a measure, I knew was true. It hinted at the strife and struggle that my notion of a Shadow had seemed to cover thinly.

"Perhaps," I murmured lamely, waiting in vain for her to say more. "But you said just now that you felt the thing was 'in layers', as it were. Do you mean each one--each influence--fighting for the upper hand?"

I used her phraseology to conceal my own poverty. Terminology, after all, was nothing, provided we could reach the idea itself.

Her eyes said yes. She had her clear conception, arrived at independently, as was her way.

And, unlike her sex, she kept it clear, unsmothered by too many words.

"One set of influences gets at me, another gets at you. It's according to our temperaments, I think." She glanced significantly at the vile portfolio. "Sometimes they are mixed--and therefore false. There has always been in me, more than in you, the pagan thing, perhaps, though never, thank God, like that."

The frank confession of course invited my own, as it was meant to do. Yet it was difficult to find the words.

"What I have felt in this place, Frances, I honestly can hardly tell you, because--er--my impressions have not arranged themselves in any definite form I can describe. The strife, the agony of vainly-sought escape, and the unrest--a sort of prison atmosphere--this I have felt at different times and with varying degrees of strength. But I find, as yet, no final label to attach. I couldn't say pagan, Christian, or anything like that, I mean, as you do. As with the blind and deaf, you may have an intensification of certain senses denied to me, or even another sense altogether in embryo--"

"Perhaps," she stopped me, anxious to keep to the point, "you feel it as Mabel does. She feels the whole thing complete."

"That also is possible," I said very slowly. I was thinking behind my words. Her odd remark that it was "big and awful" came back upon me as true. A vast sensation of distress and discomfort swept me suddenly. Pity was in it, and a fierce contempt, a savage, bitter anger as well. Fury against some sham authority was part of it.

"Frances," I said, caught unawares, and dropping all pretence, "what in the world can it be?" I looked hard at her. For some minutes neither of us spoke.

"Have you felt no desire to interpret it?" she asked presently, "Mabel did suggest my writing something about the house," was my reply, "but I've felt nothing imperative. That sort of writing is not my line, you know. My only feeling," I added, noticing that she waited for more, "is the impulse to explain, discover, get it out of me somehow, and so get rid of it. Not by writing, though--as yet." And again I repeated my former question:

"What in the world do you think it is?" My voice had become involuntarily hushed. There was awe in it. Her answer, given with slow emphasis, brought back all my reserve: the phraseology provoked me rather:--"Whatever it is, Bill, it is not of God."

I got up to go downstairs. I believe I shrugged my shoulders. "Would you like to leave, Frances? Shall we go back to town?" I suggested this at the door, and hearing no immediate reply, I turned back to look. Frances was sitting with her head bowed over and buried in her hands. The attitude horribly suggested tears. No woman, I realized, can keep back the pressure of strong emotion as long as Frances had done, without ending in a fluid collapse. I waited a moment uneasily, longing to comfort, yet afraid to act--and in this way discovered the existence of the appalling emotion in myself, hitherto but half guessed. At all costs a scene must be prevented: it would involve such exaggeration and overstatement. Brutally, such is the weakness of the ordinary man, I turned the handle to go out, but my sister then raised her head. The sunlight caught her face, framed untidily in its auburn hair, and I saw her wonderful expression with a start. Pity, tenderness, and sympathy shone in it like a flame. It was undeniable. There shone through all her features the imperishable love and yearning to sacrifice self for others which I have seen in only one type of human being. It was the great mother look.

"We must stay by Mabel and help her get it straight," she whispered, making the decision for us both.

I murmured agreement. Abashed and half ashamed, I stole softly from the room and went out into the grounds. And the first thing clearly realized when alone was this: that the long scene between us was without definite result. The exchange of confidence was really nothing but hints and vague suggestion. We had decided to stay, but it was a negative decision not to leave rather than a positive action. All our words and questions, our guesses, inferences, explanations, our most subtle allusions and insinuations, even the odious paintings themselves, were without definite result. Nothing had happened.

VI

And instinctively, once alone, I made for the places where she had painted her extraordinary pictures; I tried to see what she had seen. Perhaps, now that she had opened my mind to another view, I should be sensitive to some similar interpretation--and possibly by way of literary expression. If I were to write about the place, I asked myself, how should I treat it? I deliberately invited an interpretation in the way that came easiest to me--writing.

But in this case there came no such revelation. Looking closely at the trees and flowers, the bits of lawn and terrace, the rose-garden and corner of the house where the flaming creeper hung so thickly, I discovered nothing of the odious, unpure thing her color and grouping had unconsciously revealed. At first, that is, I discovered nothing. The reality stood there, commonplace and ugly, side by side with her distorted version of it that lay in my mind. It seemed incredible. I tried to force it, but in vain. My imagination, ploughed less deeply than hers, or to another pattern, grew different seed. Where I saw the gross soul of an overgrown suburban garden, inspired by the spirit of a vulgar, rich revivalist who loved to preach damnation, she saw this rush of pagan liberty and joy, this strange license of primitive flesh which, tainted by the other, produced the adulterated, vile result.

Certain things, however, gradually then became apparent, forcing themselves upon me, willy-nilly. They came slowly, but overwhelmingly. Not that facts had changed, or natural details altered in the grounds-- this was impossible--but that I noticed for the first time various aspects I had not noticed before--trivial enough, yet for me, just then, significant. Some I remembered from previous days; others I saw now as I wandered to and fro, uneasy, uncomfortable,--almost, it

seemed, watched by some one who took note of my impressions. The details were so foolish, the total result so formidable. I was half aware that others tried hard to make me see. It was deliberate.

My sister's phrase, "one layer got at me, another gets at you," flashed, undesired, upon me.

For I saw, as with the eyes of a child, what I can only call a goblin garden--house, grounds, trees, and flowers belonged to a goblin world that children enter through the pages of their fairy tales. And what made me first aware of it was the whisper of the wind behind me, so that I turned with a sudden start, feeling that something had moved closer. An old ash tree, ugly and ungainly, had been artificially trained to form an arbor at one end of the terrace that was a tennis lawn, and the leaves of it now went rustling together, swishing as they rose and fell. I looked at the ash tree, and felt as though I had passed that moment between doors into this goblin garden that crouched behind the real one. Below, at a deeper layer perhaps, lay hidden the one my sister had entered.

To deal with my own, however, I call it goblin, because an odd aspect of the quaint in it yet never quite achieved the picturesque. Grotesque, probably, is the truer word, for everywhere I noticed, and for the first time, this slight alteration of the natural due either to the exaggeration of some detail, or to its suppression, generally, I think, to the latter. Life everywhere appeared to me as blocked from the full delivery of its sweet and lovely message. Some counter influence stopped it--suppression; or sent it awry--exaggeration. The house itself, mere expression, of course, of a narrow, limited mind, was sheer ugliness; it required no further explanation. With the grounds and garden, so far as shape and general plan were concerned, this was also true; but that trees and flowers and other natural details should share the same deficiency perplexed my logical soul, and even dismayed it. I stood and stared, then moved about, and stood and stared again. Everywhere was this mockery of a sinister, unfinished aspect. I sought in vain to recover my normal point of view. My mind had found this goblin garden and wandered to and fro in it, unable to escape.

The change was in myself, of course, and so trivial were the details which illustrated it, that they sound absurd, thus mentioned one by one. For me, they proved it, is all I can affirm. The goblin touch lay plainly everywhere: in the forms of the trees, planted at neat intervals along the lawns; in this twisted ash that rustled just behind me; in the shadow of the gloomy wellingtonias, whose sweeping skirts obscured the grass; but especially, I noticed, in the tops and crests of them. For here, the delicate, graceful curves of last year's growth seemed to shrink back into themselves. None of them pointed upwards. Their life had failed and turned aside just when it should have become triumphant. The character of a tree reveals itself chiefly at the extremities, and it was precisely here that they all drooped and achieved this hint of goblin distortion--in the growth, that is, of the last few years. What ought to have been fairy, joyful, natural, was instead uncomely to the verge of the grotesque. Spontaneous expression was arrested. My mind perceived a goblin garden, and was caught in it. The place grimaced at me.

With the flowers it was similar, though far more difficult to detect in detail for description. I saw the smaller vegetable growth as impish, half-malicious. Even the terraces sloped ill, as though their ends had sagged since they had been so lavishly constructed; their varying angles gave a queerly bewildering aspect to their sequence that was unpleasant to the eye. One might wander among their deceptive lengths and get lost --lost among open terraces!--with the house quite close at hand. Unhomely seemed the entire garden, unable to give repose, restlessness in it everywhere, almost strife, and discord certainly.

Moreover, the garden grew into the house, the house into the garden, and in both was this idea of resistance to the natural--the spirit that says No to joy. All over it I was aware of the effort to achieve another end, the struggle to burst forth and escape into free, spontaneous expression that should be happy and natural, yet the effort forever frustrated by the weight of this dark shadow that rendered it abortive. Life crawled aside into a channel that was a cul-de-sac, then turned horribly upon itself. Instead of blossom and fruit, there were weeds. This approach of life I was conscious of-- then dismal failure. There was no fulfillment. Nothing happened.

And so, through this singular mood, I came a little nearer to understand the unpure thing that had stammered out into expression through my sister's talent. For the unpure is merely negative; it has no existence; it is but the cramped expression of what is true, stammering its way brokenly over false boundaries that seek to limit and confine. Great, full expression of anything is pure, whereas here was only the incomplete, unfinished, and therefore ugly. There was a strife and pain and desire to escape. I found myself shrinking from house and grounds as one shrinks from the touch of the mentally arrested, those in whom life has turned awry. There was almost mutilation in it.

Past items, too, now flocked to confirm this feeling that I walked, liberty captured and half-maimed, in a monstrous garden. I remembered days of rain that refreshed the countryside, but left these grounds, cracked with the summer heat, unsatisfied and thirsty; and how the big winds, that cleaned the woods and fields elsewhere, crawled here with difficulty through the dense foliage that protected The Towers from the North and West and East. They were ineffective, sluggish currents. There was no real wind. Nothing happened. I began to realize--far more clearly than in my sister's fanciful explanation about "layers"--that here were many contrary influences at work, mutually destructive of one another. House and grounds were not haunted merely; they were the arena of past thinking and feeling, perhaps of terrible, impure beliefs, each striving to suppress the others, yet no one of them achieving supremacy because no one of them was strong enough, no one of them was true. Each, moreover, tried to win me over, though only one was able to reach my mind at all. For some obscure reason--possibly because my temperament had a natural bias towards the grotesque--it was the goblin layer. With me, it was the line of least resistance....

In my own thoughts this "goblin garden" revealed, of

course, merely my personal interpretation. I felt now objectively what long ago my mind had felt subjectively. My work, essential sign of spontaneous life with me, had stopped dead; production had become impossible.

I stood now considerably closer to the cause of this sterility. The Cause, rather, turned bolder, had stepped insolently nearer. Nothing happened anywhere; house, garden, mind alike were barren, abortive, torn by the strife of frustrate impulse, ugly, hateful, sinful. Yet behind it all was still the desire of life--desire to escape--accomplish. Hope--an intolerable hope--I became startlingly aware--crowned torture.

And, realizing this, though in some part of me where Reason lost her hold, there rose upon me then another and a darker thing that caught me by the throat and made me shrink with a sense of revulsion that touched actual loathing. I knew instantly whence it came, this wave of abhorrence and disgust, for even while I saw red and felt revolt rise in me, it seemed that I grew partially aware of the layer next below the goblin. I perceived the existence of this deeper stratum. One opened the way for the other, as it were. There were so many, yet all inter-related; to admit one was to clear the way for all. If I lingered I should be caught--horribly. They struggled with such violence for supremacy among themselves, however, that this latest uprising was instantly smothered and crushed back, though not before a glimpse had been revealed to me, and the redness in my thoughts transferred itself to color my surroundings thickly and appallingly--with blood. This lurid aspect drenched the garden, smeared the terraces, lent to the very soil a tinge as of sacrificial rites, that choked the breath in me, while it seemed to fix me to the earth my feet so longed to leave. It was so revolting that at the same time I felt a dreadful curiosity as of fascination--I wished to stay. Between these contrary impulses I think I actually reeled a moment, transfixed by a fascination of the Awful. Through the lighter goblin veil I felt myself sinking down, down, down into this turgid layer that was so much more violent and so much more ancient. The upper layer, indeed, seemed fairy by comparison with this terror born of the lust for blood, thick with the anguish of human sacrificial victims.

Upper! Then I was already sinking; my feet were caught; I was actually in it! What atavistic strain, hidden deep within me, had been touched into vile response, giving this flash of intuitive comprehension, I cannot say. The coatings laid on by civilization are probably thin enough in all of us. I made a supreme effort. The sun and wind came back. I could almost swear I opened my eyes. Something very atrocious surged back into the depths, carrying with it a thought of tangled woods, of big stones standing in a circle, motion-less, white figures, the one form bound with ropes, and the ghastly gleam of the knife. Like smoke upon a battlefield, it rolled away....

I was standing on the gravel path below the second terrace when the familiar goblin garden danced back again, doubly grotesque now, doubly mocking, yet, by way of contrast, al-most welcome. My glimpse into the depths was momentary, it seems, and had passed utterly away.

The common world rushed back with a sense of glad relief, yet ominous now forever, I felt, for the knowledge of what its past had built upon. In street, in theater, in the festivities of friends, in music-room or playing field, even indeed in church--how could the memory of what I had seen and felt leave its hideous trace? The very structure of my Thought, it seemed to me, was stained.

What has been thought by others can never be obliterated until....

With a start my reverie broke and fled, scattered by a vi-olent sound that I recognized for the first time in my life as wholly desirable. The returning motor meant that my host-ess was back.

Yet, so urgent had been my temporary obsession, that my first presentation of her was--well, not as I knew her now. Floating along with a face of anguished torture I saw Ma-bel, a mere effigy captured by others' thinking, pass down into those depths of fire and blood that only just had closed beneath my feet. She dipped away. She vanished, her fading eyes turned to the last towards some savior who had failed her. And that strange intolerable hope was in her face.

The mystery of the place was pretty thick about me just then. It was the fall of dusk, and the ghost of slanting sunshine was as unreal as though badly painted. The garden stood at attention all about me. I cannot explain it, but I can tell it, I think, exactly as it happened, for it remains vivid in me forever--that, for the first time, something almost happened, myself apparently the combining link through which it pressed towards delivery:

I had already turned towards the house. In my mind were pictures--not actual thoughts--of the motor, tea on the verandah, my sister, Mabel-- when there came behind me this tumultuous, awful rush--as I left the garden. The ugliness, the pain, the striving to escape, the whole negative and suppressed agony that was the Place, focused that second into a concentrated effort to produce a result. It was a blinding tempest of long-frustrate desire that heaved at me, surging appallingly behind me like an anguished mob. I was in the act of crossing the frontier into my normal self again, when it came, catching fearfully at my skirts. I might use an entire dictionary of descriptive adjectives yet come no nearer to it than this--the conception of a huge assemblage determined to escape with me, or to snatch me back among themselves. My legs trembled for an instant, and I caught my breath-- then turned and ran as fast as possible up the ugly terraces.

At the same instant, as though the clanging of an iron gate cut short the unfinished phrase, I thought the beginning of an awful thing:

"The Damned ..."

Like this it rushed after me from that goblin garden that had sought to keep me:

"The Damned!"

For there was sound in it. I know full well it was subjective, not actually heard at all; yet somehow sound was in it--a great volume, roaring and booming thunderously, far away, and below me. The sentence dipped back into the depths that gave it birth, unfinished. Its completion was prevented. As usual, nothing happened. But it drove behind me like a hurricane as I ran towards the house, and the sound of it I can only liken to those terrible undertones you may hear

standing beside Niagara. They lie behind the mere crash of
the falling flood, within it somehow, not audible to all--felt
rather than definitely heard.

It seemed to echo back from the surface of those sagging
terraces as I flew across their sloping ends, for it was somehow underneath them. It was in the rustle of the wind that
stirred the skirts of the drooping wellingtonias. The beds of
formal flowers passed it on to the creepers, red as blood, that
crept over the unsightly building. Into the structure of the
vulgar and forbidding house it sank away; The Towers took
it home. The uncomely doors and windows seemed almost
like mouths that had uttered the words themselves, and on
the upper floors at that very moment I saw two maids in the
act of closing them again.

And on the verandah, as I arrived breathless, and shaken
in my soul, Frances and Mabel, standing by the tea table,
looked up to greet me. In the faces of both were clearly legible the signs of shock. They watched me coming, yet so full
of their own distress that they hardly noticed the state in
which I came. In the face of my hostess, however, I read another and a bigger thing than in the face of Frances. Mabel
knew. She had experienced what I had experienced. She had
heard that awful sentence I had heard but heard it not for the
first time; heard it, moreover, I verily believe, complete and
to its dreadful end.

"Bill, did you hear that curious noise just now?" Frances
asked it sharply before I could say a word. Her manner was
confused; she looked straight at me; and there was a tremor
in her voice she could not hide.

"There's wind about," I said, "wind in the trees and sweeping round the walls. It's risen rather suddenly." My voice faltered rather.

"No. It wasn't wind," she insisted, with a significance
meant for me alone, but badly hidden. "It was more like
distant thunder, we thought. How you ran too!" she added.
"What a pace you came across the terraces!"

I knew instantly from the way she said it that they both
had already heard the sound before and were anxious to
know if I had heard it, and how. My interpretation was what

they sought.

"It was a curiously deep sound, I admit. It may have been big guns at sea," I suggested, "forts or cruisers practicing. The coast isn't so very far, and with the wind in the right direction--"

The expression on Mabel's face stopped me dead.

"Like huge doors closing," she said softly in her colorless voice, "enormous metal doors shutting against a mass of people clamoring to get out." The gravity, the note of hopelessness in her tones, was shocking.

Frances had gone into the house the instant Mabel began to speak. "I'm cold," she had said; "I think I'll get a shawl." Mabel and I were alone. I believe it was the first time we had been really alone since I arrived. She looked up from the teacups, fixing her pallid eyes on mine. She had made a question of the sentence.

"You hear it like that?" I asked innocently. I purposely used the present tense.

She changed her stare from one eye to the other; it was absolutely expressionless. My sister's step sounded on the floor of the room behind us.

"If only--" Mabel began, then stopped, and my own feelings leaping out instinctively completed the sentence I felt was in her mind:

"--something would happen."

She instantly corrected me. I had caught her thought, yet somehow phrased it wrongly.

"We could escape!" She lowered her tone a little, saying it hurriedly. The "we" amazed and horrified me; but something in her voice and manner struck me utterly dumb. There was ice and terror in it. It was a dying woman speaking--a lost and hopeless soul.

In that atrocious moment I hardly noticed what was said exactly, but I remember that my sister returned with a grey shawl about her shoulders, and that Mabel said, in her ordinary voice again, "It is chilly, yes; let's have tea inside," and that two maids, one of them the grenadier, speedily carried the loaded trays into the morning-room and put a match to the logs in the great open fireplace. It was, after all, foolish to

risk the sharp evening air, for dusk was falling steadily, and even the sunshine of the day just fading could not turn autumn into summer. I was the last to come in. Just as I left the verandah a large black bird swooped down in front of me past the pillars; it dropped from overhead, swerved abruptly to one side as it caught sight of me, and flapped heavily towards the shrubberies on the left of the terraces, where it disappeared into the gloom. It flew very low, very close. And it startled me, I think because in some way it seemed like my Shadow materialized--as though the dark horror that was rising everywhere from house and garden, then settling back so thickly yet so imperceptibly upon us all, were incarnated in that whirring creature that passed between the daylight and the coming night.

I stood a moment, wondering if it would appear again, before I followed the others indoors, and as I was in the act of closing the windows after me, I caught a glimpse of a figure on the lawn. It was some distance away, on the other side of the shrubberies, in fact where the bird had vanished. But in spite of the twilight that half magnified, half obscured it, the identity was unmistakable. I knew the housekeeper's stiff walk too well to be deceived. "Mrs. Marsh taking the air," I said to myself. I felt the necessity of saying it, and I wondered why she was doing so at this particular hour. If I had other thoughts they were so vague, and so quickly and utterly suppressed, that I cannot recall them sufficiently to relate them here.

And, once indoors, it was to be expected that there would come explanation, discussion, conversation, at any rate, regarding the singular noise and its cause, some uttered evidence of the mood that had been strong enough to drive us all inside. Yet there was none. Each of us purposely, and with various skill, ignored it. We talked little, and when we did it was of anything in the world but that. Personally, I experienced a touch of that same bewilderment which had come over me during my first talk with Frances on the evening of my arrival, for I recall now the acute tension, and the hope, yet dread, that one or other of us must sooner or later introduce the subject. It did not happen, however; no reference was made to it even remotely. It was the presence of Mabel, I felt positive, that prohibited. As soon might we have discussed Death in the bedroom of a dying woman.

The only scrap of conversation I remember, where all was ordinary and commonplace, was when Mabel spoke casually to the grenadier asking why Mrs. Marsh had omitted to do something or other--what it was I forget-- and that the maid replied respectfully that "Mrs. Marsh was very sorry, but her 'and still pained her." I enquired, though so casually that I scarcely know what prompted the words, whether she had injured herself severely, and the reply, "She upset a lamp and burnt herself," was said in a tone that made me feel my curiosity was indiscreet, "but she always has an excuse for not doing things she ought to do." The little bit of conversation remained with me, and I remember particularly the quick way Frances interrupted and turned the talk upon the delinquencies of servants in general, telling incidents of her own at our flat with a volubility that perhaps seemed forced, and that certainly did not encourage general talk as it may have been intended to do. We lapsed into silence immediately she finished.

But for all our care and all our calculated silence, each knew that something had, in these last moments, come very close; it had brushed us in passing; it had retired; and I am inclined to think now that the large dark thing I saw, riding the dusk, probably bird of prey, was in some sense a symbol of it in my mind--that actually there had been no bird at all, I mean, but that my mood of apprehension and dismay had formed the vivid picture in my thoughts. It had swept past us, it had retreated, but it was now, at this moment, in hiding very close. And it was watching us.

Perhaps, too, it was mere coincidence that I encountered Mrs. Marsh, his housekeeper, several times that evening in the short interval between tea and dinner, and that on each occasion the sight of this gaunt, half-saturnine woman fed my prejudice against her. Once, on my way to the telephone, I ran into her just where the passage is somewhat jammed by a square table carrying the Chinese gong, a grandfather's clock and a box of croquet mallets. We both gave way, then

both advanced, then again gave way--simultaneously. It seemed, impossible to pass. We stepped with decision to the same side, finally colliding in the middle, while saying those futile little things, half apology, half excuse, that are inevitable at such times. In the end she stood upright against the wall for me to pass, taking her place against the very door I wished to open. It was ludicrous.

"Excuse me--I was just going in--to telephone," I explained. And she sidled off, murmuring apologies, but opening the door for me while she did so. Our hands met a moment on the handle.

There was a second's awkwardness--it was too stupid. I remembered her injury, and by way of something to say, I enquired after it. She thanked me; it was entirely healed now, but it might have been much worse; and there was something about the "mercy of the Lord" that I didn't quite catch. While telephoning, however--London call, and my attention focused on it--realized sharply that this was the first time I had spoken with her; also, that I had--touched her.

It happened to be a Sunday, and the lines were clear. I got my connection quickly, and the incident was forgotten while my thoughts went up to London. On my way upstairs, then, the woman came back into my mind, so that I recalled other things about her--how she seemed all over the house, in unlikely places often; how I had caught her sitting in the hall alone that night; how she was forever coming and going with her lugubrious visage and that untidy hair at the back that had made me laugh three years ago with the idea that it looked singed or burnt; and how the impression on my first arrival at The Towers was that this woman somehow kept alive, though its evidence was outwardly suppressed, the influence of her late employer and of his somber teachings. Somewhere with her was associated the idea of punishment, vindictiveness, revenge. I remembered again suddenly my odd notion that she sought to keep her present mistress here, a prisoner in this bleak and comfortless house, and that really, in spite of her obsequious silence, she was intensely opposed to the change of thought that had reclaimed Mabel to a happier view of life.

All this in a passing second flashed in review before me, and I discovered, or at any rate reconstructed, the real Mrs. Marsh. She was decidedly in the Shadow. More, she stood in the forefront of it, stealthily leading an assault, as it were, against The Towers and its occupants, as though, consciously or unconsciously, she labored incessantly to this hateful end.

I can only judge that some state of nervousness in me permitted the series of insignificant thoughts to assume this dramatic shape, and that what had gone before prepared the way and led her up at the head of so formidable a procession. I relate it exactly as it came to me. My nerves were doubtless somewhat on edge by now. Otherwise I should hardly have been a prey to the exaggeration at all. I seemed open to so many strange, impressions.

Nothing else, perhaps, can explain my ridiculous conversation with her, when, for the third time that evening, I came suddenly upon the woman half-way down the stairs, standing by an open window as if in the act of listening. She was dressed in black, a black shawl over her square shoulders and black gloves on her big, broad hands. Two black objects, prayer books apparently, she clasped, and on her head she wore a bonnet with shaking beads of jet. At first I did not know her, as I came running down upon her from the landing; it was only when she stood aside to let me pass that I saw her profile against the tapestry and recognized Mrs. Marsh. And to catch her on the front stairs, dressed like this, struck me as incongruous--impertinent. I paused in my dangerous descent. Through the opened window came the sound of bells-- church bells--a sound more depressing to me than superstition, and as nauseating. Though the action was ill judged, I obeyed the sudden prompting--was it a secret desire to attack, perhaps?--and spoke to her.

"Been to church, I suppose, Mrs. Marsh?" I said. "Or just going, perhaps?"

Her face, as she looked up a second to reply, was like an iron doll that moved its lips and turned its eyes, but made no other imitation of life at all.

"Some of us still goes, sir," she said unctuously.

It was respectful enough, yet the implied judgment of the rest of the world made me almost angry. A deferential insolence lay behind the affected meekness.

"For those who believe no doubt it is helpful," I smiled. "True religion brings peace and happiness, I'm sure--joy, Mrs. Marsh, joy!" I found keen satisfaction in the emphasis.

She looked at me like a knife. I cannot describe the implacable thing that shone in her fixed, stern eyes, nor the shadow of felt darkness that stole across her face. She glittered. I felt hate in her. I knew-- she knew too--who was in the thoughts of us both at that moment.

She replied softly, never forgetting her place for an instant:

"There is joy, sir--in 'eaven--over one sinner that repenteth, and in church there goes up prayer to Gawd for those 'oo--well, for the others, sir, 'oo--"

She cut short her sentence thus. The gloom about her as she said it was like the gloom about a hearse, a tomb, a darkness of great hopeless dungeons. My tongue ran on of itself with a kind of bitter satisfaction:

"We must believe there are no others, Mrs. Marsh. Salvation, you know, would be such a failure if there were. No merciful, all-foreseeing God could ever have devised such a fearful plan--"

Her voice, interrupting me, seemed to rise out of the bowels of the earth:

"They rejected the salvation when it was offered to them, sir, on earth."

"But you wouldn't have them tortured forever because of one mistake in ignorance," I said, fixing her with my eye. "Come now, would you, Mrs. Marsh? No God worth worshipping could permit such cruelty. Think a moment what it means."

She stared at me, a curious expression in her stupid eyes. It seemed to me as though the "woman" in her revolted, while yet she dared not suffer her grim belief to trip. That is, she would willingly have had it otherwise but for a terror that prevented.

"We may pray for them, sir, and we do--we may 'ope." She dropped her eyes to the carpet.

"Good, good!" I put in cheerfully, sorry now that I had spoken at all. "That's more hopeful, at any rate isn't it?"

She murmured something about Abraham's bosom, and the "time of salvation not being forever," as I tried to pass her. Then a half gesture that she made stopped me. There was something more she wished to say--to ask. She looked up furtively. In her eyes I saw the "woman" peering out through fear.

"Per'aps, sir." she faltered, as though lightning must strike her dead, "per'aps, would you think, a drop of cold water, given in His name, might moisten--?"

But I stopped her, for the foolish talk had lasted long enough. "Of course," I exclaimed, "of course. For God is love, remember, and love means charity, tolerance, sympathy, and sparing others pain," and I hurried past her, determined to end the outrageous conversation for which yet I knew myself entirely to blame. Behind me, she stood stock-still for several minutes, half bewildered, half alarmed, as I suspected. I caught the fragment of another sentence, one word of it, rather--"punishment"--but the rest escaped me. Her arrogance and condescending tolerance exasperated me, while I was at the same time secretly pleased that I might have touched some string of remorse or sympathy in her after all. Her belief was iron; she dared not let it go; yet somewhere underneath there lurked the germ of a wholesome revulsion. She would help "them"--if she dared. Her question proved it.

Half ashamed of myself, I turned and crossed the hail quickly lest I should be tempted to say more, and in me was a disagreeable sensation as though I had just left the Incurable Ward of some great hospital. A reaction caught me as of nausea. Ugh! I wanted such people cleansed by fire. They seemed to me as centers of contamination whose vicious thoughts flowed out to stain God's glorious world. I saw myself, Frances, Mabel too especially, on the rack, while that odious figure of cruelty and darkness stood over us and ordered the awful handles turned in order that we might be "saved"--forced, that is, to think and believe exactly as she thought and believed.

I found relief for my somewhat childish indignation by

letting myself loose upon the organ then. The flood of Bach and Beethoven brought back the sense of proportion. It proved, however, at the same time that there had been this growth of distortion in me, and that it had been provided apparently by my closer contact--for the first time--with that funereal personality, the woman who, like her master, believed that all holding views of God that differed from her own, must be damned eternally. It gave me, moreover, some faint clue perhaps, though a clue I was unequal of following up, to the nature of the strife and terror and frustrate influence in the house. That housekeeper had to do with it. She kept it alive. Her thought was like a spell she waved above her mistress's head.

VII

That night I was wakened by a hurried tapping at my door, and before I could answer, Frances stood beside my bed. She had switched on the light as she came in. Her hair fell straggling over her dressing gown. Her face was deathly pale, its expression so distraught it was almost haggard.

The eyes were very wide. She looked almost like another woman.

She was whispering at a great pace: "Bill, Bill, wake up, quick!"

"I am awake. What is it?" I whispered too. I was startled.

"Listen!" was all she said. Her eyes stared into vacancy.

There was not a sound in the great house. The wind had dropped, and all was still. Only the tapping seemed to continue endlessly in my brain. The clock on the mantelpiece pointed to half-past two.

"I heard nothing, Frances. What is it?" I rubbed my eyes; I had been very deeply asleep.

"Listen!" she repeated very softly, holding up one finger and turning her eyes towards the door she had left ajar. Her usual calmness had deserted her. She was in the grip of some distressing terror.

For a full minute we held our breath and listened. Then her eyes rolled round again and met my own, and her skin went even whiter than before.

"It woke me," she said beneath her breath, and moving a step nearer to my bed. "It was the Noise." Even her whisper trembled.

"The Noise!" The word repeated itself dully of its own accord. I would rather it had been anything in the world but that--earthquake, foreign cannon, collapse of the house above our heads! "The Noise, Frances! Are you sure?" I was playing really for a little time.

"It was like thunder. At first I thought it was thunder. But a minute later it came again--from underground. It's appalling." She muttered the words, her voice not properly under control.

There was a pause of perhaps a minute, and then we both spoke at once. We said foolish, obvious things that neither of us believed in for a second. The roof had fallen in, there were burglars downstairs, the safes had been blown open. It was to comfort each other as children do that we said these things; also it was to gain further time.

"There's some one in the house, of course," I heard my voice say finally, as I sprang out of bed and hurried into dressing gown and slippers. "Don't be alarmed. I'll go down and see," and from the drawer I took a pistol it was my habit to carry everywhere with me. I loaded it carefully while Frances stood stock-still beside the bed and watched. I moved towards the open door.

"You stay here, Frances," I whispered, the beating of my heart making the words uneven, "while I go down and make a search. Lock yourself in, girl. Nothing can happen to you. It was downstairs, you said?"

"Underneath," she answered faintly, pointing through the floor.

She moved suddenly between me and the door.

"Listen! Hark!" she said, the eyes in her face quite fixed; "it's coming again," and she turned her head to catch the slightest sound. I stood there watching her, and while I watched her, shook.

But nothing stirred. From the halls below rose only the whirr and quiet ticking of the numerous clocks. The blind by the open window behind us flapped out a little into the room as the draught caught it.

"I'll come with you, Bill--to the next floor," she broke the silence. "Then I'll stay with Mabel--till you come up again." The blind sank down with a long sigh as she said it.

The question jumped to my lips before I could repress it:

"Mabel is awake. She heard it too?"

I hardly know why horror caught me at her answer. All was so vague and terrible as we stood there playing the great game of this sinister house where nothing ever happened.

"We met in the passage. She was on her way to me."

What shook in me, shook inwardly. Frances, I mean, did not see it. I had the feeling just that the Noise was upon us, that any second it would boom and roar about our ears. But the deep silence held. I only heard my sister's little whisper coming across the room in answer to my question:

"Then what is Mabel doing now?"

And her reply proved that she was yielding at last beneath the dreadful tension, for she spoke at once, unable longer to keep up the pretence. With a kind of relief, as it were, she said it out, looking helplessly at me like a child:

"She is weeping and gna--"

My expression must have stopped her. I believe I clapped both hands upon her mouth, though when I realized things clearly again, I found they were covering my own ears instead. It was a moment of unutterable horror. The revulsion I felt was actually physical. It would have given me pleasure to fire off all the five chambers of my pistol into the air above my head; the sound--a definite, wholesome sound that explained itself--would have been a positive relief. Other feelings, though, were in me too, all over me, rushing to and fro. It was vain to seek their disentanglement; it was impossible. I confess that I experienced, among them, a touch of paralyzing fear--though for a moment only; it passed as sharply as it came, leaving me with a violent flush of blood to the face such as bursts of anger bring, followed abruptly by an icy perspiration over the entire body. Yet I may honestly avow that it was not ordinary personal fear I felt, nor any common dread of physical injury. It was, rather, a vast, impersonal shrinking--a sympathetic shrinking--from the agony and

terror that countless others, somewhere, somehow, felt for themselves. The first sensation of a prison overwhelmed me in that instant, of bitter strife and frenzied suffering, and the fiery torture of the yearning to escape that was yet hopelessly uttered.... It was of incredible power. It was real. The vain, intolerable hope swept over me.

I mastered myself, though hardly knowing how, and took my sister's hand. It was as cold as ice, as I led her firmly to the door and out into the passage. Apparently she noticed nothing of my so near collapse, for I caught her whisper as we went. "You are brave, Bill; splendidly brave."

The upper corridors of the great sleeping house were brightly lit; on her way to me she had turned on every electric switch her hand could reach; and as we passed the final flight of stairs to the floor below, I heard a door shut softly and knew that Mabel had been listening--waiting for us. I led my sister up to it. She knocked, and the door was opened cautiously an inch or so. The room was pitch black. I caught no glimpse of Mabel standing there. Frances turned to me with a hurried whisper, "Billy, you will be careful, won't you?" and went in. I just had time to answer that I would not be long, and Frances to reply, "You'll find us here" when the door closed and cut her sentence short before its end.

But it was not alone the closing door that took the final words. Frances--by the way she disappeared I knew it--had made a swift and violent movement into the darkness that was as though she sprang. She leaped upon that other woman who stood back among the shadows, for, simultaneously with the clipping of the sentence, another sound was also stopped--stifled, smothered, choked back lest I should also hear it. Yet not in time. I heard it--a hard and horrible sound that explained both the leap and the abrupt cessation of the whispered words.

I stood irresolute a moment. It was as though all the bones had been withdrawn from my body, so that I must sink and fall. That sound plucked them out, and plucked out my self-possession with them. I am not sure that it was a sound I had ever heard before, though children, I half remembered, made it sometimes in blind rages when they knew not what they did. In a grown-up person certainly I had never known it. I associated it with animals rather--horribly. In the history of the world, no doubt, it has been common enough, alas, but fortunately today there can be but few who know it, or would recognize it even when heard. The bones shot back into my body the same instant, but red-hot and burning; the brief instant of irresolution passed; I was torn between the desire to break down the door and enter, and to run--run for my life from a thing I dared not face.

Out of the horrid tumult, then, I adopted neither course. Without reflection, certainly without analysis of what was best to do for my sister, myself or Mabel, I took up my action where it had been interrupted. I turned from the awful door and moved slowly towards the head of the stairs.

But that dreadful little sound came with me. I believe my own teeth chattered. It seemed all over the house--in the empty halls that opened into the long passages towards the music-room, and even in the grounds outside the building. From the lawns and barren garden, from the ugly terraces themselves, it rose into the night, and behind it came a curious driving sound, incomplete, unfinished, as of wailing for deliverance, the wailing of desperate souls in anguish, the dull and dry beseeching of hopeless spirits in prison.

That I could have taken the little sound from the bedroom where I actually heard it, and spread it thus over the entire house and grounds, is evidence, perhaps, of the state my nerves were in.

The wailing assuredly was in my mind alone. But the longer I hesitated, the more difficult became my task, and, gathering up my dressing gown, lest I should trip in the darkness, I passed slowly down the staircase into the hail below. I carried neither candle nor matches; every switch in room and corridor was known to me. The covering of darkness was indeed rather comforting than otherwise, for if it prevented seeing, it also prevented being seen. The heavy pistol, knocking against my thigh as I moved, made me feel I was carrying a child's toy, foolishly. I experienced in every nerve that primitive vast dread which is the Thrill of darkness. Merely the child in me was comforted by that pistol.

The night was not entirely black; the iron bars across the glass front door were visible, and, equally, I discerned the big, stiff wooden chairs in the hall, the gaping fireplace, the upright pillars supporting the staircase, the round table in the center with its books and flower-vases, and the basket that held visitors' cards. There, too, was the stick and umbrella stand and the shelf with railway guides, directory, and telegraph forms. Clocks ticked everywhere with sounds like quiet footfalls. Light fell here and there in patches from the floor above. I stood a moment in the hall, letting my eyes grow more accustomed to the gloom, while deciding on a plan of search. I made out the ivy trailing outside over one of the big windows ... and then the tall clock by the front door made a grating noise deep down inside its body--it was the Presentation clock, large and hideous, given by the congregation of his church--and, dreading the booming strike it seemed to threaten, I made a quick decision. If others beside myself were about in the night, the sound of that striking might cover their approach.

So I tiptoed to the right, where the passage led towards the dining room. In the other direction were the morning- and drawing rooms, both little used, and various other rooms beyond that had been his, generally now kept locked. I thought of my sister, waiting upstairs with that frightened woman for my return. I went quickly, yet stealthily.

And, to my surprise, the door of the dining room was open. It had been opened. I paused on the threshold, staring about me. I think I fully expected to see a figure blocked in the shadows against the heavy sideboard, or looming on the other side beneath his portrait. But the room was empty; I felt it empty. Through the wide bow-windows that gave on to the verandah came an uncertain glimmer that even shone reflected in the polished surface of the dinner-table, and again I perceived the stiff outline of chairs, waiting tenantless all round it, two larger ones with high carved backs at either end. The monkey trees on the upper terrace, too, were visible outside against the sky, and the solemn crests of the wellingtonias on the terraces below. The enormous dock on the mantelpiece ticked very slowly, as though its machinery were running down, and I made out the pale round patch that was its face. Resisting my first inclination to turn the lights up--my hand had gone so far as to finger the friendly knob--I crossed the room so carefully that no single board creaked, nor a single chair, as I rested a hand upon its back, moved on the parquet flooring. I turned neither to the right nor left, nor did I once look back.

I went towards the long corridor filled with priceless objets d'art, that led through various antechambers into the spacious music-room, and only at the mouth of this corridor did I next halt a moment in uncertainty. For this long corridor, lit faintly by high windows on the left from the verandah, was very narrow, owing to the mass of shelves and fancy tables it contained. It was not that I feared to knock over precious things as I went, but, that, because of its ungenerous width, there would be no room to pass another person--if I met one. And the certainty had suddenly come upon me that somewhere in this corridor another person at this actual moment stood. Here, somehow, amid all this dead atmosphere of furniture and impersonal emptiness, lay the hint of a living human presence; and with such conviction did it come upon me, that my hand instinctively gripped the pistol in my pocket before I could even think. Either some one had passed along this corridor just before me, or some one lay waiting at its farther end--withdrawn or flattened into one of the little recesses, to let me pass. It was the person who had opened the door. And the blood ran from my heart as I realized it.

It was not courage that sent me on, but rather a strong impulsion from behind that made it impossible to retreat: the feeling that a throng pressed at my back, drawing nearer and nearer; that I was already half surrounded, swept, dragged, coaxed into a vast prison-house where there was wailing and gnashing of teeth, where their worm dieth not and their fire is not quenched. I can neither explain nor justify the storm of irrational emotion that swept me as I stood in that moment, staring down the length of the silent corridor towards the music-room at the far end, I can only repeat that no personal bravery sent me down it, but that the negative emotion of fear was swamped in this vast sea of pity and commiseration for others that surged upon me.

My senses, at least, were no whit confused; if anything, my brain registered impressions with keener accuracy than usual. I noticed, for instance, that the two swinging doors of baize that cut the corridor into definite lengths, making little rooms of the spaces between them, were both wide-open--in the dim light no mean achievement. Also that the fronds of a palm plant, some ten feet in front of me, still stirred gently from the air of someone who had recently gone past them. The long green leaves waved to and fro like hands. Then I went stealthily forward down the narrow space, proud even that I had this command of myself, and so carefully that my feet made no sound upon the Japanese matting on the floor.

It was a journey that seemed timeless. I have no idea how fast or slow I went, but I remember that I deliberately examined articles on each side of me, peering with particular closeness into the recesses of wall and window. I passed the first baize doors, and the passage beyond them widened out to hold shelves of books; there were sofas and small reading-tables against the wall.

It narrowed again presently, as I entered the second stretch. The windows here were higher and smaller, and marble statuettes of classical subject lined the walls, watching me like figures of the dead. Their white and shining faces saw me, yet made no sign. I passed next between the second baize doors. They, too, had been fastened back with hooks against the wall. Thus all doors were open--had been recently opened.

And so, at length, I found myself in the final widening of the corridor which formed an antechamber to the music-room itself. It had been used formerly to hold the overflow of meetings. No door separated it from the great hall beyond, but heavy curtains hung usually to close it off, and these curtains were invariably drawn. They now stood wide. And here--I can merely state the impression that came upon me--I knew myself at last surrounded. The throng that pressed behind me, also surged in front: facing me in the big room, and waiting for my entry, stood a multitude; on

either side of me, in the very air above my head, the vast assemblage paused upon my coming. The pause, however, was
momentary, for instantly the deep, tumultuous movement
was resumed that yet was silent as a cavern underground. I
felt the agony that was in it, the passionate striving, the awful
struggle to escape. The semi-darkness held beseeching faces
that fought to press themselves upon my vision, yearning yet
hopeless eyes, lips scorched and dry, mouths that opened to
implore but found no craved delivery in actual words, and a
fury of misery and hate that made the life in me stop dead,
frozen by the horror of vain pity. That intolerable, vain Hope
was everywhere.

And the multitude, it came to me, was not a single multitude, but many; for, as soon as one huge division pressed too
close upon the edge of escape, it was dragged back by another and prevented. The wild host was divided against itself.
Here dwelt the Shadow I had "imagined" weeks ago, and in
it struggled armies of lost souls as in the depths of some bot-
tomless pit whence there is no escape. The layers mingled,
fighting against themselves in endless torture. It was in this
great Shadow I had clairvoyantly seen Mabel, but about its
fearful mouth, I now was certain, hovered another figure of
darkness, a figure who sought to keep it in existence, since to
her thought were due those lampless depths of woe without
escape.... Towards me the multitudes now surged.

It was a sound and a movement that brought me back into
myself. The great dock at the farther end of the room just
then struck the hour of three. That was the sound. And the
movement--? I was aware that a figure was passing across
the distant center of the floor. Instantly I dropped back into
the arena of my little human terror. My hand again clutched
stupidly at the pistol butt. I drew back into the folds of the
heavy curtain. And the figure advanced.

I remember every detail. At first it seemed to me enor-
mous--this advancing shadow--far beyond human scale;
but as it came nearer, I measured it, though not consciously,
by the organ pipes that gleamed in faint colors, just above
its gradual soft approach. It passed them, already halfway
across the great room. I saw then that its stature was that

of ordinary men. The prolonged booming of the clock died away. I heard the footfall, shuffling upon the polished boards. I heard another sound--a voice, low and monotonous, droning as in prayer. The figure was speaking. It was a woman. And she carried in both hands before her a small object that faintly shimmered--a glass of water. And then I recognized her.

There was still an instant's time before she reached me, and I made use of it. I shrank back, flattening myself against the wall. Her voice ceased a moment, as she turned and carefully drew the curtains together behind her, dosing them with one hand. Oblivious of my presence, though she actually touched my dressing gown with the hand that pulled the cords, she resumed her dreadful, solemn march, disappearing at length down the long vista of the corridor like a shadow.

But as she passed me, her voice began again, so that I heard each word distinctly as she uttered it, her head aloft, her figure upright, as though she moved at the head of a procession:

"A drop of cold water, given in His name, shall moisten their burning tongues."

It was repeated monotonously over and over again, droning down into the distance as she went, until at length both voice and figure faded into the shadows at the farther end.

For a time, I have no means of measuring precisely, I stood in that dark corner, pressing my back against the wall, and would have drawn the curtains down to hide me had I dared to stretch an arm out. The dread that presently the woman would return passed gradually away. I realized that the air had emptied, the crowd her presence had stirred into activity had retreated; I was alone in the gloomy under-space of the odious building.... Then I remembered suddenly again the terrified women waiting for me on that upper landing; and realized that my skin was wet and freezing cold after a profuse perspiration. I prepared to retrace my steps. I remember the effort it cost me to leave the support of the wall and covering darkness of my corner, and step out into the grey light of the corridor. At first I sidled, then, find-

ing this mode of walking impossible, turned my face boldly and walked quickly, regardless that my dressing gown set the precious objects shaking as I passed. A wind that sighed mournfully against the high, small windows seemed to have got inside the corridor as well; it felt so cold; and every moment I dreaded to see the outline of the woman's figure as she waited in recess or angle against the wall for me to pass.

Was there another thing I dreaded even more? I cannot say. I only know that the first baize doors had swung to behind me, and the second ones were close at hand, when the great dim thunder caught me, pouring up with prodigious volume so that it, seemed to roll out from another world. It shook the very bowels of the building. I was closer to it than that other time, when it had followed me from the goblin garden. There was strength and hardness in it, as of metal reverberation. Some touch of numbness, almost of paralysis, must surely have been upon me that I felt no actual terror, for I remember even turning and standing still to hear it better. "That is the Noise," my thought ran stupidly, and I think I whispered it aloud; "the Doors are closing." The wind outside against the windows was audible, so it cannot have been really loud, yet to me it was the biggest, deepest sound I have ever heard, but so far away, with such awful remoteness in it, that I had to doubt my own ears at the same time. It seemed underground--the rumbling of earthquake gates that shut remorselessly within the rocky Earth--stupendous ultimate thunder. They were shut off from help again. The doors had closed.

I felt a storm of pity, an agony of bitter, futile hate sweep through me. My memory of the figure changed then. The Woman with the glass of cooling water had stepped down from Heaven; but the Man--or was it Men? --who smeared this terrible layer of belief and Thought upon the world!...

I crossed the dining room--it was fancy, of course, that held my eyes from glancing at the portrait for fear I should see it smiling approval --and so finally reached the hall, where the light from the floor above seemed now quite bright in comparison. All the doors I dosed carefully behind me; but first I had to open them. The woman had closed every one. Up the stairs, then, I actually ran, two steps at a time. My sister was standing outside Mabel's door. By her face I knew that she had also heard. There was no need to ask. I quickly made my mind up.

"There's nothing," I said, and detailed briefly my tour of search. "All is quiet and undisturbed downstairs." May God forgive me!

She beckoned to me, closing the door softly behind her. My heart beat violently a moment, then stood still.

"Mabel," she said aloud.

It was like the sentence of a judge, that one short word.

I tried to push past her and go in, but she stopped me with her arm. She was wholly mistress of herself, I saw.

"Hush!" she said in a lower voice. "I've got her round again with brandy. She's sleeping quietly now. We won't disturb her."

She drew me farther out into the landing, and as she did so, the clock in the hall below struck half-past three. I had stood, then, thirty minutes in the corridor below. "You've been such a long time." she said simply. "I feared for you," and she took my hand in her own that was cold and clammy.

VIII

And then, while that dreadful house stood listening about us in the early hours of this chill morning upon the edge of winter, she told me, with laconic brevity, things about Mabel that I heard as from a distance. There was nothing so unusual or tremendous in the short recital, nothing indeed I might not have already guessed for myself. It was the time and scene, the inference, too, that made it so afflicting: the idea that Mabel believed herself so utterly and hopelessly lost-- beyond recovery damned.

That she had loved him with so passionate a devotion that she had given her soul into his keeping, this certainly I had not divined--probably because I had never thought about it one way or the other. He had "converted" her, I knew, but that she had subscribed whole-heartedly to that most cruel and ugly of his dogmas--this was new to me, and came with a certain shock as I heard it. In love, of course, the weak-

er nature is receptive to all manner of suggestion. This man had "suggested" his pet brimstone lake so vividly that she had listened and believed. He had frightened her into heaven; and his heaven, a definite locality in the skies, had its foretaste here on earth in miniature--The Towers, house, and garden. Into his dolorous scheme of a handful saved and millions damned, his enclosure, as it were, of sheep and goats, he had swept her before she was aware of it. Her mind no longer was her own. And it was Mrs. Marsh who kept the thought-stream open, though tempered, as she deemed, with that touch of craven, superstitious mercy.

But what I found it difficult to understand, and still more difficult to accept, was that, during her year abroad, she had been so haunted with a secret dread of that hideous after-death that she had finally revolted and tried to recover that clearer state of mind she had enjoyed before the religious bully had stunned her--yet had tried in vain. She had returned to The Towers to find her soul again, only to realize that it was lost eternally. The cleaner state of mind lay then beyond recovery. In the reaction that followed the removal of his terrible "suggestion," she felt the crumbling of all that he had taught her, but searched in vain for the peace and beauty his teachings had destroyed. Nothing came to replace these. She was empty, desolate, hopeless; craving her former joy and carelessness, she found only hate and diabolical calculation. This man, whom she had loved to the point of losing her soul for him, had bequeathed to her one black and fiery thing--the terror of the damned. His thinking wrapped her in this iron garment that held her fast.

All this Frances told me, far more briefly than I have here repeated it. In her eyes and gestures and laconic sentences lay the conviction of great beating issues and of menacing drama my own description fails to recapture. It was all so incongruous and remote from the world I lived in that more than once a smile, though a smile of pity, fluttered to my lips; but a glimpse of my face in the mirror showed rather the leer of a grimace. There was no real laughter anywhere that night.

The entire adventure seemed so incredible, here, in this

twentieth century--but yet delusion, that feeble word, did not occur once in the comments my mind suggested though did not utter. I remembered that forbidding Shadow too; my sister's watercolors; the vanished personality of our hostess; the inexplicable, thundering Noise, and the figure of Mrs. Marsh in her midnight ritual that was so childish yet so horrible. I shivered in spite of my own "emancipated" cast of mind.

"There is no Mabel," were the words with which my sister sent another shower of ice down my spine. "He has killed her in his lake of fire and brimstone."

I stared at her blankly, as in a nightmare where nothing true or possible ever happened.

"He killed her in his lake of fire and brimstone," she repeated more faintly.

A desperate effort was in me to say the strong, sensible thing which should destroy the oppressive horror that grew so stiflingly about us both, but again the mirror drew the attempted smile into the merest grin, betraying the distortion that was everywhere in the place.

"You mean," I stammered beneath my breath, "that her faith has gone, but that the terror has remained?" I asked it, dully groping. I moved out of the line of the reflection in the glass.

She bowed her head as though beneath a weight; her skin was the pallor of grey ashes.

"You mean," I said louder, "that she has lost her--mind?"

"She is terror incarnate," was the whispered answer. "Mabel has lost her soul. Her soul is--there!" She pointed horribly below. "She is seeking it ...?"

The word "soul" stung me into something of my normal self again.

"But her terror, poor thing, is not--cannot be--transferable to us!" I exclaimed more vehemently. "It certainly is not convertible into feelings, sights and--even sounds!"

She interrupted me quickly, almost impatiently, speaking with that conviction by which she conquered me so easily that night.

"It is her terror that revived 'the Others.' It has brought her

into touch with them. They are loose and driving after her. Her efforts at resistance have given them also hope--that escape, after all, is possible. Day and night they strive.

"Escape! Others!" The anger fast rising in me dropped of its own accord at the moment of birth. It shrank into a shuddering beyond my control. In that moment, I think, I would have believed in the possibility of anything and everything she might tell me. To argue or contradict seemed equally futile.

"His strong belief, as also the beliefs of others who have preceded him," she replied, so sure of herself that I actually turned to look over my shoulder, "have left their shadow like a thick deposit over the house and grounds. To them, poor souls imprisoned by thought, it was hopeless as granite walls--until her resistance, her effort to dissipate it--let in light. Now, in their thousands, they are flocking to this little light, seeking escape. Her own escape, don't you see, may release them all!"

It took my breath away. Had his predecessors, former occupants of this house, also preached damnation of all the world but their own exclusive sect? Was this the explanation of her obscure talk of "layers," each striving against the other for domination? And if men are spirits, and these spirits survive, could strong Thought thus determine their condition even afterwards?

So many questions flooded into me that I selected no one of them, but stared in uncomfortable silence, bewildered, out of my depth, and acutely, painfully distressed. There was so odd a mixture of possible truth and incredible, unacceptable explanation in it all; so much confirmed, yet so much left darker than before. What she said did, indeed, offer a quasi-interpretation of my own series of abominable sensations--strife, agony, pity, hate, escape--but so far-fetched that only the deep conviction in her voice and attitude made it tolerable for a second even. I found myself in a curious state of mind. I could neither think clearly nor say a word to refute her amazing statements, whispered there beside me in the shivering hours of the early morning with only a wall between ourselves and--Mabel. Close behind her words I

remember this singular thing, however--that an atmosphere as of the Inquisition seemed to rise and stir about the room, beating awful wings of black above my head.

Abruptly, then, a moment's common sense returned to me. I faced her.

"And the Noise?" I said aloud, more firmly, "the roar of the closing doors? We have all heard that! Is that subjective too?"

Frances looked sideways about her in a queer fashion that made my flesh creep again. I spoke brusquely, almost angri-ly. I repeated the question, and waited with anxiety for her reply.

"What noise?" she asked, with the frank expression of an innocent child. "What closing doors?"

But her face turned from grey to white, and I saw that drops of perspiration glistened on her forehead. She caught at the back of a chair to steady herself, then glanced about her again with that sidelong look that made my blood run cold. I understood suddenly then. She did not take in what I said. I knew now. She was listening--for something else.

And the discovery revived in me a far stronger emotion than any mere desire for immediate explanation. Not only did I not insist upon an answer, but I was actually terrified lest she would answer. More, I felt in me a terror lest I should be moved to describe my own experiences below-stairs, thus increasing their reality and so the reality of all. She might even explain them too!

Still listening intently, she raised her head and looked me in the eyes. Her lips opened to speak. The words came to me from a great distance, it seemed, and her voice had a sound like a stone that drops into a deep well, its fate though hid-den, known.

"We are in it with her, too, Bill. We are in it with her. Our interpretations vary--because we are--in parts of it only. Ma-bel is in it--all."

The desire for violence came over me. If only she would say a definite thing in plain King's English! If only I could find it in me to give utterance to what shouted so loud within me! If only--the same old cry-- something would happen! For

all this elliptic talk that dazed my mind left obscurity everywhere. Her atrocious meaning, nonetheless, flashed through
me, though vanishing before it wholly divulged itself.

It brought a certain reaction with it. I found my tongue.
Whether I actually believed what I said is more than I can
swear to; that it seemed to me wise at the moment is all I remember. My mind was in a state of obscure perception less
than that of normal consciousness.

"Yes, Frances, I believe that what you say is the truth, and
that we are in it with her"--I meant to say I with loud, hostile
emphasis, but instead I whispered it lest she should hear the
trembling of my voice-- "and for that reason, my dear sister,
we leave tomorrow, you and I-- today, rather, since it is long
past midnight--we leave this house of the damned. We go
back to London."

Frances looked up, her face distraught almost beyond recognition. But it was not my words that caused the tumult in
her heart. It was a sound-- the sound she had been listening for--so faint I barely caught it myself, and had she not
pointed I could never have known the direction whence it
came. Small and terrible it rose again in the stillness of the
night, the sound of gnashing teeth. And behind it came an-
other--the tread of stealthy footsteps. Both were just outside
the door.

The room swung round me for a second. My first instinct
to prevent my sister going out--she had dashed past me
frantically to the door--gave place to another when I saw
the expression in her eyes. I followed her lead instead; it was
surer than my own. The pistol in my pocket swung uselessly
against my thigh. I was flustered beyond belief and ashamed
that I was so.

"Keep close to me, Frances," I said huskily, as the door
swung wide and a shaft of light fell upon a figure moving
rapidly. Mabel was going down the corridor. Beyond her, in
the shadows on the staircase, a second figure stood beckon-
ing, scarcely visible.

"Before they get her! Quick!" was screamed into my ears,
and our arms were about her in the same moment. It was
a horrible scene. Not that Mabel struggled in the least, but

that she collapsed as we caught her and fell with her dead weight, as of a corpse, limp, against us. And her teeth began again. They continued, even beneath the hand that Frances clapped upon her lips....

We carried her back into her own bedroom, where she lay down peacefully enough. It was so soon over.... The rapidity of the whole thing robbed it of reality almost. It had the swiftness of something remembered rather than of something witnessed. She slept again so quickly that it was almost as if we had caught her sleepwalking. I cannot say. I asked no questions at the time; I have asked none since; and my help was needed as little as the protection of my pistol. Frances was strangely competent and collected.... I lingered for some time uselessly by the door, till at length, looking up with a sigh, she made a sign for me to go.

"I shall wait in your room next door," I whispered, "till you come." But, though going out, I waited in the corridor instead, so as to hear the faintest call for help. In that dark corridor upstairs I waited, but not long. It may have been fifteen minutes when Frances reappeared, locking the door softly behind her. Leaning over the banisters, I saw her.

"I'll go in again about six o'clock," she whispered, "as soon as it gets light. She is sound asleep now. Please don't wait. If anything happens I'll call--you might leave your door ajar, perhaps."

And she came up, looking like a ghost.

But I saw her first safely into bed, and the rest of the night I spent in an armchair close to my opened door, listening for the slightest sound. Soon after five o'clock I heard Frances fumbling with the key, and, peering over the railing again, I waited till she reappeared and went back into her own room. She closed her door. Evidently she was satisfied that all was well.

Then, and then only, did I go to bed myself, but not to sleep. I could not get the scene out of my mind, especially that odious detail of it which I hoped and believed my sister had not seen--the still, dark figure of the housekeeper waiting on the stairs below--waiting, of course, for Mabel.

IX

It seems I became a mere spectator after that; my sister's lead was so assured for one thing, and, for another, the responsibility of leaving Mabel alone--Frances laid it bodily upon my shoulders--was a little more than I cared about. Moreover, when we all three met later in the day, things went on so exactly as before, so absolutely without friction or distress, that to present a sudden, obvious excuse for cutting our visit short seemed ill-judged. And on the lowest grounds it would have been desertion. At any rate, it was beyond my powers, and Frances was quite firm that she must stay. We therefore did stay. Things that happen in the night always seem exaggerated and distorted when the sun shines brightly next morning; no one can reconstruct the terror of a nightmare afterwards, nor comprehend why it seemed so overwhelming at the time.

I slept till ten o'clock, and when I rang for breakfast, a note from my sister lay upon the tray, its message of counsel couched in a calm and comforting strain. Mabel, she assured me, was herself again and remembered nothing of what had happened; there was no need of any violent measures; I was to treat her exactly as if I knew nothing. "And, if you don't mind, Bill, let us leave the matter unmentioned between ourselves as well. Discussion exaggerates; such things are best not talked about. I'm sorry I disturbed you so unnecessarily; I was stupidly excited. Please forget all the things I said at the moment." She had written "nonsense" first instead of "things," then scratched it out. She wished to convey that hysteria had been abroad in the night, and I readily gulped the explanation down, though it could not satisfy me in the smallest degree.

There was another week of our visit still, and we stayed it out to the end without disaster. My desire to leave at times became that frantic thing, desire to escape; but I controlled it, kept silent, watched and wondered. Nothing happened. As before, and everywhere, there was no sequence of development, no connection between cause and effect; and climax, none whatever. The thing swayed up and down, backwards and forwards like a great loose curtain in the wind, 

and I could only vaguely surmise what caused the draught or why there was a curtain at all. A novelist might mold the queer material into coherent sequence that would be interesting but could not be true.

It remains, therefore, not a story but a history. Nothing happened.

Perhaps my intense dislike of the fall of darkness was due wholly to my stirred imagination, and perhaps my anger when I learned that Frances now occupied a bed in our hostess's room was unreasonable. Nerves were unquestionably on edge. I was forever on the lookout for some event that should make escape imperative, but yet that never presented itself. I slept lightly, left my door ajar to catch the slightest sound, even made stealthy tours of the house below-stairs while everybody dreamed in their beds. But I discovered nothing; the doors were always locked; I neither saw the housekeeper again in unreasonable times and places, nor heard a footstep in the passages and halls. The Noise was never once repeated. That horrible, ultimate thunder, my intensest dread of all, lay withdrawn into the abyss whence it had twice arisen. And though in my thoughts it was sternly denied existence, the great black reason for the fact afflicted me unbelievably. Since Mabel's fruitless effort to escape, the Doors kept closed remorselessly. She had failed; they gave up hope. For this was the explanation that haunted the region of my mind where feelings stir and hint before they clothe themselves in actual language. Only I firmly kept it there; it never knew expression.

But, if my ears were open, my eyes were opened too, and it were idle to pretend that I did not notice a hundred details that were capable of sinister interpretation had I been weak enough to yield. Some protective barrier had fallen into ruins round me, so that Terror stalked behind the general collapse, feeling for me through all the gaping fissures. Much of this, I admit, must have been merely the elaboration of those sensations I had first vaguely felt, before subsequent events and my talks with Frances had dramatized them into living thoughts. I therefore leave them unmentioned in this history, just as my mind left them unmentioned in that interminable final week. Our life went on precisely as before--Mabel unreal and outwardly so still; Frances, secretive, anxious, tactful to the point of slyness, and keen to save to the point of self-forgetfulness.

There were the same stupid meals, the same wearisome long evenings, the stifling ugliness of house and grounds, the Shadow settling in so thickly that it seemed almost a visible, tangible thing. I came to feel the only friendly things in all this hostile, cruel place were the robins that hopped boldly over the monstrous terraces and even up to the windows of the unsightly house itself. The robins alone knew joy; they danced, believing no evil thing was possible in all God's radiant world. They believed in everybody; their god's plan of life had no room in it for hell, damnation, and lakes of brimstone. I came to love the little birds. Had Samuel Franklyn known them, he might have preached a different sermon, bequeathing love in place of terror!

Most of my time I spent writing; but it was a pretence at best, and rather a dangerous one besides. For it stirred the mind to production, with the result that other things came pouring in as well. With reading it was the same. In the end I found an aggressive, deliberate resistance to be the only way of feasible defense. To walk far afield was out of the question, for it meant leaving my sister too long alone, so that my exercise was confined to nearer home. My saunters in the grounds, however, never surprised the goblin garden again. It was close at hand, but I seemed unable to get wholly into it. Too many things assailed my mind for any one to hold exclusive possession, perhaps.

Indeed, all the interpretations, all the "layers," to use my sister's phrase, slipped in by turns and lodged there for a time. They came day and night, and though my reason denied them entrance they held their own as by a kind of squatter's right. They stirred moods already in me, that is, and did not introduce entirely new ones; for every mind conceals ancestral deposits that have been cultivated in turn along the whole line of its descent. Any day a chance shower may cause this one or that to blossom. Thus it came to me, at any rate. After darkness the Inquisition paced the empty corridors and set up ghastly apparatus in the dismal halls; and once, in the library, there swept over me that easy and delicious conviction that by confessing my wickedness I could resume it later, since Confession is expression, and expression brings relief and leaves one ready to accumulate again. And in such mood I felt bitter and unforgiving towards all others who thought differently. Another time it was a Pagan thing that assaulted me--so trivial yet oh, so significant at the time--when I dreamed that a herd of centaurs rolled up with a great stamping of hoofs round the house to destroy it, and then woke to hear the horses tramping across the field below the lawns; they neighed ominously and their noisy panting was audible as if it were just outside my windows.

But the tree episode, I think, was the most curious of all--except, perhaps, the incident with the children which I shall mention in a moment--for its closeness to reality was so unforgettable.

Outside the east window of my room stood a giant wellingtonia on the lawn, its head rising level with the upper sash. It grew some twenty feet away, planted on the highest terrace, and I often saw it when closing my curtains for the night, noticing how it drew its heavy skirts about it, and how the light from other windows threw glimmering streaks and patches that turned it into the semblance of a towering, solemn image. It stood there then so strikingly, somehow like a great old-world idol, that it claimed attention. Its appearance was curiously formidable. Its branches rustled without visibly moving and it had a certain portentous, forbidding air, so grand and dark and monstrous in the night that I was always glad when my curtains shut it out. Yet, once in bed, I had never thought about it one way or the other, and by day had certainly never sought it out.

One night, then, as I went to bed and closed this window against a cutting easterly wind, I saw--that there were two of these trees. A brother wellingtonia rose mysteriously beside it, equally huge, equally towering, equally monstrous. The menacing pair of them faced me there upon the lawn. But in this new arrival lay a strange suggestion that frightened me before I could argue it away. Exact counterpart of its giant companion, it revealed also that gross, odious quality that all my sister's paintings held. I got the odd impression that the rest of these trees, stretching away dimly in a troop over the farther lawns, were similar, and that, led by this enormous pair, they had all moved boldly closer to my windows. At the same moment a blind was drawn down over an upper room; the second tree disappeared into the surrounding darkness.

It was, of course, this chance light that had brought it into the field of vision, but when the black shutter dropped over it, hiding it from view, the manner of its vanishing produced the queer effect that it had slipped into its companion--almost that it had been an emanation of the one I so disliked, and not really a tree at all! In this way the garden turned vehicle for expressing what lay behind it all ...!

The behavior of the doors, the little, ordinary doors, seems scarcely worth mention at all, their queer way of opening and shutting of their own accord; for this was accountable in a hundred natural ways, and to tell the truth, I never caught one in the act of moving. Indeed, only after frequent repetitions did the detail force itself upon me, when, having noticed one, I noticed all. It produced, however, the unpleasant impression of a continual coming and going in the house, as though, screened cleverly and purposely from actual sight, some one in the building held constant invisible intercourse with--others.

Upon detailed descriptions of these uncertain incidents I do not venture, individually so trivial, but taken all together so impressive and so insolent. But the episode of the children, mentioned above, was different. And I give it because it showed how vividly the intuitive child-mind received the impression--one impression, at any rate--of what was in the air. It may be told in a very few words. I believe they were the coachman's children, and that the man had been in Mr. Franklyn's service; but of neither point am I quite positive.

I heard screaming in the rose-garden that runs along the stable walls-- it was one afternoon not far from the tea-hour--and on hurrying up I found a little girl of nine or ten fastened with ropes to a rustic seat, and two other children-- boys, one about twelve and one much younger-- gathering sticks beneath the climbing rose trees. The girl was white and frightened, but the others were laughing and talking among themselves so busily while they picked that they did not notice my abrupt arrival. Some game, I understood, was in progress, but a game that had become too serious for the happiness of the prisoner, for there was a fear in the girl's eyes that was a very genuine fear indeed. I unfastened her at once; the ropes were so loosely and clumsily knotted that they had not hurt her skin; it was not that which made her pale. She collapsed a moment upon the bench, then picked up her tiny skirts and dived away at full speed into the safety of the stable-yard.

There was no response to my brief comforting, but she ran as though for her life, and I divined that some horrid boys' cruelty had been afoot. It was probably mere thoughtless-ness, as cruelty with children usually is, but something in me decided to discover exactly what it was.

And the boys, not one whit alarmed at my intervention, merely laughed shyly when I explained that their prison-er had escaped, and told me frankly what their "gime" had been. There was no vestige of shame in them, nor any idea, of course, that they aped a monstrous reality.

That it was mere pretence was neither here nor there. To them, though make-believe, it was a make-believe of something that was right and natural and in no sense cruel. Grown-ups did it too. It was necessary for her good.

"We was going to burn her up, sir," the older one informed me, answering my "Why?" with the explanation, "Because she wouldn't believe what we wanted 'er to believe."

And, game though it was, the feeling of reality about the little episode was so arresting, so terrific in some way, that only with difficulty did I confine my admonitions on this occasion to mere words. The boys slunk off, frightened in their turn, yet not, I felt, convinced that they had erred in principle. It was their inheritance. They had breathed it in with the atmosphere of their bringing-up. They would re-new the salutary torture when they could--till she "believed" as they did.

I went back into the house, afflicted with a passion of mingled pity and distress impossible to describe, yet on my short way across the garden was attacked by other moods in turn, each more real and bitter than its predecessor. I received the whole series, as it were, at once. I felt like a diver rising to the surface through layers of water at different temperatures, though here the natural order was reversed, and the cooler strata were uppermost, the heated ones below. Thus, I was caught by the goblin touch of the willows that fringed the field; by the sensuous curving of the twisted ash that formed a gateway to the little grove of sapling oaks where fauns and satyrs lurked to play in the moonlight before Pagan altars; and by the cloaking darkness, next, of the copse of stunted pines, close gathered each to each, where hooded figures stalked behind an awful cross. The episode with the children seemed to have opened me like a knife. The whole Place rushed at me.

I suspect this synthesis of many moods produced in me that climax of loathing and disgust which made me feel the limit of bearable emotion had been reached, so that I made straight to find Frances in order to convince her that at any rate I must leave. For, although this was our last day in the house, and we had arranged to go next day, the dread was in me that she would still find some persuasive reason for staying on. And an unexpected incident then made my dread unnecessary. The front door was open and a cab stood in the drive; a tall, elderly man was gravely talking in the hall with the parlor maid we called the Grenadier. He held a piece of paper in his hand. "I have called to see the house," I heard him say, as I ran up the stairs to Frances, who was peering like an inquisitive child over the banisters....

"Yes," she told me with a sigh, I know not whether of resignation or relief, "the house is to be let or sold. Mabel has decided. Some Society or other, I believe--"

I was overjoyed: this made our leaving right and possible. "You never told me, Frances!"

"Mabel only heard of it a few days ago. She told me herself this morning. It is a chance, she says. Alone she cannot get it 'straight'.

"Defeat?" I asked, watching her closely.

"She thinks she has found a way out. It's not a family, you see, it's a Society, a sort of Community--they go in for thought--"

"A Community!" I gasped. "You mean religious?"

She shook her head. "Not exactly," she said smiling, "but some kind of association of men and women who want a headquarters in the country--a place where they can write and meditate--think--mature their plans and all the rest--I don't know exactly what."

"Utopian dreamers?" I asked, yet feeling an immense relief come over me as I heard. But I asked in ignorance, not cynically. Frances would know. She knew all this kind of thing.

"No, not that exactly," she smiled. "Their teachings are grand and simple--old as the world too, really--the basis of every religion before men's minds perverted them with their manufactured creeds--"

Footsteps on the stairs, and the sound of voices, interrupted our odd impromptu conversation, as the Grenadier came up, followed by the tall, grave gentleman who was being shown over the house. My sister drew me along the corridor towards her room, where she went in and closed the door behind me, yet not before I had stolen a good look at the caller-- long enough, at least, for his face and general appearance to have made a definite impression on me. For something strong and peaceful emanated from his presence; he moved with such quiet dignity; the glance of his eyes was so steady and reassuring, that my mind labeled him instantly as a type of man one would turn to in an emergency and not be disappointed. I had seen him but for a passing moment, but I had seen him twice, and the way he walked down the passage, looking competently about him, conveyed the same impression as when I saw him standing at the door-- fearless, tolerant, wise. "A sincere and kindly character," I judged instantly, "a man whom some big kind of love has trained in sweetness towards the world; no hate in him anywhere." A great deal, no doubt, to read in so brief a glance! Yet his voice confirmed my intuition, a deep and very gentle voice, great firmness in it too.

"Have I become suddenly sensitive to people's atmospheres in this extraordinary fashion?" I asked myself, smiling, as I stood in the room and heard the door close behind me. "Have I developed some clairvoyant faculty here?" At any other time I should have mocked.

And I sat down and faced my sister, feeling strangely comforted and at peace for the first time since I had stepped beneath The Towers' roof a month ago. Frances, I then saw, was smiling a little as she watched me.

"You know him?" I asked.

"You felt it too?" was her question in reply. "No," she added, "I don't know him--beyond the fact that he is a leader in the Movement and has devoted years and money to its objects. Mabel felt the same thing in him that you have felt--and jumped at it."

"But you've seen him before?" I urged, for the certainty was in me that he was no stranger to her.

She shook her head. "He called one day early this week, when you were out. Mabel saw him. I believe--" she hesitated a moment, as though expecting me to stop her with my usual impatience of such subjects--"I believe he has explained everything to her--the beliefs he embodies, she declares, are her salvation--might be, rather, if she could adopt them."

"Conversion again!" For I remembered her riches, and how gladly a Society would gobble them.

"The layers I told you about," she continued calmly, shrugging her shoulders slightly--"the deposits that are left behind by strong thinking and real belief--but especially by ugly, hateful belief, because, you see--unfortunately there's more vital passion in that sort--"

"Frances, I don't understand a bit," I said out loud, but said it a little humbly, for the impression the man had left was still strong upon me and I was grateful for the steady sense of peace and comfort he had somehow introduced. The horrors had been so dreadful. My nerves, doubtless, were more than a little overstrained. Absurd as it must sound, I classed him in my mind with the robins, the happy, confiding robins who believed in everybody and thought no evil! I laughed a moment at my ridiculous idea, and my sister, encouraged by this sign of patience in me, continued more fluently.

"Of course you don't understand, Bill? Why should you? You've never thought about such things. Needing no creed yourself, you think all creeds are rubbish."

"I'm open to conviction--I'm tolerant," I interrupted.

"You're as narrow as Sam Franklyn, and as crammed with prejudice," she answered, knowing that she had me at her mercy.

"Then, pray, what may be his, or his Society's beliefs?" I asked, feeling no desire to argue, "and how are they going to prove your Mabel's salvation? Can they bring beauty into all this aggressive hate and ugliness?"

"Certain hope and peace," she said, "that peace which is understanding, and that understanding which explains all creeds and therefore tolerates them."

"Toleration! The one word a religious man loathes above all others! His pet word is damnation--"

"Tolerates them," she repeated patiently, unperturbed by my explosion, "because it includes them all."

"Fine, if true" I admitted, "very fine. But how, pray, does it include them all?"

"Because the key-word, the motto, of their Society is, 'There is no religion higher than Truth,' and it has no single dogma of any kind. Above all," she went on, "because it claims that no individual can be 'lost.' It teaches universal salvation. To damn outsiders is uncivilized, childish, impure. Some take longer than others--it's according to the way they think and live--but all find peace, through development, in the end. What the creeds call a hopeless soul, it regards as a soul having further to go. There is no damnation--"

"Well, well," I exclaimed, feeling that she rode her hobby horse too wildly, too roughly over me, "but what is the bearing of all this upon this dreadful place, and upon Mabel? I'll admit that there is this atmosphere--this--er--inexplicable horror in the house and grounds, and that if not of damnation exactly, it is certainly damnable. I'm not too prejudiced to deny that, for I've felt it myself."

To my relief she was brief. She made her statement, leaving me to take it or reject it as I would.

"The thought and belief its former occupants--have left behind. For there has been coincidence here, a coincidence that must be rare. The site on which this modern house now stands was Roman, before that Early Britain, with burial mounds, before that again, Druid--the Druid stones still lie in that copse below the field, the Tumuli among the ilexes behind the drive. The older building Sam Franklyn altered and practically pulled down was a monastery; he changed the chapel into a meeting hall, which is now the music room; but, before he came here, the house was occupied by Manetti, a violent Catholic without tolerance or vision; and in the interval between these two, Julius Weinbaum had it, Hebrew of most rigid orthodox type imaginable--so they all have left their--"

"Even so," I repeated, yet interested to hear the rest, "what of it?"

"Simply this," said Frances with conviction, "that each in turn has left his layer of concentrated thinking and belief behind him; because each believed intensely, absolutely, beyond the least weakening of any doubt --the kind of strong belief and thinking that is rare anywhere today, the kind that wills, impregnates objects, saturates the atmosphere, haunts, in a word. And each, believing he was utterly and finally right, damned with equally positive conviction the rest of the world. One and all preached that implicitly if not explicitly. It's the root of every creed. Last of the bigoted, grim series came Samuel Franklyn."

I listened in amazement that increased as she went on. Up to this point her explanation was so admirable. It was, indeed, a pretty study in psychology if it were true.

"Then why does nothing ever happen?" I enquired mildly. "A place so thickly haunted ought to produce a crop of no ordinary results!"

"There lies the proof," she went on in a lowered voice, "the proof of the horror and the ugly reality. The thought and belief of each occupant in turn kept all the others under. They gave no sign of life at the time. But the results of thinking never die. They crop out again the moment there's an opening. And, with the return of Mabel in her negative state, believing nothing positive herself the place for the first time found itself free to reproduce its buried stores.

"Damnation, hell-fire, and the rest--the most permanent and vital thought of all those creeds, since it was applied to the majority of the world--broke loose again, for there was no restraint to hold it back. Each sought to obtain its former supremacy. None conquered. There results a pandemonium of hate and fear, of striving to escape, of agonized, bitter warring to find safety, peace--salvation. The place is saturated by that appalling stream of thinking--the terror of the damned. It concentrated upon Mabel, whose negative attitude furnished the channel of deliverance. You and I, according to our sympathy with her, were similarly involved. Nothing happened, because no one layer could ever gain the supremacy."

I was so interested--I dare not say amused--that I stared in silence while she paused a moment, afraid that she would draw rein and end the fairy tale too soon.

"The beliefs of this man, of his Society rather, vigorously thought and therefore vigorously given out here, will put the whole place straight. It will act as a solvent. These vitriolic layers actively denied, will fuse and disappear in the stream of gentle, tolerant sympathy which is love. For each member, worthy of the name, loves the world, and all creeds go into the melting-pot; Mabel, too, if she joins them out of real conviction, will find salvation--"

"Thinking, I know, is of the first importance," I objected, "but don't you, perhaps, exaggerate the power of feeling and emotion which in religion are au fond always hysterical?"

"What is the world," she told me, "but thinking and feeling? An individual's world is entirely what that individual thinks and believes --interpretation. There is no other. And unless he really thinks and really believes, he has no permanent world at all. I grant that few people think, and still fewer believe, and that most take ready-made suits and make them do. Only the strong make their own things; the lesser fry, Mabel among them, are merely swept up into what has been manufactured for them. They get along somehow. You and I have made for ourselves, Mabel has not. She is a nonentity,

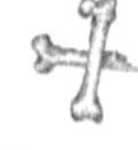

and when her belief is taken from her, she goes with it."

It was not in me just then to criticize the evasion, or pick out the sophistry from the truth. I merely waited for her to continue.

"None of us have Truth, my dear Frances," I ventured presently, seeing that she kept silent.

"Precisely," she answered, "but most of us have beliefs. And what one believes and thinks affects the world at large. Consider the legacy of hatred and cruelty involved in the doctrines men have built into their creeds where the sine qua non of salvation is absolute acceptance of one particular set of views or else perishing everlastingly--for only by repudiating history can they disavow it--"

"You're not quite accurate," I put in. "Not all the creeds teach damnation, do they? Franklyn did, of course, but the others are a bit modernized now surely?"

"Trying to get out of it," she admitted, "perhaps they are, but damnation of unbelievers--of most of the world, that is--is their rather favorite idea if you talk with them."

"I never have."

She smiled. "But I have," she said significantly, "so, if you consider what the various occupants of this house have so strongly held and thought and believed, you need not be surprised that the influence they have left behind them should be a dark and dreadful legacy. For thought, you know, does leave--"

The opening of the door, to my great relief, interrupted her, as the Grenadier led in the visitor to see the room. He bowed to both of us with a brief word of apology, looked round him, and withdrew, and with his departure the conversation between us came naturally to an end. I followed him out. Neither of us in any case, I think, cared to argue further.

And, so far as I am aware, the curious history of The Towers ends here too. There was no climax in the story sense. Nothing ever really happened. We left next morning for London. I only know that the Society in question took the house and have since occupied it to their entire satisfaction, and that Mabel, who became a member shortly afterwards,

now stays there frequently when in need of repose from the arduous and unselfish labors she took upon herself under its aegis. She dined with us only the other night, here in our tiny Chelsea flat, and a jollier, saner, more interesting and happy guest I could hardly wish for. She was vital--in the best sense; the lay figure had come to life. I found it difficult to believe she was the same woman whose fearful effigy had floated down those dreary corridors and almost disappeared in the depths of that atrocious Shadow.

What her beliefs were now I was wise enough to leave un-questioned, and Frances, to my great relief, kept the conver-sation well away from such inappropriate topics. It was clear, however, that the woman had in herself some secret source of joy, that she was now an aggressive, positive force, sure of herself, and apparently afraid of nothing in heaven or hell. She radiated something very like hope and courage about her, and talked as though the world were a glorious place and everybody in it kind and beautiful. Her optimism was certainly infectious.

The Towers were mentioned only in passing. The name of Marsh came up-- not the Marsh, it so happened, but a name in some book that was being discussed--and I was unable to restrain myself. Curiosity was too strong. I threw out a casual enquiry Mabel could leave unanswered if she wished. But there was no desire to avoid it. Her reply was frank and smiling.

"Would you believe it? She married," Mabel told me, though obviously surprised that I remembered the house-keeper at all; "and is happy as the day is long. She's found her right niche in life. A sergeant--"

"The army!" I ejaculated.

"Salvation Army," she explained merrily.

Frances exchanged a glance with me. I laughed too, for the information took me by surprise. I cannot say why exactly, but I expected at least to hear that the woman had met some dreadful end, not impossibly by burning.

"And The Towers, now called the Rest House," Mabel chat-tered on, "seems to me the most peaceful and delightful spot in England--"

"Really," I said politely.

"When I lived there in the old days--while you were there, perhaps, though I won't be sure."

Mabel went on, "the story got abroad that it was haunted. Wasn't it odd? A less likely place for a ghost I've never seen. Why, it had no atmosphere at all." She said this to Frances, glancing up at me with a smile that apparently had no hidden meaning. "Did you notice anything queer about it when you were there?"

This was plainly addressed to me.

"I found it--er--difficult to settle down to anything," I said, after an instant's hesitation. "I couldn't work there--"

"But I thought you wrote that wonderful book on the Deaf and Blind while you stayed with me," she asked innocently.

I stammered a little. "Oh no, not then. I only made a few notes--er--at The Towers. My mind, oddly enough, refused to produce at all down there. But--why do you ask? Did anything--was anything supposed to happen there?"

She looked searchingly into my eyes a moment before she answered:

"Not that I know of," she said simply.

ANCIENT LIGHTS

From Southwater, where he left the train, the road led due west. That he knew; for the rest he trusted to luck, being one of those born walkers who dislike asking the way. He had that instinct, and as a rule it served him well. "A mile or so due west along the sandy road till you come to a stile on the right; then across the fields. You'll see the red house straight before you." He glanced at the post-card's instructions once again, and once again he tried to decipher the scratched-out sentence—without success. It had been so elaborately inked over that no word was legible. Inked-out sentences in a letter were always enticing. He wondered what it was that had to be so very carefully obliterated.

The afternoon was boisterous, with a tearing, shouting wind that blew from the sea, across the Sussex weald. Massive clouds with rounded, piled-up edges, cannoned across gaping spaces of blue sky. Far away the line of Downs swept the horizon, like an arriving wave. Chanctonbury Ring rode their crest—a scudding ship, hull down before the wind. He took his hat off and walked rapidly, breathing great draughts of air with delight and exhilaration. The road was deserted; no horsemen, bicycles, or motors; not even a tradesman's cart; no single walker. But anyhow he would never have asked the way. Keeping a sharp eye for the stile, he pounded along, while the wind tossed the cloak against his face, and made waves across the blue puddles in the yellow road. The trees showed their under leaves of white. The bracken and the high new grass bent all one way. Great life was in the day, high spirits and dancing everywhere. And for a Croydon surveyor's clerk just out of an office this was like a holiday at the sea.

It was a day for high adventure, and his heart rose up to meet the mood of Nature. His umbrella with the silver ring ought to have been a sword, and his brown shoes should have been top-boots with spurs upon the heels. Where hid the enchanted Castle and the princess with the hair of sunny gold? His horse...

The stile came suddenly into view and nipped adventure in the bud. Everyday clothes took him prisoner again. He was a surveyor's clerk, middle-aged, earning three pounds a week, coming from Croydon to see about a client's proposed alterations in a wood—something to ensure a better view from the dining-room window. Across the fields, perhaps a mile away, he saw the red house gleaming in the sunshine; and resting on the stile a moment to get his breath he noticed a copse of oak and hornbeam on the right. "Aha," he told himself "so that must be the wood he wants to cut down to improve the view? I'll 'ave a look at it." There were boards up, of course, but there was an inviting little path as well. "I'm not a trespasser," he said; "it's part of my business, this is." He scrambled awkwardly over the gate and entered the copse. A little round would bring him to the field again.

But the moment he passed among the trees the wind ceased shouting and a stillness dropped upon the world. So dense was the growth that the sunshine only came through in isolated patches. The air was close. He mopped his forehead and put his green felt hat on, but a low branch knocked it off again at once, and as he stooped an elastic twig swung back and stung his face. There were flowers along both edges of the little path; glades opened on either side; ferns curved about in damper corners, and the smell of earth and foliage was rich and sweet. It was cooler here. What an enchanting little wood, he thought, turning down a small green glade where the sunshine flickered like silver wings. How it danced and fluttered and moved about! He put a dark blue flower in his buttonhole. Again his hat, caught by an oak branch as he rose, was knocked from his head, falling across his eyes. And this time he did not put it on again. Swinging his umbrella, he walked on with uncovered head, whistling rather loudly as he went. But the thickness of the trees hardly encouraged whistling, and something of his gaiety and high spirits seemed to leave him. He suddenly found himself treading circumspectly and with caution. The stillness in the wood was so peculiar.

There was a rustle among the ferns and leaves and something shot across the path ten yards ahead, stopped abruptly an instant with head cocked sideways to stare, then dived again beneath the underbrush with the speed of a shadow. He started like a frightened child, laughing the next second that a mere pheasant could have made him jump. In the distance he heard wheels upon the road, and wondered why the sound was pleasant. "Good old butcher's cart," he said to himself—then realised that he was going in the wrong direction and had somehow got turned round. For the road should be behind him, not in front.

And he hurriedly took another narrow glade that lost itself in greenness to the right. "That's my direction, of course," he said; "the trees has mixed me up a bit, it seems"—then found himself abruptly by the gate he had first climbed over. He had merely made a circle. Surprise became almost discomfiture then. And a man, dressed like a gamekeeper in browny green, leaned against the gate, hitting his legs with a switch. "I'm making for Mr. Lumley's farm," explained the walker. "This is his wood, I believe—" then stopped dead, because it was no man at all, but merely an effect of light and shade and foliage. He stepped back to reconstruct the singular illusion, but the wind shook the branches roughly here on the edge of the wood and the foliage refused to reconstruct the figure. The leaves all rustled strangely. And just then the sun went behind a cloud, making the whole wood look otherwise. Yet how the mind could be thus doubly deceived was indeed remarkable, for it almost seemed to him the man had answered, spoken—or was this the shuffling noise the branches made?—and had pointed with his switch to the notice-board upon the nearest tree. The words rang on in his head, but of course he had imagined them: "No, it's not his wood. It's ours." And some village wit, moreover, had changed the lettering on the weather-beaten board, for it read quite plainly, "Trespassers will be persecuted."

And while the astonished clerk read the words and chuckled, he said to himself, thinking what a tale he'd have to tell his wife and children later—"The blooming wood has tried to chuck me out. But I'll go in again. Why, it's only a matter of a square acre at most. I'm bound to reach the fields on the other side if I keep straight on." He remembered his position in the office. He had a certain dignity to maintain.

The cloud passed from below the sun, and light splashed suddenly in all manner of unlikely places. The man went straight on. He felt a touch of puzzling confusion somewhere; this way the copse had of shifting from sunshine into shadow doubtless troubled sight a little. To his relief at last, a new glade opened through the trees and disclosed the fields with a glimpse of the red house in the distance at the far end. But a little wicket gate that stood across the path had first to be climbed, and as he scrambled heavily over—for it would not open—he got the astonishing feeling that it slid off sideways beneath his weight, and towards the wood. Like the moving staircases at Harrod's and Earl's Court, it began to glide off with him. It was quite horrible. He made a violent effort to get down before it carried him into the trees, but his feet became entangled with the bars and umbrella, so that he fell heavily upon the farther side, arms spread across the grass and nettles, boots clutched between the first and second bars. He lay there a moment like a man crucified upside down, and while he struggled to get disentangled—feet, bars, and umbrella formed a regular net—he saw the little man in browny green go past him with extreme rapidity through the wood. The man was laughing. He passed across the glade some fifty yards away, and he was not alone this time. A companion like himself went with him. The clerk, now upon his feet again, watched them disappear into the gloom of green beyond. "They're tramps, not gamekeepers," he said to himself, half mortified, half angry. But his heart was thumping dreadfully, and he dared not utter all his thought.

He examined the wicket gate, convinced it was a trick gate somehow—then went hurriedly on again, disturbed beyond belief to see that the glade no longer opened into fields, but curved away to the right. What in the world had happened to him? His sight was so utterly at fault. Again the sun flamed out abruptly and lit the floor of the wood with pools of silver, and at the same moment a violent gust of wind passed shouting overhead. Drops fell clattering everywhere upon the leaves, making a sharp pattering as of many footsteps. The whole copse shuddered and went moving.

"Rain, by George," thought the clerk, and feeling for his umbrella, discovered he had lost it. He turned back to the gate and found it lying on the farther side. To his amazement he saw the fields at the far end of the glade, the red house, too, ashine in the sunset. He laughed then, for, of course, in his struggle with the gate, he had somehow got turned round—had fallen back instead of forwards. Climbing over, this time quite easily, he retraced his steps. The silver band, he saw, had been torn from the umbrella. No doubt his foot, a nail, or something had caught in it and ripped it off. The clerk began to run; he felt extraordinarily dismayed.

But, while he ran, the entire wood ran with him, round him, to and fro, trees shifting like living things, leaves folding and unfolding, trunks darting backwards and forwards, and branches disclosing enormous empty spaces, then closing up again before he could look into them. There were footsteps everywhere, and laughing, crying voices, and crowds of figures gathering just behind his back till the glade, he knew, was thick with moving life. The wind in his ears, of course, produced the voices and the laughter, while sun and clouds, plunging the copse alternately in shadow and bright dazzling light, created the figures. But he did not like it, and went as fast as ever his sturdy legs could take him. He was frightened now. This was no story for his wife and children. He ran like the wind. But his feet made no sound upon the soft mossy turf.

Then, to his horror, he saw that the glade grew narrow, nettles and weeds stood thick across it, it dwindled down into a tiny path, and twenty yards ahead it stopped finally and melted off among the trees. What the trick gate had failed to achieve, this twisting glade accomplished easily— carried him in bodily among the dense and crowding trees.

There was only one thing to do—turn sharply and dash back again, run headlong into the life that followed at his back, followed so closely too that now it almost touched him, pushing him in. And with reckless courage this was what he did. It seemed a fearful thing to do. He turned with a sort of violent spring, head down and shoulders forward, hands stretched before his face. He made the plunge; like a hunted creature he charged full tilt the other way, meeting the wind now in his face.

Good Lord! The glade behind him had closed up as well; there was no longer any path at all. Turning round and round, like an animal at bay, he searched for an opening, a way of escape, searched frantically, breathlessly, terrified now in his bones. But foliage surrounded him, branches blocked the way; the trees stood close and still, unshaken by a breath of wind; and the sun dipped that moment behind a great black cloud. The entire wood turned dark and silent. It watched him.

Perhaps it was this final touch of sudden blackness that made him act so foolishly, as though he had really lost his head. At any rate, without pausing to think, he dashed headlong in among the trees again. There was a sensation of being stiflingly surrounded and entangled, and that he must break out at all costs—out and away into the open of the blessed fields and air. He did this ill-considered thing, and apparently charged straight into an oak that deliberately moved into his path to stop him. He saw it shift across a good full yard, and being a measuring man, accustomed to theodolite and chain, he ought to know. He fell, saw stars, and felt a thousand tiny fingers tugging and pulling at his hands and neck and ankles. The stinging nettles, no doubt, were responsible for this. He thought of it later. At the moment it felt diabolically calculated.

But another remarkable illusion was not so easily explained. For all in a moment, it seemed, the entire wood went sliding past him with a thick deep rustling of leaves and laughter, myriad footsteps, and tiny little active, energetic shapes; two men in browny green gave him a mighty hoist — and he opened his eyes to find himself lying in the meadow beside the stile where first his incredible adventure had begun. The wood stood in its usual place and stared down upon him in the sunlight. There was the red house in the distance as before. Above him grinned the weather-beaten notice-board: "Trespassers will be prosecuted."

Dishevelled in mind and body, and a good deal shaken in his official soul, the clerk walked slowly across the fields. But on the way he glanced once more at the postcard of instructions, and saw with dull amazement that the inked-out sentence was quite legible after all beneath the scratches made across it: "There is a short cut through the wood — the wood I want cut down — if you care to take it." Only care" was so badly written, it looked more like another word; the "c" was uncommonly like "d."

"That's the copse that spoils my view of the Downs, you see," his client explained to him later, pointing across the fields, and referring to the ordnance map beside him. "I want it cut down and a path made so and so." His finger indicated direction on the map. "The Fairy Wood—it's still called, and it's far older than this house. Come now, if you're ready, Mr. Thomas, we might go out and have a look at it. . ."

THE WILLOWS

I

After leaving Vienna, and long before you come to Budapest, the Danube enters a region of singular loneliness and desolation, where its waters spread away on all sides regardless of a main channel, and the country becomes a swamp for miles upon miles, covered by a vast sea of low willow-bushes. On the big maps this deserted area is painted in a fluffy blue, growing fainter in color as it leaves the banks, and across it may be seen in large straggling letters the word Sumpfe, meaning marshes.

In high flood this great acreage of sand, shingle-beds, and willow-grown islands is almost topped by the water, but in normal seasons the bushes bend and rustle in the free winds, showing their silver leaves to the sunshine in an ever-moving plain of bewildering beauty. These willows never attain to the dignity of trees; they have no rigid trunks; they remain humble bushes, with rounded tops and soft outline, swaying on slender stems that answer to the least pressure of the wind; supple as grasses, and so continually shifting that they somehow give the impression that the entire plain is moving and alive. For the wind sends waves rising and falling over the whole surface, waves of leaves instead of waves of water, green swells like the sea, too, until the branches turn and lift, and then silvery white as their underside turns to the sun.

Happy to slip beyond the control of the stern banks, the Danube here wanders about at will among the intricate network of channels intersecting the islands everywhere with broad avenues down which the waters pour with a shouting sound; making whirlpools, eddies, and foaming rapids; tearing at the sandy banks; carrying away masses of shore and willow-clumps; and forming new islands innumerably which shift daily in size and shape and possess at best an impermanent life, since the flood-time obliterates their very existence.

Properly speaking, this fascinating part of the river's life begins soon after leaving Pressburg, and we, in our Canadian canoe, with gipsy tent and frying-pan on board, reached it on the crest of a rising flood about mid-July. That very same morning, when the sky was reddening before sunrise, we had slipped swiftly through still-sleeping Vienna, leaving it a couple of hours later a mere patch of smoke against the blue hills of the Wienerwald on the horizon; we had breakfasted below Fischeramend under a grove of birch trees roaring in the wind; and had then swept on the tearing current past Orth, Hainburg, Petronell (the old Roman Carnuntum of Marcus Aurelius), and so under the frowning heights of Thelsen on a spur of the Carpathians, where the March steals in quietly from the left and the frontier is crossed between Austria and Hungary.

Racing along at twelve kilometers an hour soon took us well into Hungary, and the muddy waters--sure sign of flood--sent us aground on many a shingle-bed, and twisted us like a cork in many a sudden belching whirlpool before the towers of Pressburg (Hungarian, Poszony) showed against the sky; and then the canoe, leaping like a spirited horse, flew at top speed under the grey walls, negotiated safely the sunken chain of the Fliegende Brucke ferry, turned the corner sharply to the left, and plunged on yellow foam into the wilderness of islands, sandbanks, and swamp-land beyond--the land of the willows.

The change came suddenly, as when a series of bioscope pictures snaps down on the streets of a town and shifts without warning into the scenery of lake and forest. We entered the land of desolation on wings, and in less than half an hour there was neither boat nor fishing-hut nor red roof, nor any single sign of human habitation and civilization within sight. The sense of remoteness from the world of humankind, the utter isolation, the fascination of this singular world of willows, winds, and waters, instantly laid its spell upon us both, so that we allowed laughingly to one another that we ought by rights to have held some special kind of passport to admit us, and that we had, somewhat audaciously, come without asking leave into a separate little kingdom of wonder and magic--a kingdom that was reserved for the use of others who had a right to it, with everywhere unwritten warnings to trespassers for those who had the imagination to discover them.

Though still early in the afternoon, the ceaseless buffetings of a most tempestuous wind made us feel weary, and we at once began casting about for a suitable camping-ground for the night. But the bewildering character of the islands made landing difficult; the swirling flood carried us in shore and then swept us out again; the willow branches tore our hands as we seized them to stop the canoe, and we pulled many a yard of sandy bank into the water before at length we shot with a great sideways blow from the wind into a backwater and managed to beach the bows in a cloud of spray. Then we lay panting and laughing after our exertions on the hot yellow sand, sheltered from the wind, and in the full blaze of a scorching sun, a cloudless blue sky above, and an immense army of dancing, shouting willow bushes, closing in from all sides, shining with spray and clapping their thousand little hands as though to applaud the success of our efforts.

"What a river!" I said to my companion, thinking of all the way we had traveled from the source in the Black Forest, and how he had often been obliged to wade and push in the upper shallows at the beginning of June.

"Won't stand much nonsense now, will it?" he said, pulling the canoe a little farther into safety up the sand, and then composing himself for a nap.

I lay by his side, happy and peaceful in the bath of the elements--water, wind, sand, and the great fire of the sun--thinking of the long journey that lay behind us, and of the great stretch before us to the Black Sea, and how lucky I was to have such a delightful and charming traveling companion as my friend, the Swede.

We had made many similar journeys together, but the Danube, more than any other river I knew, impressed us from the very beginning with its aliveness. From its tiny bubbling entry into the world among the pinewood gardens of Donaueschingen, until this moment when it began to play the great river-game of losing itself among the deserted swamps, unobserved, unrestrained, it had seemed to us like following the growth of some living creature. Sleepy at first, but later developing violent desires as it became conscious of its deep soul, it rolled, like some huge fluid being, through all the countries we had passed, holding our little craft on its mighty shoulders, playing roughly with us sometimes, yet always friendly and well-meaning, 'til at length we had come inevitably to regard it as a Great Personage.

How, indeed, could it be otherwise, since it told us so much of its secret life? At night we heard it singing to the moon as we lay in our tent, uttering that odd sibilant note peculiar to itself and said to be caused by the rapid tearing of the pebbles along its bed, so great is its hurrying speed. We knew, too, the voice of its gurgling whirlpools, suddenly bubbling up on a surface previously quite calm; the roar of its shallows and swift rapids; its constant steady thundering below all mere surface sounds; and that ceaseless tearing of its icy waters at the banks. How it stood up and shouted when the rains fell flat upon its face! And how its laughter roared out when the wind blew up-stream and tried to stop its growing speed! We knew all its sounds and voices, its tumblings and foamings, its unnecessary splashing against the bridges; that self-conscious chatter when there were hills to look on; the affected dignity of its speech when it passed through the little towns, far too important to laugh; and all these faint, sweet whisperings when the sun caught it fairly in some slow curve and poured down upon it till the steam rose.

It was full of tricks, too, in its early life before the great world knew it. There were places in the upper reaches among the Swabian forests, when yet the first whispers of its destiny had not reached it, where it elected to disappear through holes in the ground, to appear again on the other side of the porous limestone hills and start a new river with another name; leaving, too, so little water in its own bed that we had to climb out and wade and push the canoe through

miles of shallows.

And a chief pleasure, in those early days of its irresponsible youth, was to lie low, like Brer Fox, just before the little turbulent tributaries came to join it from the Alps, and to refuse to acknowledge them when in, but to run for miles side by side, the dividing line well marked, the very levels different, the Danube utterly declining to recognize the newcomer. Below Passau, however, it gave up this particular trick, for there the Inn comes in with a thundering power impossible to ignore, and so pushes and incommodes the parent river that there is hardly room for them in the long twisting gorge that follows, and the Danube is shoved this way and that against the cliffs, and forced to hurry itself with great waves and much dashing to and fro in order to get through in time. And during the fight our canoe slipped down from its shoulder to its breast, and had the time of its life among the struggling waves. But the Inn taught the old river a lesson, and after Passau it no longer pretended to ignore new arrivals.

This was many days back, of course, and since then we had come to know other aspects of the great creature, and across the Bavarian wheat plain of Straubing she wandered so slowly under the blazing June sun that we could well imagine only the surface inches were water, while below there moved, concealed as by a silken mantle, a whole army of Undines, passing silently and unseen down to the sea, and very leisurely too, lest they be discovered.

Much, too, we forgave her because of her friendliness to the birds and animals that haunted the shores. Cormorants lined the banks in lonely places in rows like short black palings; grey crows crowded the shingle-beds; storks stood fishing in the vistas of shallower water that opened up between the islands, and hawks, swans, and marsh birds of all sorts filled the air with glinting wings and singing, petulant cries. It was impossible to feel annoyed with the river's vagaries after seeing a deer leap with a splash into the water at sunrise and swim past the bows of the canoe; and often we saw fawns peering at us from the underbrush, or looked straight into the brown eyes of a stag as we charged full tilt round a

corner and entered another reach of the river. Foxes, too,

everywhere haunted the banks, tripping daintily among the driftwood and disappearing so suddenly that it was impossible to see how they managed it.

But now, after leaving Pressburg, everything changed a little, and the Danube became more serious. It ceased trifling. It was half-way to the Black Sea, within seeming distance almost of other, stranger countries where no tricks would be permitted or understood. It became suddenly grown-up, and claimed our respect and even our awe. It broke out into three arms, for one thing, that only met again a hundred kilometers farther down, and for a canoe there were no indications which one was intended to be followed.

"If you take a side channel," said the Hungarian officer we met in the Pressburg shop while buying provisions, "you may find yourselves, when the flood subsides, forty miles from anywhere, high and dry, and you may easily starve. There are no people, no farms, no fishermen. I warn you not to continue. The river, too, is still rising, and this wind will increase."

The rising river did not alarm us in the least, but the matter of being left high and dry by a sudden subsidence of the waters might be serious, and we had consequently laid in an extra stock of provisions. For the rest, the officer's prophecy held true, and the wind, blowing down a perfectly clear sky, increased steadily till it reached the dignity of a westerly gale.

It was earlier than usual when we camped, for the sun was a good hour or two from the horizon, and leaving my friend still asleep on the hot sand, I wandered about in desultory examination of our hotel. The island, I found, was less than an acre in extent, a mere sandy bank standing some two or three feet above the level of the river. The far end, pointing into the sunset, was covered with flying spray which the tremendous wind drove off the crests of the broken waves. It was triangular in shape, with the apex up stream.

I stood there for several minutes, watching the impetuous crimson flood bearing down with a shouting roar, dashing in waves against the bank as though to sweep it bodily away, and then swirling by in two foaming streams on either side.

The ground seemed to shake with the shock and rush, while the furious movement of the willow bushes as the wind poured over them increased the curious illusion that the island itself actually moved. Above, for a mile or two, I could see the great river descending upon me; it was like looking up the slope of a sliding hill, white with foam, and leaping up everywhere to show itself to the sun.

The rest of the island was too thickly grown with willows to make walking pleasant, but I made the tour, nevertheless. From the lower end the light, of course, changed, and the river looked dark and angry. Only the backs of the flying waves were visible, streaked with foam, and pushed forcibly by the great puffs of wind that fell upon them from behind. For a short mile it was visible, pouring in and out among the islands, and then disappearing with a huge sweep into the willows, which closed about it like a herd of monstrous antediluvian creatures crowding down to drink. They made me think of gigantic sponge-like growths that sucked the river up into themselves. They caused it to vanish from sight. They herded there together in such overpowering numbers.

Altogether it was an impressive scene, with its utter loneliness, its bizarre suggestion; and as I gazed, long and curiously, a singular emotion began to stir somewhere in the depths of me. Midway in my delight of the wild beauty, there crept, unbidden and unexplained, a curious feeling of disquietude, almost of alarm.

A rising river, perhaps, always suggests something of the ominous; many of the little islands I saw before me would probably have been swept away by the morning; this resistless, thundering flood of water touched the sense of awe. Yet I was aware that my uneasiness lay deeper far than the emotions of awe and wonder. It was not that I felt. Nor had it directly to do with the power of the driving wind--this shouting hurricane that might almost carry up a few acres of willows into the air and scatter them like so much chaff over the landscape. The wind was simply enjoying itself, for nothing rose out of the flat landscape to stop it, and I was conscious of sharing its great game with a kind of pleasurable excitement. Yet this novel emotion had nothing to do with the wind. Indeed, so vague was the sense of distress I experienced, that it was impossible to trace it to its source and deal with it accordingly, though I was aware somehow that it had to do with my realization of our utter insignificance before this unrestrained power of the elements about me. The huge-grown river had something to do with it too--a vague, unpleasant idea that we had somehow trifled with these great elemental forces in whose power we lay helpless every hour of the day and night. For here, indeed, they were gigantically at play together, and the sight appealed to the imagination.

But my emotion, so far as I could understand it, seemed to attach itself more particularly to the willow bushes, to these acres and acres of willows, crowding, so thickly growing there, swarming everywhere the eye could reach, pressing upon the river as though to suffocate it, standing in dense array mile after mile beneath the sky, watching, waiting, listening. And, apart quite from the elements, the willows connected themselves subtly with my malaise, attacking the mind insidiously somehow by reason of their vast numbers, and contriving in some way or other to represent to the imagination a new and mighty power, a power, moreover, not altogether friendly to us.

Great revelations of nature, of course, never fail to impress in one way or another, and I was no stranger to moods of the kind. Mountains overawe and oceans terrify, while the mystery of great forests exercises a spell peculiarly its own. But all these, at one point or another, somewhere link on intimately with human life and human experience. They stir comprehensible, even if alarming, emotions. They tend on the whole to exalt.

With this multitude of willows, however, it was something far different, I felt. Some essence emanated from them that besieged the heart. A sense of awe awakened, true, but of awe touched somewhere by a vague terror. Their serried ranks, growing everywhere darker about me as the shadows deepened, moving furiously yet softly in the wind, woke in me the curious and unwelcome suggestion that we had trespassed here upon the borders of an alien world, a world where we were intruders, a world where we were not wanted or invited to remain--where we ran grave risks perhaps!

The feeling, however, though it refused to yield its meaning entirely to analysis, did not at the time trouble me by passing into menace. Yet it never left me quite, even during the very practical business of putting up the tent in a hurricane of wind and building a fire for the stew-pot. It remained, just enough to bother and perplex, and to rob a most delightful camping-ground of a good portion of its charm. To my companion, however, I said nothing, for he was a man I considered devoid of imagination. In the first place, I could never have explained to him what I meant, and in the second, he would have laughed stupidly at me if I had.

There was a slight depression in the center of the island, and here we pitched the tent. The surrounding willows broke the wind a bit.

"A poor camp," observed the imperturbable Swede when at last the tent stood upright, "no stones and precious little firewood. I'm for moving on early tomorrow--eh? This sand won't hold anything."

But the experience of a collapsing tent at midnight had taught us many devices, and we made the cozy gipsy house as safe as possible, and then set about collecting a store of wood to last till bed-time. Willow bushes drop no branches, and driftwood was our only source of supply. We hunted the shores pretty thoroughly. Everywhere the banks were crumbling as the rising flood tore at them and carried away great portions with a splash and a gurgle.

"The island's much smaller than when we landed," said the accurate Swede. "It won't last long at this rate. We'd better drag the canoe close to the tent, and be ready to start at a moment's notice. I shall sleep in my clothes."

He was a little distance off, climbing along the bank, and I heard his rather jolly laugh as he spoke.

"By Jove!" I heard him call, a moment later, and turned to see what had caused his exclamation. But for the moment he was hidden by the willows, and I could not find him.

"What in the world's this?" I heard him cry again, and this time his voice had become serious.

I ran up quickly and joined him on the bank. He was look-ing over the river, pointing at something in the water.

"Good heavens, it's a man's body!" he cried excitedly. "Look!"

A black thing, turning over and over in the foaming waves, swept rapidly past. It kept disappearing and coming up to the surface again. It was about twenty feet from the shore, and just as it was opposite to where we stood it lurched round and looked straight at us. We saw its eyes reflecting the sunset, and gleaming an odd yellow as the body turned over. Then it gave a swift, gulping plunge, and dived out of sight in a flash.

"An otter, by gad!" we exclaimed in the same breath, laughing.

It was an otter, alive, and out on the hunt; yet it had looked exactly like the body of a drowned man turning helplessly in the current. Far below it came to the surface once again, and we saw its black skin, wet and shining in the sunlight.

Then, too, just as we turned back, our arms full of drift-wood, another thing happened to recall us to the river bank. This time it really was a man, and what was more, a man in a boat. Now a small boat on the Danube was an unusual sight at any time, but here in this deserted region, and at flood time, it was so unexpected as to constitute a real event. We stood and stared.

Whether it was due to the slanting sunlight, or the refrac-tion from the wonderfully illumined water, I cannot say, but, whatever the cause, I found it difficult to focus my sight properly upon the flying apparition. It seemed, however, to be a man standing upright in a sort of flat-bottomed boat, steering with a long oar, and being carried down the oppo-site shore at a tremendous pace. He apparently was looking across in our direction, but the distance was too great and the light too uncertain for us to make out very plainly what he was about. It seemed to me that he was gesticulating and making signs at us. His voice came across the water to us shouting something furiously, but the wind drowned it so that no single word was audible. There was something cu-rious about the whole appearance--man, boat, signs, voice-

-that made an impression on me out of all proportion to its cause.

"He's crossing himself!" I cried. "Look, he's making the sign of the Cross!"

"I believe you're right," the Swede said, shading his eyes with his hand and watching the man out of sight. He seemed to be gone in a moment, melting away down there into the sea of willows where the sun caught them in the bend of the river and turned them into a great crimson wall of beauty. Mist, too, had begun to ruse, so that the air was hazy.

"But what in the world is he doing at nightfall on this flooded river?" I said, half to myself. "Where is he going at such a time, and what did he mean by his signs and shouting? D'you think he wished to warn us about something?"

"He saw our smoke, and thought we were spirits probably," laughed my companion. "These Hungarians believe in all sorts of rubbish; you remember the shopwoman at Pressburg warning us that no one ever landed here because it belonged to some sort of beings outside man's world! I suppose they believe in fairies and elementals, possibly demons, too. That peasant in the boat saw people on the islands for the first time in his life," he added, after a slight pause, "and it scared him, that's all."

The Swede's tone of voice was not convincing, and his manner lacked something that was usually there. I noted the change instantly while he talked, though without being able to label it precisely.

"If they had enough imagination," I laughed loudly--I remember trying to make as much noise as I could--"they might well people a place like this with the old gods of antiquity. The Romans must have haunted all this region more or less with their shrines and sacred groves and elemental deities."

The subject dropped and we returned to our stew-pot, for my friend was not given to imaginative conversation as a rule. Moreover, just then I remember feeling distinctly glad that he was not imaginative; his stolid, practical nature suddenly seemed to me welcome and comforting. It was an admirable temperament, I felt; he could steer down rapids like

a red Indian, shoot dangerous bridges and whirlpools better than any white man I ever saw in a canoe. He was a grand fellow for an adventurous trip, a tower of strength when untoward things happened. I looked at his strong face and light curly hair as he staggered along under his pile of driftwood (twice the size of mine!), and I experienced a feeling of relief. Yes, I was distinctly glad just then that the Swede was--what he was, and that he never made remarks that suggested more than they said.

"The river's still rising, though," he added, as if following out some thoughts of his own, and dropping his load with a gasp. "This island will be under water in two days if it goes on."

"I wish the wind would go down," I said. "I don't care a fig for the river."

The flood, indeed, had no terrors for us; we could get off at ten minutes' notice, and the more water the better we liked it. It meant an increasing current and the obliteration of the treacherous shingle-beds that so often threatened to tear the bottom out of our canoe.

Contrary to our expectations, the wind did not go down with the sun. It seemed to increase with the darkness, howling overhead and shaking the willows round us like straws. Curious sounds accompanied it sometimes, like the explosion of heavy guns, and it fell upon the water and the island in great flat blows of immense power. It made me think of the sounds a planet must make, could we only hear it, driving along through space.

But the sky kept wholly clear of clouds, and soon after supper the full moon rose up in the east and covered the river and the plain of shouting willows with a light like the day.

We lay on the sandy patch beside the fire, smoking, listening to the noises of the night round us, and talking happily of the journey we had already made, and of our plans ahead. The map lay spread in the door of the tent, but the high wind made it hard to study, and presently we lowered the curtain and extinguished the lantern. The firelight was enough to smoke and see each other's faces by, and the sparks flew about overhead like fireworks. A few yards beyond, the river

gurgled and hissed, and from time to time a heavy splash announced the falling away of further portions of the bank.

Our talk, I noticed, had to do with the faraway scenes and incidents of our first camps in the Black Forest, or of other subjects altogether remote from the present setting, for neither of us spoke of the actual moment more than was necessary--almost as though we had agreed tacitly to avoid discussion of the camp and its incidents. Neither the otter nor the boatman, for instance, received the honor of a single mention, though ordinarily these would have furnished discussion for the greater part of the evening. They were, of course, distinct events in such a place.

The scarcity of wood made it a business to keep the fire going, for the wind, that drove the smoke in our faces wherever we sat, helped at the same time to make a forced draught. We took it in turn to make some foraging expeditions into the darkness, and the quantity the Swede brought back always made me feel that he took an absurdly long time finding it; for the fact was I did not care much about being left alone, and yet it always seemed to be my turn to grub about among the bushes or scramble along the slippery banks in the moonlight. The long day's battle with wind and water--such wind and such water!--had tired us both, and an early bed was the obvious program. Yet neither of us made the move for the tent. We lay there, tending the fire, talking in desultory fashion, peering about us into the dense willow bushes, and listening to the thunder of wind and river. The loneliness of the place had entered our very bones, and silence seemed natural, for after a bit the sound of our voices became a trifle unreal and forced; whispering would have been the fitting mode of communication, I felt, and the human voice, always rather absurd amid the roar of the elements, now carried with it something almost illegitimate. It was like talking out loud in church, or in some place where it was not lawful, perhaps not quite safe, to be overheard.

The eeriness of this lonely island, set among a million willows, swept by a hurricane, and surrounded by hurrying deep waters, touched us both, I fancy. Untrodden by man, almost unknown to man, it lay there beneath the moon, remote from human influence, on the frontier of another world, an alien world, a world tenanted by willows only and the souls of willows. And we, in our rashness, had dared to invade it, even to make use of it! Something more than the power of its mystery stirred in me as I lay on the sand, feet to fire, and peered up through the leaves at the stars. For the last time I rose to get firewood.

"When this has burnt up," I said firmly, "I shall turn in," and my companion watched me lazily as I moved off into the surrounding shadows.

For an unimaginative man I thought he seemed unusually receptive that night, unusually open to suggestion of things other than sensory. He too was touched by the beauty and loneliness of the place. I was not altogether pleased, I re-member, to recognize this slight change in him, and instead of immediately collecting sticks, I made my way to the far point of the island where the moonlight on plain and river could be seen to better advantage. The desire to be alone had come suddenly upon me; my former dread returned in force; there was a vague feeling in me I wished to face and probe to the bottom.

When I reached the point of sand jutting out among the waves, the spell of the place descended upon me with a posi-tive shock. No mere "scenery" could have produced such an effect. There was something more here, something to alarm.

I gazed across the waste of wild waters; I watched the whis-pering willows; I heard the ceaseless beating of the tireless wind; and, one and all, each in its own way, stirred in me this sensation of a strange distress. But the willows especially; for ever they went on chattering and talking among themselves, laughing a little, shrilly crying out, sometimes sighing--but what it was they made so much to-do about belonged to the secret life of the great plain they inhabited. And it was utter-ly alien to the world I knew, or to that of the wild yet kindly elements. They made me think of a host of beings from an-other plane of life, another evolution altogether, perhaps, all discussing a mystery known only to themselves. I watched them moving busily together, oddly shaking their big bushy heads, twirling their myriad leaves even when there was no wind. They moved of their own will as though alive, and they touched, by some incalculable method, my own keen sense of the horrible.

There they stood in the moonlight, like a vast army surrounding our camp, shaking their innumerable silver spears defiantly, formed all ready for an attack.

The psychology of places, for some imaginations at least, is very vivid; for the wanderer, especially, camps have their "note" either of welcome or rejection. At first it may not always be apparent, because the busy preparations of tent and cooking prevent, but with the first pause--after supper usually--it comes and announces itself. And the note of this willow-camp now became unmistakably plain to me; we were interlopers, trespassers; we were not welcomed. The sense of unfamiliarity grew upon me as I stood there watching. We touched the frontier of a region where our presence was resented. For a night's lodging we might perhaps be tolerated; but for a prolonged and inquisitive stay--No! by all the gods of the trees and wilderness, no! We were the first human influences upon this island, and we were not wanted. The willows were against us.

Strange thoughts like these, bizarre fancies, borne I know not whence, found lodgment in my mind as I stood listening. What, I thought, if, after all, these crouching willows proved to be alive; if suddenly they should rise up, like a swarm of living creatures, marshaled by the gods whose territory we had invaded, sweep towards us off the vast swamps, booming overhead in the night--and then settle down! As I looked it was so easy to imagine they actually moved, crept nearer, retreated a little, huddled together in masses, hostile, waiting for the great wind that should finally start them a-running. I could have sworn their aspect changed a little, and their ranks deepened and pressed more closely together.

The melancholy shrill cry of a night-bird sounded overhead, and suddenly I nearly lost my balance as the piece of bank I stood upon fell with a great splash into the river, undermined by the flood. I stepped back just in time, and went on hunting for firewood again, half laughing at the odd fancies that crowded so thickly into my mind and cast their spell upon me. I recalled the Swede's remark about moving on next day, and I was just thinking that I fully agreed with him, when I turned with a start and saw the subject of my thoughts standing immediately in front of me. He was quite close. The roar of the elements had covered his approach.

II

"You've been gone so long," he shouted above the wind, "I thought something must have happened to you."

But there was that in his tone, and a certain look in his face as well, that conveyed to me more than his usual words, and in a flash I understood the real reason for his coming. It was because the spell of the place had entered his soul too, and he did not like being alone.

"River still rising," he cried, pointing to the flood in the moonlight, "and the wind's simply awful."

He always said the same things, but it was the cry for companionship that gave the real importance to his words.

"Lucky," I cried back, "our tent's in the hollow. I think it'll hold all right." I added something about the difficulty of finding wood, in order to explain my absence, but the wind caught my words and flung them across the river, so that he did not hear, but just looked at me through the branches, nodding his head.

"Lucky if we get away without disaster!" he shouted, or words to that effect; and I remember feeling half angry with him for putting the thought into words, for it was exactly what I felt myself. There was disaster impending somewhere, and the sense of presentiment lay unpleasantly upon me.

We went back to the fire and made a final blaze, poking it up with our feet. We took a last look round. But for the wind the heat would have been unpleasant. I put this thought into words, and I remember my friend's reply struck me oddly: that he would rather have the heat, the ordinary July weather, than this "diabolical wind."

Everything was snug for the night; the canoe lying turned over beside the tent, with both yellow paddles beneath her; the provision sack hanging from a willow-stem, and the washed-up dishes removed to a safe distance from the fire, all ready for the morning meal.

We smothered the embers of the fire with sand, and then turned in. The flap of the tent door was up, and I saw the branches and the stars and the white moonlight. The shaking willows and the heavy buffetings of the wind against our taut little house were the last things I remembered as sleep came down and covered all with its soft and delicious forgetfulness.

Suddenly I found myself lying awake, peering from my sandy mattress through the door of the tent. I looked at my watch pinned against the canvas, and saw by the bright moonlight that it was past twelve o'clock--the threshold of a new day--and I had therefore slept a couple of hours. The Swede was asleep still beside me; the wind howled as before; something plucked at my heart and made me feel afraid. There was a sense of disturbance in my immediate neighborhood.

I sat up quickly and looked out. The trees were swaying violently to and fro as the gusts smote them, but our little bit of green canvas lay snugly safe in the hollow, for the wind passed over it without meeting enough resistance to make it vicious. The feeling of disquietude did not pass, however, and I crawled quietly out of the tent to see if our belongings were safe. I moved carefully so as not to waken my companion. A curious excitement was on me.

I was half-way out, kneeling on all fours, when my eye first took in that the tops of the bushes opposite, with their moving tracery of leaves, made shapes against the sky. I sat back on my haunches and stared. It was incredible, surely, but there, opposite and slightly above me, were shapes of some indeterminate sort among the willows, and as the branches swayed in the wind they seemed to group themselves about these shapes, forming a series of monstrous outlines that shifted rapidly beneath the moon. Close, about fifty feet in front of me, I saw these things.

My first instinct was to waken my companion, that he too might see them, but something made me hesitate--the sudden realization, probably, that I should not welcome corroboration; and meanwhile I crouched there staring in 

amazement with smarting eyes. I was wide awake. I remember saying to myself that I was not dreaming.

They first became properly visible, these huge figures, just within the tops of the bushes--immense, bronze-colored, moving, and wholly independent of the swaying of the branches. I saw them plainly and noted, now I came to examine them more calmly, that they were very much larger than human, and indeed that something in their appearance proclaimed them to be not human at all. Certainly they were not merely the moving tracery of the branches against the moonlight. They shifted independently. They rose upwards in a continuous stream from earth to sky, vanishing utterly as soon as they reached the dark of the sky. They were interlaced one with another, making a great column, and I saw their limbs and huge bodies melting in and out of each other, forming this serpentine line that bent and swayed and twisted spirally with the contortions of the wind-tossed trees. They were nude, fluid shapes, passing up the bushes, within the leaves almost--rising up in a living column into the heavens. Their faces I never could see. Unceasingly they poured upwards, swaying in great bending curves, with a hue of dull bronze upon their skins.

I stared, trying to force every atom of vision from my eyes. For a long time I thought they must every moment disappear and resolve themselves into the movements of the branches and prove to be an optical illusion. I searched everywhere for a proof of reality, when all the while I understood quite well that the standard of reality had changed. For the longer I looked the more certain I became that these figures were real and living, though perhaps not according to the standards that the camera and the biologist would insist upon.

Far from feeling fear, I was possessed with a sense of awe and wonder such as I have never known. I seemed to be gazing at the personified elemental forces of this haunted and primeval region. Our intrusion had stirred the powers of the place into activity. It was we who were the cause of the disturbance, and my brain filled to bursting with stories and legends of the spirits and deities of places that have been acknowledged and worshipped by men in all ages of

the world's history. But, before I could arrive at any possible explanation, something impelled me to go farther out, and I crept forward on the sand and stood upright. I felt the ground still warm under my bare feet; the wind tore at my hair and face; and the sound of the river burst upon my ears with a sudden roar. These things, I knew, were real, and proved that my senses were acting normally. Yet the figures still rose from earth to heaven, silent, majestically, in a great spiral of grace and strength that overwhelmed me at length with a genuine deep emotion of worship. I felt that I must fall down and worship--absolutely worship.

Perhaps in another minute I might have done so, when a gust of wind swept against me with such force that it blew me sideways, and I nearly stumbled and fell. It seemed to shake the dream violently out of me. At least it gave me another point of view somehow. The figures still remained, still ascended into heaven from the heart of the night, but my reason at last began to assert itself. It must be a subjective experience, I argued--none the less real for that, but still subjective. The moonlight and the branches combined to work out these pictures upon the mirror of my imagination, and for some reason I projected them outwards and made them appear objective. I knew this must be the case, of course. I took courage, and began to move forward across the open patches of sand. By Jove, though, was it all hallucination? Was it merely subjective? Did not my reason argue in the old futile way from the little standard of the known?

I only know that great column of figures ascended darkly into the sky for what seemed a very long period of time, and with a very complete measure of reality as most men are accustomed to gauge reality. Then suddenly they were gone!

And, once they were gone and the immediate wonder of their great presence had passed, fear came down upon me with a cold rush. The esoteric meaning of this lonely and haunted region suddenly flamed up within me, and I began to tremble dreadfully. I took a quick look round--a look of horror that came near to panic--calculating vainly ways of escape; and then, realizing how helpless I was to achieve anything really effective, I crept back silently into the tent and lay down again upon my sandy mattress, first lowering the door-curtain to shut out the sight of the willows in the moonlight, and then burying my head as deeply as possible beneath the blankets to deaden the sound of the terrifying wind.

As though further to convince me that I had not been dreaming, I remember that it was a long time before I fell again into a troubled and restless sleep; and even then only the upper crust of me slept, and underneath there was something that never quite lost consciousness, but lay alert and on the watch.

But this second time I jumped up with a genuine start of terror. It was neither the wind nor the river that woke me, but the slow approach of something that caused the sleeping portion of me to grow smaller and smaller till at last it vanished altogether, and I found myself sitting bolt upright--listening.

Outside there was a sound of multitudinous little patterings. They had been coming, I was aware, for a long time, and in my sleep they had first become audible. I sat there nervously wide awake as though I had not slept at all. It seemed to me that my breathing came with difficulty, and that there was a great weight upon the surface of my body. In spite of the hot night, I felt clammy with cold and shivered. Something surely was pressing steadily against the sides of the tent and weighing down upon it from above. Was it the body of the wind? Was this the pattering rain, the dripping of the leaves? The spray blown from the river by the wind and gathering in big drops? I thought quickly of a dozen things.

Then suddenly the explanation leaped into my mind: a bough from the poplar, the only large tree on the island, had fallen with the wind. Still half caught by the other branches, it would fall with the next gust and crush us, and meanwhile its leaves brushed and tapped upon the tight canvas surface of the tent. I raised a loose flap and rushed out, calling to the Swede to follow.

But when I got out and stood upright I saw that the tent was free. There was no hanging bough; there was no rain or

spray; nothing approached.

A cold, grey light filtered down through the bushes and lay on the faintly gleaming sand. Stars still crowded the sky directly overhead, and the wind howled magnificently, but the fire no longer gave out any glow, and I saw the east reddening in streaks through the trees. Several hours must have passed since I stood there before watching the ascending figures, and the memory of it now came back to me horribly, like an evil dream. Oh, how tired it made me feel, that ceaseless raging wind! Yet, though the deep lassitude of a sleepless night was on me, my nerves were tingling with the activity of an equally tireless apprehension, and all idea of repose was out of the question. The river I saw had risen further. Its thunder filled the air, and a fine spray made itself felt through my thin sleeping shirt.

Yet nowhere did I discover the slightest evidence of anything to cause alarm. This deep, prolonged disturbance in my heart remained wholly unaccounted for.

My companion had not stirred when I called him, and there was no need to waken him now. I looked about me carefully, noting everything; the turned-over canoe; the yellow paddles--two of them, I'm certain; the provision sack and the extra lantern hanging together from the tree; and, crowding everywhere about me, enveloping all, the willows, those endless, shaking willows. A bird uttered its morning cry, and a string of duck passed with whirring flight overhead in the twilight. The sand whirled, dry and stinging, about my bare feet in the wind.

I walked round the tent and then went out a little way into the bush, so that I could see across the river to the farther landscape, and the same profound yet indefinable emotion of distress seized upon me again as I saw the interminable sea of bushes stretching to the horizon, looking ghostly and unreal in the wan light of dawn. I walked softly here and there, still puzzling over that odd sound of infinite pattering, and of that pressure upon the tent that had wakened me. It must have been the wind, I reflected--the wind bearing upon the loose, hot sand, driving the dry particles smartly against the taut canvas--the wind dropping heavily upon

our fragile roof.

Yet all the time my nervousness and malaise increased appreciably.

I crossed over to the farther shore and noted how the coast-line had altered in the night, and what masses of sand the river had torn away. I dipped my hands and feet into the cool current, and bathed my forehead. Already there was a glow of sunrise in the sky and the exquisite freshness of coming day. On my way back I passed purposely beneath the very bushes where I had seen the column of figures rising into the air, and midway among the clumps I suddenly found myself overtaken by a sense of vast terror. From the shadows a large figure went swiftly by. Someone passed me, as sure as ever man did....

It was a great staggering blow from the wind that helped me forward again, and once out in the more open space, the sense of terror diminished strangely. The winds were about and walking, I remember saying to myself, for the winds often move like great presences under the trees. And altogether the fear that hovered about me was such an unknown and immense kind of fear, so unlike anything I had ever felt before, that it woke a sense of awe and wonder in me that did much to counteract its worst effects; and when I reached a high point in the middle of the island from which I could see the wide stretch of river, crimson in the sunrise, the whole magical beauty of it all was so overpowering that a sort of wild yearning woke in me and almost brought a cry up into the throat.

But this cry found no expression, for as my eyes wandered from the plain beyond to the island round me and noted our little tent half hidden among the willows, a dreadful discovery leaped out at me, compared to which my terror of the walking winds seemed as nothing at all.

For a change, I thought, had somehow come about in the arrangement of the landscape. It was not that my point of vantage gave me a different view, but that an alteration had apparently been effected in the relation of the tent to the willows, and of the willows to the tent. Surely the bushes now crowded much closer--unnecessarily, unpleasantly close.

They had moved nearer.

Creeping with silent feet over the shifting sands, drawing imperceptibly nearer by soft, unhurried movements, the willows had come closer during the night. But had the wind moved them, or had they moved of themselves? I recalled the sound of infinite small patterings and the pressure upon the tent and upon my own heart that caused me to wake in terror. I swayed for a moment in the wind like a tree, finding it hard to keep my upright position on the sandy hillock. There was a suggestion here of personal agency, of deliberate intention, of aggressive hostility, and it terrified me into a sort of rigidity.

Then the reaction followed quickly. The idea was so bizarre, so absurd, that I felt inclined to laugh. But the laughter came no more readily than the cry, for the knowledge that my mind was so receptive to such dangerous imaginings brought the additional terror that it was through our minds and not through our physical bodies that the attack would come, and was coming.

The wind buffeted me about, and, very quickly it seemed, the sun came up over the horizon, for it was after four o'clock, and I must have stood on that little pinnacle of sand longer than I knew, afraid to come down to close quarters with the willows. I returned quietly, creepily, to the tent, first taking another exhaustive look round and--yes, I confess it--making a few measurements. I paced out on the warm sand the distances between the willows and the tent, making a note of the shortest distance particularly.

I crawled stealthily into my blankets. My companion, to all appearances, still slept soundly, and I was glad that this was so. Provided my experiences were not corroborated, I could find strength somehow to deny them, perhaps. With the daylight I could persuade myself that it was all a subjective hallucination, a fantasy of the night, a projection of the excited imagination.

Nothing further came in to disturb me, and I fell asleep almost at once, utterly exhausted, yet still in dread of hearing again that weird sound of multitudinous pattering, or of feeling the pressure upon my heart that had made it difficult to breathe.

The sun was high in the heavens when my companion woke me from a heavy sleep and announced that the porridge was cooked and there was just time to bathe. The grateful smell of frizzling bacon entered the tent door.

"River still rising," he said, "and several islands out in midstream have disappeared altogether. Our own island's much smaller."

"Any wood left?" I asked sleepily.

"The wood and the island will finish tomorrow in a dead heat," he laughed, "but there's enough to last us till then."

I plunged in from the point of the island, which had indeed altered a lot in size and shape during the night, and was swept down in a moment to the landing-place opposite the tent. The water was icy, and the banks flew by like the country from an express train. Bathing under such conditions was an exhilarating operation, and the terror of the night seemed cleansed out of me by a process of evaporation in the brain. The sun was blazing hot; not a cloud showed itself anywhere; the wind, however, had not abated one little jot.

Quite suddenly then the implied meaning of the Swede's words flashed across me, showing that he no longer wished to leave post-haste, and had changed his mind. "Enough to last till tomorrow"--he assumed we should stay on the island another night. It struck me as odd. The night before he was so positive the other way. How had the change come about?

Great crumblings of the banks occurred at breakfast, with heavy splashings and clouds of spray which the wind brought into our frying-pan, and my fellow-traveler talked incessantly about the difficulty the Vienna-Pesth steamers must have to find the channel in flood. But the state of his mind interested and impressed me far more than the state of the river or the difficulties of the steamers. He had changed somehow since the evening before. His manner was different--a trifle excited, a trifle shy, with a sort of suspicion about his voice and gestures. I hardly know how to describe it now in cold blood, but at the time I remember being quite certain of one thing--that he had become frightened?

He ate very little breakfast, and for once omitted to smoke

his pipe. He had the map spread open beside him, and kept studying its markings.

"We'd better get off sharp in an hour," I said presently, feeling for an opening that must bring him indirectly to a partial confession at any rate. And his answer puzzled me uncomfortably: "Rather! If they'll let us."

"Who'll let us? The elements?" I asked quickly, with affected indifference.

"The powers of this awful place, whoever they are," he replied, keeping his eyes on the map. "The gods are here, if they are anywhere at all in the world."

"The elements are always the true immortals," I replied, laughing as naturally as I could manage, yet knowing quite well that my face reflected my true feelings when he looked up gravely at me and spoke across the smoke:

"We shall be fortunate if we get away without further disaster."

This was exactly what I had dreaded, and I screwed myself up to the point of the direct question. It was like agreeing to allow the dentist to extract the tooth; it had to come anyhow in the long run, and the rest was all pretence.

"Further disaster! Why, what's happened?"

"For one thing--the steering paddle's gone," he said quietly.

"The steering paddle gone!" I repeated, greatly excited, for this was our rudder, and the Danube in flood without a rudder was suicide. "But what--"

"And there's a tear in the bottom of the canoe," he added, with a genuine little tremor in his voice.

I continued staring at him, able only to repeat the words in his face somewhat foolishly. There, in the heat of the sun, and on this burning sand, I was aware of a freezing atmosphere descending round us. I got up to follow him, for he merely nodded his head gravely and led the way towards the tent a few yards on the other side of the fireplace. The canoe still lay there as I had last seen her in the night, ribs uppermost, the paddles, or rather, the paddle, on the sand beside her.

"There's only one," he said, stooping to pick it up. "And here's the rent in the base-board."

It was on the tip of my tongue to tell him that I had clearly noticed two paddles a few hours before, but a second impulse made me think better of it, and I said nothing. I approached to see.

There was a long, finely made tear in the bottom of the canoe where a little slither of wood had been neatly taken clean out; it looked as if the tooth of a sharp rock or snag had eaten down her length, and investigation showed that the hole went through. Had we launched out in her without observing it we must inevitably have foundered. At first the water would have made the wood swell so as to close the hole, but once out in mid-stream the water must have poured in, and the canoe, never more than two inches above the surface, would have filled and sunk very rapidly.

"There, you see an attempt to prepare a victim for the sacrifice," I heard him saying, more to himself than to me, "two victims rather," he added as he bent over and ran his fingers along the slit.

I began to whistle--a thing I always do unconsciously when utterly nonplussed--and purposely paid no attention to his words. I was determined to consider them foolish.

"It wasn't there last night," he said presently, straightening up from his examination and looking anywhere but at me.

"We must have scratched her in landing, of course," I stopped whistling to say. "The stones are very sharp."

I stopped abruptly, for at that moment he turned round and met my eye squarely. I knew just as well as he did how impossible my explanation was. There were no stones, to begin with.

"And then there's this to explain too," he added quietly, handing me the paddle and pointing to the blade.

A new and curious emotion spread freezingly over me as I took and examined it. The blade was scraped down all over, beautifully scraped, as though someone had sand-papered it with care, making it so thin that the first vigorous stroke must have snapped it off at the elbow.

"One of us walked in his sleep and did this thing," I said feebly, "or--or it has been filed by the constant stream of sand particles blown against it by the wind, perhaps."

"Ah," said the Swede, turning away, laughing a little, "you can explain everything."

"The same wind that caught the steering paddle and flung it so near the bank that it fell in with the next lump that crumbled," I called out after him, absolutely determined to find an explanation for everything he showed me.

"I see," he shouted back, turning his head to look at me before disappearing among the willow bushes.

Once alone with these perplexing evidences of personal agency, I think my first thoughts took the form of "One of us must have done this thing, and it certainly was not I." But my second thought decided how impossible it was to suppose, under all the circumstances, that either of us had done it. That my companion, the trusted friend of a dozen similar expeditions, could have knowingly had a hand in it, was a suggestion not to be entertained for a moment. Equally absurd seemed the explanation that this imperturbable and densely practical nature had suddenly become insane and was busied with insane purposes.

Yet the fact remained that what disturbed me most, and kept my fear actively alive even in this blaze of sunshine and wild beauty, was the clear certainty that some curious alteration had come about in his mind--that he was nervous, timid, suspicious, aware of goings on he did not speak about, watching a series of secret and hitherto unmentionable events--waiting, in a word, for a climax that he expected, and, I thought, expected very soon. This grew up in my mind intuitively--I hardly knew how.

I made a hurried examination of the tent and its surroundings, but the measurements of the night remained the same. There were deep hollows formed in the sand I now noticed for the first time, basin-shaped and of various depths and sizes, varying from that of a tea-cup to a large bowl. The wind, no doubt, was responsible for these miniature craters, just as it was for lifting the paddle and tossing it towards the water. The rent in the canoe was the only thing that seemed quite inexplicable; and, after all, it was conceivable that a sharp point had caught it when we landed. The examination I made of the shore did not assist this theory, but all the same I clung to it with that diminishing portion of my intelligence which I called my "reason." An explanation of some kind was an absolute necessity, just as some working explanation of the universe is necessary--however absurd--to the happiness of every individual who seeks to do his duty in the world and face the problems of life. The simile seemed to me at the time an exact parallel.

I at once set the pitch melting, and presently the Swede joined me at the work, though under the best conditions in the world the canoe could not be safe for traveling till the following day. I drew his attention casually to the hollows in the sand.

"Yes," he said, "I know. They're all over the island. But you can explain them, no doubt!"

"Wind, of course," I answered without hesitation. "Have you never watched those little whirlwinds in the street that twist and twirl everything into a circle? This sand's loose enough to yield, that's all."

He made no reply, and we worked on in silence for a bit. I watched him surreptitiously all the time, and I had an idea he was watching me. He seemed, too, to be always listening attentively to something I could not hear, or perhaps for something that he expected to hear, for he kept turning about and staring into the bushes, and up into the sky, and out across the water where it was visible through the openings among the willows. Sometimes he even put his hand to his ear and held it there for several minutes. He said nothing to me, however, about it, and I asked no questions. And meanwhile, as he mended that torn canoe with the skill and address of a red Indian, I was glad to notice his absorption in the work, for there was a vague dread in my heart that he would speak of the changed aspect of the willows. And, if he had noticed that, my imagination could no longer be held a sufficient explanation of it.

III

At length, after a long pause, he began to talk.

"Queer thing," he added in a hurried sort of voice, as though he wanted to say something and get it over. "Queer

thing. I mean, about that otter last night.”

I had expected something so totally different that he caught me with surprise, and I looked up sharply.

“Shows how lonely this place is. Otters are awfully shy things--”

“I don’t mean that, of course,” he interrupted. “I mean--do you think--did you think it really was an otter?”

“What else, in the name of Heaven, what else?”

“You know, I saw it before you did, and at first it seemed-- so much bigger than an otter.”

“The sunset as you looked up-stream magnified it, or something,” I replied.

He looked at me absently a moment, as though his mind were busy with other thoughts.

“It had such extraordinary yellow eyes,” he went on half to himself.

“That was the sun too,” I laughed, a trifle boisterously. “I suppose you’ll wonder next if that fellow in the boat--”

I suddenly decided not to finish the sentence. He was in the act again of listening, turning his head to the wind, and something in the expression of his face made me halt. The subject dropped, and we went on with our caulking. Apparently he had not noticed my unfinished sentence. Five minutes later, however, he looked at me across the canoe, the smoking pitch in his hand, his face exceedingly grave.

“I did rather wonder, if you want to know,” he said slowly, “what that thing in the boat was. I remember thinking at the time it was not a man. The whole business seemed to rise quite suddenly out of the water.”

I laughed again boisterously in his face, but this time there was impatience, and a strain of anger too, in my feeling.

“Look here now,” I cried, “this place is quite queer enough without going out of our way to imagine things! That boat was an ordinary boat, and the man in it was an ordinary man, and they were both going down-stream as fast as they could lick. And that otter was an otter, so don’t let’s play the fool about it!”

He looked steadily at me with the same grave expression. He was not in the least annoyed. I took courage from his

silence.

"And, for Heaven's sake," I went on, "don't keep pretending you hear things, because it only gives me the jumps, and there's nothing to hear but the river and this cursed old thundering wind."

"You fool!" he answered in a low, shocked voice, "you utter fool. That's just the way all victims talk. As if you didn't understand just as well as I do!" he sneered with scorn in his voice, and a sort of resignation. "The best thing you can do is to keep quiet and try to hold your mind as firm as possible. This feeble attempt at self-deception only makes the truth harder when you're forced to meet it."

My little effort was over, and I found nothing more to say, for I knew quite well his words were true, and that I was the fool, not he. Up to a certain stage in the adventure he kept ahead of me easily, and I think I felt annoyed to be out of it, to be thus proved less psychic, less sensitive than himself to these extraordinary happenings, and half ignorant all the time of what was going on under my very nose. He knew from the very beginning, apparently. But at the moment I wholly missed the point of his words about the necessity of there being a victim, and that we ourselves were destined to satisfy the want. I dropped all pretence thenceforward, but thenceforward likewise my fear increased steadily to the climax.

"But you're quite right about one thing," he added, before the subject passed, "and that is that we're wiser not to talk about it, or even to think about it, because what one thinks finds expression in words, and what one says, happens."

That afternoon, while the canoe dried and hardened, we spent trying to fish, testing the leak, collecting wood, and watching the enormous flood of rising water. Masses of driftwood swept near our shores sometimes, and we fished for them with long willow branches. The island grew perceptibly smaller as the banks were torn away with great gulps and splashes. The weather kept brilliantly fine till about four o'clock, and then for the first time for three days the wind showed signs of abating. Clouds began to gather in the south-west, spreading thence slowly over the sky.

This lessening of the wind came as a great relief, for the incessant roaring, banging, and thundering had irritated our nerves. Yet the silence that came about five o'clock with its sudden cessation was in a manner quite as oppressive. The booming of the river had everything in its own way then; it filled the air with deep murmurs, more musical than the wind noises, but infinitely more monotonous. The wind held many notes, rising, falling always beating out some sort of great elemental tune; whereas the river's song lay between three notes at most--dull pedal notes, that held a lugubrious quality foreign to the wind, and somehow seemed to me, in my then nervous state, to sound wonderfully well the music of doom.

It was extraordinary, too, how the withdrawal suddenly of bright sunlight took everything out of the landscape that made for cheerfulness; and since this particular landscape had already managed to convey the suggestion of something sinister, the change of course was all the more unwelcome and noticeable. For me, I know, the darkening outlook became distinctly more alarming, and I found myself more than once calculating how soon after sunset the full moon would get up in the east, and whether the gathering clouds would greatly interfere with her lighting of the little island.

With this general hush of the wind--though it still indulged in occasional brief gusts--the river seemed to me to grow blacker, the willows to stand more densely together. The latter, too, kept up a sort of independent movement of their own, rustling among themselves when no wind stirred, and shaking oddly from the roots upwards. When common objects in this way be come charged with the suggestion of horror, they stimulate the imagination far more than things of unusual appearance; and these bushes, crowding huddled about us, assumed for me in the darkness a bizarre grotesquerie of appearance that lent to them somehow the aspect of purposeful and living creatures. Their very ordinariness, I felt, masked what was malignant and hostile to us. The forces of the region drew nearer with the coming of night. They were focusing upon our island, and more particularly upon ourselves. For thus, somehow, in the terms of the imagination, did my really indescribable sensations in this extraordinary place present themselves.

I had slept a good deal in the early afternoon, and had thus recovered somewhat from the exhaustion of a disturbed night, but this only served apparently to render me more susceptible than before to the obsessing spell of the haunting. I fought against it, laughing at my feelings as absurd and childish, with very obvious physiological explanations, yet, in spite of every effort, they gained in strength upon me so that I dreaded the night as a child lost in a forest must dread the approach of darkness.

The canoe we had carefully covered with a waterproof sheet during the day, and the one remaining paddle had been securely tied by the Swede to the base of a tree, lest the wind should rob us of that too. From five o'clock onwards I busied myself with the stew-pot and preparations for dinner, it being my turn to cook that night. We had potatoes, onions, bits of bacon fat to add flavor, and a general thick residue from former stews at the bottom of the pot; with black bread broken up into it the result was most excellent, and it was followed by a stew of plums with sugar and a brew of strong tea with dried milk. A good pile of wood lay close at hand, and the absence of wind made my duties easy. My companion sat lazily watching me, dividing his attentions between cleaning his pipe and giving useless advice--an admitted privilege of the off-duty man. He had been very quiet all the afternoon, engaged in re-caulking the canoe, strengthening the tent ropes, and fishing for driftwood while I slept. No more talk about undesirable things had passed between us, and I think his only remarks had to do with the gradual destruction of the island, which he declared was not fully a third smaller than when we first landed.

The pot had just begun to bubble when I heard his voice calling to me from the bank, where he had wandered away without my noticing. I ran up.

"Come and listen," he said, "and see what you make of it." He held his hand cupwise to his ear, as so often before.

"Now do you hear anything?" he asked, watching me curiously.

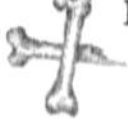

We stood there, listening attentively together. At first I heard only the deep note of the water and the hissings rising from its turbulent surface. The willows, for once, were motionless and silent. Then a sound began to reach my ears faintly, a peculiar sound--something like the humming of a distant gong. It seemed to come across to us in the darkness from the waste of swamps and willows opposite. It was repeated at regular intervals, but it was certainly neither the sound of a bell nor the hooting of a distant steamer. I can liken it to nothing so much as to the sound of an immense gong, suspended far up in the sky, repeating incessantly its muffled metallic note, soft and musical, as it was repeatedly struck. My heart quickened as I listened.

"I've heard it all day," said my companion. "While you slept this afternoon it came all round the island. I hunted it down, but could never get near enough to see--to localize it correctly. Sometimes it was overhead, and sometimes it seemed under the water. Once or twice, too, I could have sworn it was not outside at all, but within myself--you know--the way a sound in the fourth dimension is supposed to come."

I was too much puzzled to pay much attention to his words. I listened carefully, striving to associate it with any known familiar sound I could think of, but without success. It changed in the direction, too, coming nearer, and then sinking utterly away into remote distance. I cannot say that it was ominous in quality, because to me it seemed distinctly musical, yet I must admit it set going a distressing feeling that made me wish I had never heard it.

"The wind blowing in those sand-funnels," I said determined to find an explanation, "or the bushes rubbing together after the storm perhaps."

"It comes off the whole swamp," my friend answered. "It comes from everywhere at once." He ignored my explanations. "It comes from the willow bushes somehow--"

"But now the wind has dropped," I objected. "The willows can hardly make a noise by themselves, can they?"

His answer frightened me, first because I had dreaded it, and secondly, because I knew intuitively it was true.

"It is because the wind has dropped we now hear it. It was

drowned before. It is the cry, I believe, of the--"

I dashed back to my fire, warned by the sound of bubbling that the stew was in danger, but determined at the same time to escape further conversation. I was resolute, if possible, to avoid the exchanging of views. I dreaded, too, that he would begin about the gods, or the elemental forces, or something else disquieting, and I wanted to keep myself well in hand for what might happen later. There was another night to be faced before we escaped from this distressing place, and there was no knowing yet what it might bring forth.

"Come and cut up bread for the pot," I called to him, vigorously stirring the appetizing mixture. That stew-pot held sanity for us both, and the thought made me laugh.

He came over slowly and took the provision sack from the tree, fumbling in its mysterious depths, and then emptying the entire contents upon the ground-sheet at his feet.

"Hurry up!" I cried; "it's boiling."

The Swede burst out into a roar of laughter that startled me. It was forced laughter, not artificial exactly, but mirthless.

"There's nothing here!" he shouted, holding his sides.

"Bread, I mean."

"It's gone. There is no bread. They've taken it!"

I dropped the long spoon and ran up. Everything the sack had contained lay upon the ground-sheet, but there was no loaf.

The whole dead weight of my growing fear fell upon me and shook me. Then I burst out laughing too. It was the only thing to do: and the sound of my laughter also made me understand his. The stain of psychical pressure caused it-- this explosion of unnatural laughter in both of us; it was an effort of repressed forces to seek relief; it was a temporary safety-valve. And with both of us it ceased quite suddenly.

"How criminally stupid of me!" I cried, still determined to be consistent and find an explanation. "I clean forgot to buy a loaf at Pressburg. That chattering woman put everything out of my head, and I must have left it lying on the counter or--"

"The oatmeal, too, is much less than it was this morning,"

the Swede interrupted.

Why in the world need he draw attention to it? I thought angrily.

"There's enough for tomorrow," I said, stirring vigorously, "and we can get lots more at Komorn or Gran. In twenty-four hours we shall be miles from here."

"I hope so--to God," he muttered, putting the things back into the sack, "unless we're claimed first as victims for the sacrifice," he added with a foolish laugh. He dragged the sack into the tent, for safety's sake, I suppose, and I heard him mumbling to himself, but so indistinctly that it seemed quite natural for me to ignore his words.

Our meal was beyond question a gloomy one, and we ate it almost in silence, avoiding one another's eyes, and keeping the fire bright. Then we washed up and prepared for the night, and, once smoking, our minds unoccupied with any definite duties, the apprehension I had felt all day long became more and more acute. It was not then active fear, I think, but the very vagueness of its origin distressed me far more that if I had been able to ticket and face it squarely. The curious sound I have likened to the note of a gong became now almost incessant, and filled the stillness of the night with a faint, continuous ringing rather than a series of distinct notes. At one time it was behind and at another time in front of us. Sometimes I fancied it came from the bushes on our left, and then again from the clumps on our right. More often it hovered directly overhead like the whirring of wings. It was really everywhere at once, behind, in front, at our sides and over our heads, completely surrounding us. The sound really defies description. But nothing within my knowledge is like that ceaseless muffled humming rising off the deserted world of swamps and willows.

We sat smoking in comparative silence, the strain growing every minute greater. The worst feature of the situation seemed to me that we did not know what to expect, and could therefore make no sort of preparation by way of defense. We could anticipate nothing. My explanations made in the sunshine, moreover, now came to haunt me with their foolish and wholly unsatisfactory nature, and it was more and more

clear to us that some kind of plain talk with my companion was inevitable, whether I liked it or not. After all, we had to spend the night together, and to sleep in the same tent side by side. I saw that I could not get along much longer without the support of his mind, and for that, of course, plain talk was imperative. As long as possible, however, I postponed this little climax, and tried to ignore or laugh at the occasional sentences he flung into the emptiness.

Some of these sentences, moreover, were confoundedly disquieting to me, coming as they did to corroborate much that I felt myself; corroboration, too--which made it so much more convincing--from a totally different point of view. He composed such curious sentences, and hurled them at me in such an inconsequential sort of way, as though his main line of thought was secret to himself, and these fragments were mere bits he found it impossible to digest. He got rid of them by uttering them. Speech relieved him. It was like being sick.

"There are things about us, I'm sure, that make for disorder, disintegration, destruction, our destruction," he said once, while the fire blazed between us. "We've strayed out of a safe line somewhere."

And, another time, when the gong sounds had come nearer, ringing much louder than before, and directly over our heads, he said as though talking to himself:

"I don't think a gramophone would show any record of that. The sound doesn't come to me by the ears at all. The vibrations reach me in another manner altogether, and seem to be within me, which is precisely how a fourth dimensional sound might be supposed to make itself heard."

I purposely made no reply to this, but I sat up a little closer to the fire and peered about me into the darkness. The clouds were massed all over the sky, and no trace of moonlight came through. Very still, too, everything was, so that the river and the frogs had things all their own way.

"It has that about it," he went on, "which is utterly out of common experience. It is unknown. Only one thing describes it really; it is a non-human sound; I mean a sound outside humanity."

Having rid himself of this indigestible morsel, he lay quiet for a time, but he had so admirably expressed my own feeling that it was a relief to have the thought out, and to have confined it by the limitation of words from dangerous wandering to and fro in the mind.

The solitude of that Danube camping-place, can I ever forget it? The feeling of being utterly alone on an empty planet! My thoughts ran incessantly upon cities and the haunts of men. I would have given my soul, as the saying is, for the "feel" of those Bavarian villages we had passed through by the score; for the normal, human commonplaces; peasants drinking beer, tables beneath the trees, hot sunshine, and a ruined castle on the rocks behind the red-roofed church. Even the tourists would have been welcome.

Yet what I felt of dread was no ordinary ghostly fear. It was infinitely greater, stranger, and seemed to arise from some dim ancestral sense of terror more profoundly disturbing than anything I had known or dreamed of. We had "strayed," as the Swede put it, into some region or some set of conditions where the risks were great, yet unintelligible to us; where the frontiers of some unknown world lay close about us. It was a spot held by the dwellers in some outer space, a sort of peep-hole whence they could spy upon the earth, themselves unseen, a point where the veil between had worn a little thin. As the final result of too long a sojourn here, we should be carried over the border and deprived of what we called "our lives," yet by mental, not physical, processes. In that sense, as he said, we should be the victims of our adventure--a sacrifice.

It took us in different fashion, each according to the measure of his sensitiveness and powers of resistance. I translated it vaguely into a personification of the mightily disturbed elements, investing them with the horror of a deliberate and malefic purpose, resentful of our audacious intrusion into their breeding-place; whereas my friend threw it into the unoriginal form at first of a trespass on some ancient shrine, some place where the old gods still held sway, where the emotional forces of former worshippers still clung, and the ancestral portion of him yielded to the old pagan spell.

At any rate, here was a place unpolluted by men, kept clean

by the winds from coarsening human influences, a place where spiritual agencies were within reach and aggressive. Never, before or since, have I been so attacked by indescribable suggestions of a "beyond region," of another scheme of life, another revolution not parallel to the human. And in the end our minds would succumb under the weight of the awful spell, and we should be drawn across the frontier into their world.

Small things testified to the amazing influence of the place, and now in the silence round the fire they allowed themselves to be noted by the mind. The very atmosphere had proved itself a magnifying medium to distort every indication: the otter rolling in the current, the hurrying boatman making signs, the shifting willows, one and all had been robbed of its natural character, and revealed in something of its other aspect--as it existed across the border to that other region. And this changed aspect I felt was now not merely to me, but to the race. The whole experience whose verge we touched was unknown to humanity at all. It was a new order of experience, and in the true sense of the word unearthly.

"It's the deliberate, calculating purpose that reduces one's courage to zero," the Swede said suddenly, as if he had been actually following my thoughts. "Otherwise imagination might count for much. But the paddle, the canoe, the lessening food--"

"Haven't I explained all that once?" I interrupted viciously.

"You have," he answered dryly; "you have indeed."

He made other remarks too, as usual, about what he called the "plain determination to provide a victim"; but, having now arranged my thoughts better, I recognized that this was simply the cry of his frightened soul against the knowledge that he was being attacked in a vital part, and that he would be somehow taken or destroyed. The situation called for a courage and calmness of reasoning that neither of us could compass, and I have never before been so clearly conscious of two persons in me--the one that explained everything, and the other that laughed at such foolish explanations, yet was horribly afraid.

Meanwhile, in the pitchy night the fire died down and the

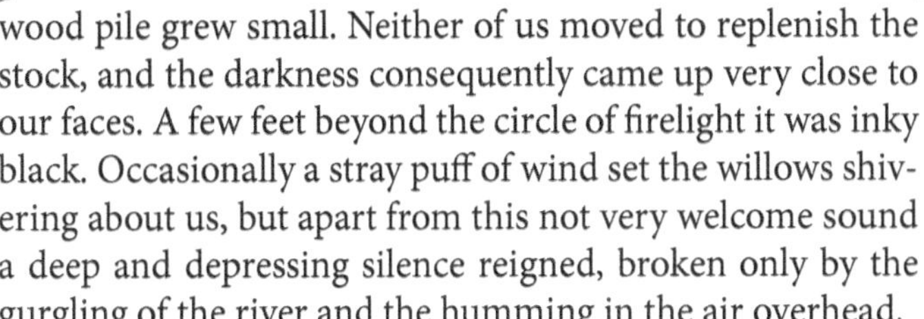

wood pile grew small. Neither of us moved to replenish the stock, and the darkness consequently came up very close to our faces. A few feet beyond the circle of firelight it was inky black. Occasionally a stray puff of wind set the willows shivering about us, but apart from this not very welcome sound a deep and depressing silence reigned, broken only by the gurgling of the river and the humming in the air overhead.

We both missed, I think, the shouting company of the winds.

At length, at a moment when a stray puff prolonged itself as though the wind were about to rise again, I reached the point for me of saturation, the point where it was absolutely necessary to find relief in plain speech, or else to betray myself by some hysterical extravagance that must have been far worse in its effect upon both of us. I kicked the fire into a blaze, and turned to my companion abruptly. He looked up with a start.

"I can't disguise it any longer," I said; "I don't like this place, and the darkness, and the noises, and the awful feelings I get. There's something here that beats me utterly. I'm in a blue funk, and that's the plain truth. If the other shore was--different, I swear I'd be inclined to swim for it!"

The Swede's face turned very white beneath the deep tan of sun and wind. He stared straight at me and answered quietly, but his voice betrayed his huge excitement by its unnatural calmness. For the moment, at any rate, he was the strong man of the two. He was more phlegmatic, for one thing.

"It's not a physical condition we can escape from by running away," he replied, in the tone of a doctor diagnosing some grave disease; "we must sit tight and wait. There are forces close here that could kill a herd of elephants in a second as easily as you or I could squash a fly. Our only chance is to keep perfectly still. Our insignificance perhaps may save us."

I put a dozen questions into my expression of face, but found no words. It was precisely like listening to an accurate description of a disease whose symptoms had puzzled me.

"I mean that so far, although aware of our disturbing pres-

ence, they have not found us--not 'located' us, as the Americans say," he went on. "They're blundering about like men hunting for a leak of gas. The paddle and canoe and provisions prove that. I think they feel us, but cannot actually see us. We must keep our minds quiet--it's our minds they feel. We must control our thoughts, or it's all up with us."

"Death, you mean?" I stammered, icy with the horror of his suggestion.

"Worse--by far," he said. "Death, according to one's belief, means either annihilation or release from the limitations of the senses, but it involves no change of character. You don't suddenly alter just because the body's gone. But this means a radical alteration, a complete change, a horrible loss of oneself by substitution--far worse than death, and not even annihilation. We happen to have camped in a spot where their region touches ours, where the veil between has worn thin"--horrors! he was using my very own phrase, my actual words--"so that they are aware of our being in their neighborhood."

"But who are aware?" I asked.

I forgot the shaking of the willows in the windless calm, the humming overhead, everything except that I was waiting for an answer that I dreaded more than I can possibly explain.

He lowered his voice at once to reply, leaning forward a little over the fire, an indefinable change in his face that made me avoid his eyes and look down upon the ground.

"All my life," he said, "I have been strangely, vividly conscious of another region--not far removed from our own world in one sense, yet wholly different in kind--where great things go on unceasingly, where immense and terrible personalities hurry by, intent on vast purposes compared to which earthly affairs, the rise and fall of nations, the destinies of empires, the fate of armies and continents, are all as dust in the balance; vast purposes, I mean, that deal directly with the soul, and not indirectly with more expressions of the soul--"

"I suggest just now--" I began, seeking to stop him, feeling as though I was face to face with a madman. But he instantly

overbore me with his torrent that had to come.

"You think," he said, "it is the spirit of the elements, and I thought perhaps it was the old gods. But I tell you now it is--neither. These would be comprehensible entities, for they have relations with men, depending upon them for worship or sacrifice, whereas these beings who are now about us have absolutely nothing to do with mankind, and it is mere chance that their space happens just at this spot to touch our own."

The mere conception, which his words somehow made so convincing, as I listened to them there in the dark stillness of that lonely island, set me shaking a little all over. I found it impossible to control my movements.

"And what do you propose?" I began again.

"A sacrifice, a victim, might save us by distracting them until we could get away," he went on, "just as the wolves stop to devour the dogs and give the sleigh another start. But--I see no chance of any other victim now."

I stared blankly at him. The gleam in his eye was dreadful. Presently he continued.

IV

"It's the willows, of course. The willows mask the others, but the others are feeling about for us. If we let our minds betray our fear, we're lost, lost utterly." He looked at me with an expression so calm, so determined, so sincere, that I no longer had any doubts as to his sanity. He was as sane as any man ever was. "If we can hold out through the night," he added, "we may get off in the daylight unnoticed, or rather, undiscovered."

"But you really think a sacrifice would--"

That gong-like humming came down very close over our heads as I spoke, but it was my friend's scared face that really stopped my mouth.

"Hush!" he whispered, holding up his hand. "Do not mention them more than you can help. Do not refer to them by name. To name is to reveal; it is the inevitable clue, and our only hope lies in ignoring them, in order that they may

ignore us."

"Even in thought?" He was extraordinarily agitated.

"Especially in thought. Our thoughts make spirals in their world. We must keep them out of our minds at all costs if possible."

I raked the fire together to prevent the darkness having everything its own way. I never longed for the sun as I longed for it then in the awful blackness of that summer night.

"Were you awake all last night?" he went on suddenly.

"I slept badly a little after dawn," I replied evasively, trying to follow his instructions, which I knew instinctively were true, "but the wind, of course--"

"I know. But the wind won't account for all the noises."

"Then you heard it too?"

"The multiplying countless little footsteps I heard," he said, adding, after a moment's hesitation, "and that other sound--"

"You mean above the tent, and the pressing down upon us of something tremendous, gigantic?"

He nodded significantly.

"It was like the beginning of a sort of inner suffocation?" I said.

"Partly, yes. It seemed to me that the weight of the atmosphere had been altered--had increased enormously, so that we should have been crushed."

"And that," I went on, determined to have it all out, pointing upwards where the gong-like note hummed ceaselessly, rising and falling like wind. "What do you make of that?"

"It's their sound," he whispered gravely. "It's the sound of their world, the humming in their region. The division here is so thin that it leaks through somehow. But, if you listen carefully, you'll find it's not above so much as around us. It's in the willows. It's the willows themselves humming, because here the willows have been made symbols of the forces that are against us."

I could not follow exactly what he meant by this, yet the thought and idea in my mind were beyond question the thought and idea in his. I realized what he realized, only with less power of analysis than his. It was on the tip of my tongue to tell him at last about my hallucination of the as-

cending figures and the moving bushes, when he suddenly thrust his face again close into mine across the firelight and began to speak in a very earnest whisper. He amazed me by his calmness and pluck, his apparent control of the situation. This man I had for years deemed unimaginative, stolid!

"Now listen," he said. "The only thing for us to do is to go on as though nothing had happened, follow our usual habits, go to bed, and so forth; pretend we feel nothing and notice nothing. It is a question wholly of the mind, and the less we think about them the better our chance of escape. Above all, don't think, for what you think happens!"

"All right," I managed to reply, simply breathless with his words and the strangeness of it all; "all right, I'll try, but tell me one more thing first. Tell me what you make of those hollows in the ground all about us, those sand-funnels?"

"No!" he cried, forgetting to whisper in his excitement. "I dare not, simply dare not, put the thought into words. If you have not guessed I am glad. Don't try to. They have put it into my mind; try your hardest to prevent their putting it into yours."

He sank his voice again to a whisper before he finished, and I did not press him to explain. There was already just about as much horror in me as I could hold. The conversation came to an end, and we smoked our pipes busily in silence.

Then something happened, something unimportant apparently, as the way is when the nerves are in a very great state of tension, and this small thing for a brief space gave me an entirely different point of view. I chanced to look down at my sand-shoe--the sort we used for the canoe--and something to do with the hole at the toe suddenly recalled to me the London shop where I had bought them, the difficulty the man had in fitting me, and other details of the uninteresting but practical operation. At once, in its train, followed a wholesome view of the modern skeptical world I was accustomed to move in at home. I thought of roast beef, and ale, motor-cars, policemen, brass bands, and a dozen other things that proclaimed the soul of ordinariness or utility. The effect was immediate and astonishing even to myself. Psychologically, I suppose, it was simply a sudden and violent reaction after the strain of living in an atmosphere of things that to the normal consciousness must seem impossible and incredible. But, whatever the cause, it momentarily lifted the spell from my heart, and left me for the short space of a minute feeling free and utterly unafraid. I looked up at my friend opposite.

"You damned old pagan!" I cried, laughing aloud in his face. "You imaginative idiot! You superstitious idolater! You--"

I stopped in the middle, seized anew by the old horror. I tried to smother the sound of my voice as something sacrilegious. The Swede, of course, heard it too--the strange cry overhead in the darkness--and that sudden drop in the air as though something had come nearer.

He had turned ashen white under the tan. He stood bolt upright in front of the fire, stiff as a rod, staring at me.

"After that," he said in a sort of helpless, frantic way, "we must go! We can't stay now; we must strike camp this very instant and go on--down the river."

He was talking, I saw, quite wildly, his words dictated by abject terror--the terror he had resisted so long, but which had caught him at last.

"In the dark?" I exclaimed, shaking with fear after my hysterical outburst, but still realizing our position better than he did. "Sheer madness! The river's in flood, and we've only got a single paddle. Besides, we only go deeper into their country! There's nothing ahead for fifty miles but willows, willows, willows!"

He sat down again in a state of semi-collapse. The positions, by one of those kaleidoscopic changes nature loves, were suddenly reversed, and the control of our forces passed over into my hands. His mind at last had reached the point where it was beginning to weaken.

"What on earth possessed you to do such a thing?" he whispered with the awe of genuine terror in his voice and face.

I crossed round to his side of the fire. I took both his hands in mine, kneeling down beside him and looking straight

into his frightened eyes.

"We'll make one more blaze," I said firmly, "and then turn in for the night. At sunrise we'll be off full speed for Komorn. Now, pull yourself together a bit, and remember your own advice about not thinking fear!"

He said no more, and I saw that he would agree and obey. In some measure, too, it was a sort of relief to get up and make an excursion into the darkness for more wood. We kept close together, almost touching, groping among the bushes and along the bank. The humming overhead never ceased, but seemed to me to grow louder as we increased our distance from the fire. It was shivery work!

We were grubbing away in the middle of a thickish clump of willows where some driftwood from a former flood had caught high among the branches, when my body was seized in a grip that made me half drop upon the sand. It was the Swede. He had fallen against me, and was clutching me for support. I heard his breath coming and going in short gasps.

"Look! By my soul!" he whispered, and for the first time in my experience I knew what it was to hear tears of terror in a human voice. He was pointing to the fire, some fifty feet away. I followed the direction of his finger, and I swear my heart missed a beat.

There, in front of the dim glow, something was moving.

I saw it through a veil that hung before my eyes like the gauze drop-curtain used at the back of a theater--hazily a little. It was neither a human figure nor an animal. To me it gave the strange impression of being as large as several animals grouped together, like horses, two or three, moving slowly. The Swede, too, got a similar result, though expressing it differently, for he thought it was shaped and sized like a clump of willow bushes, rounded at the top, and moving all over upon its surface--"coiling upon itself like smoke," he said afterwards.

"I watched it settle downwards through the bushes," he sobbed at me. "Look, by God! It's coming this way! Oh, oh!"--he gave a kind of whistling cry. "They've found us."

I gave one terrified glance, which just enabled me to see that the shadowy form was swinging towards us through the bushes, and then I collapsed backwards with a crash into the branches. These failed, of course, to support my weight, so that with the Swede on top of me we fell in a struggling heap upon the sand. I really hardly knew what was happening. I was conscious only of a sort of enveloping sensation of icy fear that plucked the nerves out of their fleshly covering, twisted them this way and that, and replaced them quivering. My eyes were tightly shut; something in my throat choked me; a feeling that my consciousness was expanding, extending out into space, swiftly gave way to another feeling that I was losing it altogether, and about to die.

An acute spasm of pain passed through me, and I was aware that the Swede had hold of me in such a way that he hurt me abominably. It was the way he caught at me in falling.

But it was the pain, he declared afterwards, that saved me; it caused me to forget them and think of something else at the very instant when they were about to find me. It concealed my mind from them at the moment of discovery, yet just in time to evade their terrible seizing of me. He himself, he says, actually swooned at the same moment, and that was what saved him.

I only know that at a later date, how long or short is impossible to say, I found myself scrambling up out of the slippery network of willow branches, and saw my companion standing in front of me holding out a hand to assist me. I stared at him in a dazed way, rubbing the arm he had twisted for me. Nothing came to me to say, somehow.

"I lost consciousness for a moment or two," I heard him say. "That's what saved me. It made me stop thinking about them."

"You nearly broke my arm in two," I said, uttering my only connected thought at the moment. A numbness came over me.

"That's what saved you!" he replied. "Between us, we've managed to set them off on a false tack somewhere. The humming has ceased. It's gone--for the moment at any rate!"

A wave of hysterical laughter seized me again, and this time spread to my friend too--great healing gusts of shaking

laughter that brought a tremendous sense of relief in their train. We made our way back to the fire and put the wood on so that it blazed at once. Then we saw that the tent had fallen over and lay in a tangled heap upon the ground.

We picked it up, and during the process tripped more than once and caught our feet in sand.

"It's those sand-funnels," exclaimed the Swede, when the tent was up again and the firelight lit up the ground for several yards about us. "And look at the size of them!"

All round the tent and about the fireplace where we had seen the moving shadows there were deep funnel-shaped hollows in the sand, exactly similar to the ones we had already found over the island, only far bigger and deeper, beautifully formed, and wide enough in some instances to admit the whole of my foot and leg.

Neither of us said a word. We both knew that sleep was the safest thing we could do, and to bed we went accordingly without further delay, having first thrown sand on the fire and taken the provision sack and the paddle inside the tent with us. The canoe, too, we propped in such a way at the end of the tent that our feet touched it, and the least motion would disturb and wake us.

In case of emergency, too, we again went to bed in our clothes, ready for a sudden start.

It was my firm intention to lie awake all night and watch, but the exhaustion of nerves and body decreed otherwise, and sleep after a while came over me with a welcome blanket of oblivion. The fact that my companion also slept quickened its approach. At first he fidgeted and constantly sat up, asking me if I "heard this" or "heard that." He tossed about on his cork mattress, and said the tent was moving and the river had risen over the point of the island, but each time I went out to look I returned with the report that all was well, and finally he grew calmer and lay still. Then at length his breathing became regular and I heard unmistakable sounds of snoring--the first and only time in my life when snoring has been a welcome and calming influence.

This, I remember, was the last thought in my mind before dozing off.

A difficulty in breathing woke me, and I found the blanket over my face. But something else besides the blanket was pressing upon me, and my first thought was that my companion had rolled off his mattress on to my own in his sleep. I called to him and sat up, and at the same moment it came to me that the tent was surrounded. That sound of multitudinous soft pattering was again audible outside, filling the night with horror.

I called again to him, louder than before. He did not answer, but I missed the sound of his snoring, and also noticed that the flap of the tent was down. This was the unpardonable sin. I crawled out in the darkness to hook it back securely, and it was then for the first time I realized positively that the Swede was not here. He had gone.

I dashed out in a mad run, seized by a dreadful agitation, and the moment I was out I plunged into a sort of torrent of humming that surrounded me completely and came out of every quarter of the heavens at once. It was that same familiar humming--gone mad! A swarm of great invisible bees might have been about me in the air. The sound seemed to thicken the very atmosphere, and I felt that my lungs worked with difficulty.

But my friend was in danger, and I could not hesitate.

The dawn was just about to break, and a faint whitish light spread upwards over the clouds from a thin strip of clear horizon. No wind stirred. I could just make out the bushes and river beyond, and the pale sandy patches. In my excitement I ran frantically to and fro about the island, calling him by name, shouting at the top of my voice the first words that came into my head. But the willows smothered my voice, and the humming muffled it, so that the sound only traveled a few feet round me. I plunged among the bushes, tripping headlong, tumbling over roots, and scraping my face as I tore this way and that among the preventing branches.

Then, quite unexpectedly, I came out upon the island's point and saw a dark figure outlined between the water and the sky. It was the Swede. And already he had one foot in the river! A moment more and he would have taken the plunge.

I threw myself upon him, flinging my arms about his

waist and dragging him shorewards with all my strength. Of course he struggled furiously, making a noise all the time just like that cursed humming, and using the most outland-ish phrases in his anger about "going inside to Them," and "taking the way of the water and the wind," and God only knows what more besides, that I tried in vain to recall af-terwards, but which turned me sick with horror and amaze-ment as I listened. But in the end I managed to get him into the comparative safety of the tent, and flung him breathless and cursing upon the mattress where I held him until the fit had passed.

I think the suddenness with which it all went and he grew calm, coinciding as it did with the equally abrupt cessation of the humming and pattering outside--I think this was al-most the strangest part of the whole business perhaps. For he had just opened his eyes and turned his tired face up to me so that the dawn threw a pale light upon it through the doorway, and said, for all the world just like a frightened child:

"My life, old man--it's my life I owe you. But it's all over now anyhow. They've found a victim in our place!"

Then he dropped back upon his blankets and went to sleep literally under my eyes. He simply collapsed, and began to snore again as healthily as though nothing had happened and he had never tried to offer his own life as a sacrifice by drowning. And when the sunlight woke him three hours later--hours of ceaseless vigil for me--it became so clear to me that he remembered absolutely nothing of what he had attempted to do, that I deemed it wise to hold my peace and ask no dangerous questions.

He woke naturally and easily, as I have said, when the sun was already high in a windless hot sky, and he at once got up and set about the preparation of the fire for breakfast. I followed him anxiously at bathing, but he did not attempt to plunge in, merely dipping his head and making some re-mark about the extra coldness of the water.

"River's falling at last," he said, "and I'm glad of it."

"The humming has stopped too," I said.

He looked up at me quietly with his normal expression.

Evidently he remembered everything except his own attempt at suicide.

"Everything has stopped," he said, "because--"

He hesitated. But I knew some reference to that remark he had made just before he fainted was in his mind, and I was determined to know it.

"Because 'They've found another victim'?" I said, forcing a little laugh.

"Exactly," he answered, "exactly! I feel as positive of it as though--as though--I feel quite safe again, I mean," he finished.

He began to look curiously about him. The sunlight lay in hot patches on the sand. There was no wind. The willows were motionless. He slowly rose to feet.

"Come," he said; "I think if we look, we shall find it."

He started off on a run, and I followed him. He kept to the banks, poking with a stick among the sandy bays and caves and little back-waters, myself always close on his heels.

"Ah!" he exclaimed presently, "ah!"

The tone of his voice somehow brought back to me a vivid sense of the horror of the last twenty-four hours, and I hurried up to join him. He was pointing with his stick at a large black object that lay half in the water and half on the sand. It appeared to be caught by some twisted willow roots so that the river could not sweep it away. A few hours before the spot must have been under water.

"See," he said quietly, "the victim that made our escape possible!"

And when I peered across his shoulder I saw that his stick rested on the body of a man. He turned it over. It was the corpse of a peasant, and the face was hidden in the sand. Clearly the man had been drowned, but a few hours before, and his body must have been swept down upon our island somewhere about the hour of the dawn--at the very time the fit had passed.

"We must give it a decent burial, you know."

"I suppose so," I replied. I shuddered a little in spite of myself, for there was something about the appearance of that poor drowned man that turned me cold.

The Swede glanced up sharply at me, an undecipherable expression on his face, and began clambering down the bank. I followed him more leisurely. The current, I noticed, had torn away much of the clothing from the body, so that the neck and part of the chest lay bare.

Halfway down the bank my companion suddenly stopped and held up his hand in warning; but either my foot slipped, or I had gained too much momentum to bring myself quickly to a halt, for I bumped into him and sent him forward with a sort of leap to save himself. We tumbled together on to the hard sand so that our feet splashed into the water. And, before anything could be done, we had collided a little heavily against the corpse.

The Swede uttered a sharp cry. And I sprang back as if I had been shot.

At the moment we touched the body there rose from its surface the loud sound of humming--the sound of several hummings--which passed with a vast commotion as of winged things in the air about us and disappeared upwards into the sky, growing fainter and fainter till they finally ceased in the distance. It was exactly as though we had disturbed some living yet invisible creatures at work.

My companion clutched me, and I think I clutched him, but before either of us had time properly to recover from the unexpected shock, we saw that a movement of the current was turning the corpse round so that it became released from the grip of the willow roots. A moment later it had turned completely over, the dead face uppermost, staring at the sky. It lay on the edge of the main stream. In another moment it would be swept away.

The Swede started to save it, shouting again something I did not catch about a "proper burial"--and then abruptly dropped upon his knees on the sand and covered his eyes with his hands. I was beside him in an instant.

I saw what he had seen.

For just as the body swung round to the current the face and the exposed chest turned full towards us, and showed plainly how the skin and flesh were indented with small hollows, beautifully formed, and exactly similar in shape and kind to the sand-funnels that we had found all over the island.

"Their mark!" I heard my companion mutter under his breath. "Their awful mark!"

And when I turned my eyes again from his ghastly face to the river, the current had done its work, and the body had been swept away into mid-stream and was already beyond our reach and almost out of sight, turning over and over on the waves like an otter.

THE KIT-BAG

When the words 'Not Guilty' sounded through the crowded courtroom that dark December afternoon, Arthur Wilbraham, the great criminal K.C., and leader for the triumphant defence, was represented by his junior; but Johnson, his private secretary, carried the verdict across to his chambers like lightning.

'It's what we expected, I think,' said the barrister, without emotion; 'and, personally, I am glad the case is over.' There was no particular sign of pleasure that his defence of John Turk, the murderer, on a plea of insanity, had been successful, for no doubt he felt, as everybody who had watched the face felt, that no man had ever better deserved the gallows.

'I'm glad too,' said Johnson. He had sat in the court for ten days watching the face of the man who had carried out with callous detail one of the most brutal and cold-blooded murders of recent years.

The counsel glanced up at his secretary. They were more than employer and employed; for family and other reasons, they were friends. 'Ah, I remember, yes,' he said with a kind smile, 'and you want to get away for Christmas. You're going to skate and ski in the Alps, aren't you? If I was your age I'd come with you.'

Johnson laughed shortly. He was a young man of twenty-six, with a delicate face like a girl's. 'I can catch the morning boat now,' he said; 'but that's not the reason I'm glad the trial is over. I'm glad it's over because I've seen the last of that man's dreadful face. It positively haunted me. That white skin, with the black hair brushed low over the forehead, is a thing I shall never forget, and the description of the way the dismembered body was crammed and packed with lime into that——'

'Don't dwell on it, my dear fellow,' interrupted the other,

looking at him curiously out of his keen eyes, 'don't think about it. Such pictures have a trick of coming back when one least wants them.' He paused a moment. 'Now go,' he added presently, 'and enjoy your holiday. I shall want all your energy for my Parliamentary work when you get back. And don't break your neck skiing.'

Johnson shook hands and took his leave. At the door he turned suddenly.

'I knew there was something I wanted to ask you,' he said. 'Would you mind lending me one of your kit-bags? It's too late to get one tonight, and I leave in the morning before the shops are open.'

'Of course; I'll send Henry over with it to your rooms. You shall have it the moment I get home.'

'I promise to take great care of it,' said Johnson gratefully, delighted to think that within thirty hours he would be nearing the brilliant sunshine of the high Alps in winter. The thought of that criminal court was like an evil dream in his mind.

He dined at his club and went on to Bloomsbury, where he occupied the top floor in one of those old, gaunt houses in which the rooms are large and lofty. The floor below his own was vacant and unfurnished, and below that were other lodgers whom he did not know. It was cheerless, and he looked forward heartily to a change. The night was even more cheerless: it was miserable, and few people were about. A cold, sleety rain was driving down the streets before the keenest east wind he had ever felt. It howled dismally among the big, gloomy houses of the great squares, and when he reached his rooms he heard it whistling and shouting over the world of black roofs beyond his windows.

In the hall he met his landlady, shading a candle from the draughts with her thin hand. 'This come by a man from Mr Wilbr'im's, sir.'

She pointed to what was evidently the kit-bag, and Johnson thanked her and took it upstairs with him. 'I shall be going abroad in the morning for ten days, Mrs Monks,' he said. 'I'll leave an address for letters.'

'And I hope you'll 'ave a merry Christmas, sir,' she said, in

a raucous, wheezy voice that suggested spirits, 'and better weather than this.'

'I hope so too,' replied her lodger, shuddering a little as the wind went roaring down the street outside.

When he got upstairs he heard the sleet volleying against the window panes. He put his kettle on to make a cup of hot coffee, and then set about putting a few things in order for his absence. 'And now I must pack—such as my packing is,' he laughed to himself, and set to work at once.

He liked the packing, for it brought the snow mountains so vividly before him, and made him forget the unpleasant scenes of the past ten days. Besides, it was not elaborate in nature. His friend had lent him the very thing—a stout canvas kit-bag, sack-shaped, with holes round the neck for the brass bar and padlock. It was a bit shapeless, true, and not much to look at, but its capacity was unlimited, and there was no need to pack carefully. He shoved in his waterproof coat, his fur cap and gloves, his skates and climbing boots, his sweaters, snow-boots, and ear-caps; and then on the top of these he piled his woollen shirts and underwear, his thick socks, puttees, and knickerbockers. The dress-suit came next, in case the hotel people dressed for dinner, and then, thinking of the best way to pack his white shirts, he paused a moment to reflect. 'That's the worst of these kit-bags,' he mused vaguely, standing in the centre of the sitting-room, where he had come to fetch some string.

It was after ten o'clock. A furious gust of wind rattled the windows as though to hurry him up, and he thought with pity of the poor Londoners whose Christmas would be spent in such a climate, whilst he was skimming over snowy slopes in bright sunshine, and dancing in the evening with rosy-cheeked girls—— Ah! that reminded him; he must put in his dancing-pumps and evening socks. He crossed over from his sitting-room to the cupboard on the landing where he kept his linen.

And as he did so he heard someone coming up the stairs. He stood still a moment on the landing to listen. It was Mrs Monks's step, he thought; she must be coming up with the last post. But then the steps ceased suddenly, and he heard no more. They were at least two flights down, and he came to the conclusion they were too heavy to be those of his bibulous landlady. No doubt they belonged to a late lodger who had mistaken his floor. He went into his bedroom and packed his pumps and dress-shirts as best he could.

The kit-bag by this time was two-thirds full, and stood upright on its own base like a sack of flour. For the first time he noticed that it was old and dirty, the canvas faded and worn, and that it had obviously been subjected to rather rough treatment. It was not a very nice bag to have sent him—certainly not a new one, or one that his chief valued. He gave the matter a passing thought, and went on with his packing. Once or twice, however, he caught himself wondering who it could have been wandering down below, for Mrs Monks had not come up with letters, and the floor was empty and unfurnished. From time to time, moreover, he was almost certain he heard a soft tread of someone padding about over the bare boards—cautiously, stealthily, as silently as possible—and, further, that the sounds had been lately coming distinctly nearer.

For the first time in his life he began to feel a little creepy. Then, as though to emphasize this feeling, an odd thing happened: as he left the bedroom, having just packed his recalcitrant white shirts, he noticed that the top of the kit-bag lopped over towards him with an extraordinary resemblance to a human face. The canvas fell into a fold like a nose and forehead, and the brass rings for the padlock just filled the position of the eyes. A shadow—or was it a travel stain? for he could not tell exactly—looked like hair. It gave him rather a turn, for it was so absurdly, so outrageously, like the face of John Turk, the murderer.

He laughed, and went into the front room, where the light was stronger.

'That horrid case has got on my mind,' he thought; 'I shall be glad of a change of scene and air.' In the sitting-room, however, he was not pleased to hear again that stealthy tread upon the stairs, and to realize that it was much closer than before, as well as unmistakably real. And this time he got up and went out to see who it could be creeping about on the upper staircase at so late an hour.

But the sound ceased; there was no one visible on the stairs. He went to the floor below, not without trepidation, and turned on the electric light to make sure that no one was hiding in the empty rooms of the unoccupied suite. There was not a stick of furniture large enough to hide a dog. Then he called over the banisters to Mrs Monks, but there was no answer, and his voice echoed down into the dark vault of the house, and was lost in the roar of the gale that howled outside. Everyone was in bed and asleep—everyone except himself and the owner of this soft and stealthy tread.

'My absurd imagination, I suppose,' he thought. 'It must have been the wind after all, although—it seemed so very real and close, I thought.' He went back to his packing. It was by this time getting on towards midnight. He drank his coffee up and lit another pipe—the last before turning in.

It is difficult to say exactly at what point fear begins, when the causes of that fear are not plainly before the eyes. Impressions gather on the surface of the mind, film by film, as ice gathers upon the surface of still water, but often so lightly that they claim no definite recognition from the consciousness. Then a point is reached where the accumulated impressions become a definite emotion, and the mind realizes that something has happened. With something of a start, Johnson suddenly recognized that he felt nervous— oddly nervous; also, that for some time past the causes of this feeling had been gathering slowly in his mind, but that he had only just reached the point where he was forced to acknowledge them.

It was a singular and curious malaise that had come over him, and he hardly knew what to make of it. He felt as though he were doing something that was strongly objected to by another person, another person, moreover, who had some right to object. It was a most disturbing and disagreeable feeling, not unlike the persistent promptings of conscience: almost, in fact, as if he were doing something he knew to be wrong. Yet, though he searched vigorously and honestly in his mind, he could nowhere lay his finger upon the secret of this growing uneasiness, and it perplexed him. More, it

distressed and frightened him.

'Pure nerves, I suppose,' he said aloud with a forced laugh. 'Mountain air will cure all that! Ah,' he added, still speaking to himself, 'and that reminds me—my snow-glasses.'

He was standing by the door of the bedroom during this brief soliloquy, and as he passed quickly towards the sitting-room to fetch them from the cupboard he saw out of the corner of his eye the indistinct outline of a figure standing on the stairs, a few feet from the top. It was someone in a stooping position, with one hand on the banisters, and the face peering up towards the landing. And at the same moment he heard a shuffling footstep. The person who had been creeping about below all this time had at last come up to his own floor. Who in the world could it be? And what in the name of Heaven did he want?

Johnson caught his breath sharply and stood stock still. Then, after a few seconds' hesitation, he found his courage, and turned to investigate. The stairs, he saw to his utter amazement, were empty; there was no one. He felt a series of cold shivers run over him, and something about the muscles of his legs gave a little and grew weak. For the space of several minutes he peered steadily into the shadows that congregated about the top of the staircase where he had seen the figure, and then he walked fast—almost ran, in fact—into the light of the front room; but hardly had he passed inside the doorway when he heard someone come up the stairs behind him with a quick bound and go swiftly into his bedroom. It was a heavy, but at the same time a stealthy footstep—the tread of somebody who did not wish to be seen. And it was at this precise moment that the nervousness he had hitherto experienced leaped the boundary line, and entered the state of fear, almost of acute unreasoning fear. Before it turned into terror there was a further boundary to cross, and beyond that again lay the region of pure horror. Johnson's position was an unenviable one.

'By Jove! That was someone on the stairs, then,' he muttered, his flesh crawling all over; 'and whoever it was has now gone into my bedroom.' His delicate, pale face turned absolutely white, and for some minutes he hardly knew what

to think or do. Then he realized intuitively that delay only set a premium upon fear; and he crossed the landing boldly and went straight into the other room, where, a few seconds before, the steps had disappeared.

'Who's there? Is that you, Mrs Monks?' he called aloud, as he went, and heard the first half of his words echo down the empty stairs, while the second half fell dead against the curtains in a room that apparently held no other human figure than his own.

'Who's there?' he called again, in a voice unnecessarily loud and that only just held firm. 'What do you want here?'

The curtains swayed very slightly, and, as he saw it, his heart felt as if it almost missed a beat; yet he dashed forward and drew them aside with a rush. A window, streaming with rain, was all that met his gaze. He continued his search, but in vain; the cupboards held nothing but rows of clothes, hanging motionless; and under the bed there was no sign of anyone hiding. He stepped backwards into the middle of the room, and, as he did so, something all but tripped him up. Turning with a sudden spring of alarm he saw—the kit-bag.

'Odd!' he thought. 'That's not where I left it!' A few moments before it had surely been on his right, between the bed and the bath; he did not remember having moved it. It was very curious. What in the world was the matter with everything? Were all his senses gone queer? A terrific gust of wind tore at the windows, dashing the sleet against the glass with the force of small gunshot, and then fled away howling dismally over the waste of Bloomsbury roofs. A sudden vision of the Channel next day rose in his mind and recalled him sharply to realities.

'There's no one here at any rate; that's quite clear!' he exclaimed aloud. Yet at the time he uttered them he knew perfectly well that his words were not true and that he did not believe them himself. He felt exactly as though someone was hiding close about him, watching all his movements, trying to hinder his packing in some way. 'And two of my senses,' he added, keeping up the pretence, 'have played me the most absurd tricks: the steps I heard and the figure I saw were both entirely imaginary.'

He went back to the front room, poked the fire into a blaze, and sat down before it to think. What impressed him more than anything else was the fact that the kit-bag was no longer where he had left it. It had been dragged nearer to the door.

What happened afterwards that night happened, of course, to a man already excited by fear, and was perceived by a mind that had not the full and proper control, therefore, of the senses. Outwardly, Johnson remained calm and master of himself to the end, pretending to the very last that everything he witnessed had a natural explanation, or was merely delusions of his tired nerves. But inwardly, in his very heart, he knew all along that someone had been hiding downstairs in the empty suite when he came in, that this person had watched his opportunity and then stealthily made his way up to the bedroom, and that all he saw and heard afterwards, from the moving of the kit-bag to—well, to the other things this story has to tell—were caused directly by the presence of this invisible person.

And it was here, just when he most desired to keep his mind and thoughts controlled, that the vivid pictures received day after day upon the mental plates exposed in the courtroom of the Old Bailey, came strongly to light and developed themselves in the dark room of his inner vision. Unpleasant, haunting memories have a way of coming to life again just when the mind least desires them—in the silent watches of the night, on sleepless pillows, during the lonely hours spent by sick and dying beds. And so now, in the same way, Johnson saw nothing but the dreadful face of John Turk, the murderer, lowering at him from every corner of his mental field of vision; the white skin, the evil eyes, and the fringe of black hair low over the forehead. All the pictures of those ten days in court crowded back into his mind unbidden, and very vivid.

'This is all rubbish and nerves,' he exclaimed at length, springing with sudden energy from his chair. 'I shall finish my packing and go to bed. I'm overwrought, overtired. No doubt, at this rate I shall hear steps and things all night!'

But his face was deadly white all the same. He snatched

up his field-glasses and walked across to the bedroom, humming a music-hall song as he went—a trifle too loud to be natural; and the instant he crossed the threshold and stood within the room something turned cold about his heart, and he felt that every hair on his head stood up.

The kit-bag lay close in front of him, several feet nearer to the door than he had left it, and just over its crumpled top he saw a head and face slowly sinking down out of sight as though someone were crouching behind it to hide, and at the same moment a sound like a long-drawn sigh was distinctly audible in the still air about him between the gusts of the storm outside.

Johnson had more courage and will-power than the girlish indecision of his face indicated; but at first such a wave of terror came over him that for some seconds he could do nothing but stand and stare. A violent trembling ran down his back and legs, and he was conscious of a foolish, almost a hysterical, impulse to scream aloud. That sigh seemed in his very ear, and the air still quivered with it. It was unmistakably a human sigh.

'Who's there?' he said at length, finding his voice; but though he meant to speak with loud decision, the tones came out instead in a faint whisper, for he had partly lost the control of his tongue and lips.

He stepped forward, so that he could see all round and over the kit-bag. Of course there was nothing there, nothing but the faded carpet and the bulging canvas sides. He put out his hands and threw open the mouth of the sack where it had fallen over, being only three parts full, and then he saw for the first time that round the inside, some six inches from the top, there ran a broad smear of dull crimson. It was an old and faded blood stain. He uttered a scream, and drew back his hands as if they had been burnt. At the same moment the kit-bag gave a faint, but unmistakable, lurch forward towards the door.

Johnson collapsed backwards, searching with his hands for the support of something solid, and the door, being further behind him than he realized, received his weight just in time to prevent his falling, and shut to with a resounding bang. At the same moment the swinging of his left arm accidentally touched the electric switch, and the light in the room went out.

It was an awkward and disagreeable predicament, and if Johnson had not been possessed of real pluck he might have done all manner of foolish things. As it was, however, he pulled himself together, and groped furiously for the little brass knob to turn the light on again. But the rapid closing of the door had set the coats hanging on it a-swinging, and his fingers became entangled in a confusion of sleeves and pockets, so that it was some moments before he found the switch. And in those few moments of bewilderment and terror two things happened that sent him beyond recall over the boundary into the region of genuine horror—he distinctly heard the kit-bag shuffling heavily across the floor in jerks, and close in front of his face sounded once again the sigh of a human being.

In his anguished efforts to find the brass button on the wall he nearly scraped the nails from his fingers, but even then, in those frenzied moments of alarm—so swift and alert are the impressions of a mind keyed-up by a vivid emotion—he had time to realize that he dreaded the return of the light, and that it might be better for him to stay hidden in the merciful screen of darkness. It was but the impulse of a moment, however, and before he had time to act upon it he had yielded automatically to the original desire, and the room was flooded again with light.

But the second instinct had been right. It would have been better for him to have stayed in the shelter of the kind darkness. For there, close before him, bending over the half-packed kit-bag, clear as life in the merciless glare of the electric light, stood the figure of John Turk, the murderer. Not three feet from him the man stood, the fringe of black hair marked plainly against the pallor of the forehead, the whole horrible presentment of the scoundrel, as vivid as he had seen him day after day in the Old Bailey, when he stood there in the dock, cynical and callous, under the very shadow of the gallows.

In a flash Johnson realized what it all meant: the dirty

and much-used bag; the smear of crimson within the top; the dreadful stretched condition of the bulging sides. He remembered how the victim's body had been stuffed into a canvas bag for burial, the ghastly, dismembered fragments forced with lime into this very bag; and the bag itself produced as evidence—— It all came back to him as clear as day. . . .

Very softly and stealthily his hand groped behind him for the handle of the door, but before he could actually turn it the very thing that he most of all dreaded came about, and John Turk lifted his devil's face and looked at him. At the same moment that heavy sigh passed through the air of the room, formulated somehow into words: 'It's my bag. And I want it.'

Johnson just remembered clawing the door open, and then falling in a heap upon the floor of the landing, as he tried frantically to make his way into the front room.

He remained unconscious for a long time, and it was still dark when he opened his eyes and realized that he was lying, stiff and bruised, on the cold boards. Then the memory of what he had seen rushed back into his mind, and he promptly fainted again. When he woke the second time the wintry dawn was just beginning to peep in at the windows, painting the stairs a cheerless, dismal grey, and he managed to crawl into the front room, and cover himself with an overcoat in the armchair, where at length he fell asleep.

A great clamour woke him. He recognized Mrs Monks's voice, loud and voluble.

'What! You ain't been to bed, sir! Are you ill, or has anything 'appened? And there's an urgent gentleman to see you, though it ain't seven o'clock yet, and——'

'Who is it?' he stammered. 'I'm all right, thanks. Fell asleep in my chair, I suppose.'

'Someone from Mr Wilb'rim's, and he says he ought to see you quick before you go abroad, and I told him——'

'Show him up, please, at once,' said Johnson, whose head was whirling, and his mind was still full of dreadful visions.

Mr Wilbraham's man came in with many apologies, and explained briefly and quickly that an absurd mistake had been made, and that the wrong kit-bag had been sent over the night before.

'Henry somehow got hold of the one that came over from the courtroom, and Mr Wilbraham only discovered it when he saw his own lying in his room, and asked why it had not gone to you,' the man said.

'Oh!' said Johnson stupidly.

'And he must have brought you the one from the murder case instead, sir, I'm afraid,' the man continued, without the ghost of an expression on his face. 'The one John Turk packed the dead body in. Mr Wilbraham's awful upset about it, sir, and told me to come over first thing this morning with the right one, as you were leaving by the boat.'

He pointed to a clean-looking kit-bag on the floor, which he had just brought. 'And I was to bring the other one back, sir,' he added casually.

For some minutes Johnson could not find his voice. At last he pointed in the direction of his bedroom. 'Perhaps you would kindly unpack it for me. Just empty the things out on the floor.'

The man disappeared into the other room, and was gone for five minutes. Johnson heard the shifting to and fro of the bag, and the rattle of the skates and boots being unpacked.

'Thank you, sir,' the man said, returning with the bag folded over his arm. 'And can I do anything more to help you, sir?'

'What is it?' asked Johnson, seeing that he still had something he wished to say.

The man shuffled and looked mysterious. 'Beg pardon, sir, but knowing your interest in the Turk case, I thought you'd maybe like to know what's happened——'

'Yes.'

'John Turk killed hisself last night with poison immediately on getting his release, and he left a note for Mr Wilbraham saying as he'd be much obliged if they'd have him put away, same as the woman he murdered, in the old kit-bag.'

'What time—did he do it?' asked Johnson.

'Ten o'clock last night, sir, the warder says.'

THE OCCUPANT OF THE ROOM

He arrived late at night by the yellow diligence, stiff and cramped after the toilsome ascent of three slow hours. The village, a single mass of shadow, was already asleep. Only in front of the little hotel was there noise and light and bustle—for a moment. The horses, with tired, slouching gait, crossed the road and disappeared into the stable of their own accord, their harness trailing in the dust; and the lumbering diligence stood for the night where they had dragged it—the body of a great yellow-sided beetle with broken legs.

In spite of his physical weariness the schoolmaster, revelling in the first hours of his ten-guinea holiday, felt exhilarated. For the high Alpine valley was marvellously still; stars twinkled over the torn ridges of the Dent du Midi where spectral snows gleamed against rocks that looked like solid ink; and the keen air smelt of pine forests, dew-soaked pastures, and freshly sawn wood. He took it all in with a kind of bewildered delight for a few minutes, while the other three passengers gave directions about their luggage and went to their rooms. Then he turned and walked over the coarse matting into the glare of the hall, only just able to resist stopping to examine the big mountain map that hung upon the wall by the door.

And, with a sudden disagreeable shock, he came down from the ideal to the actual. For at the inn—the only inn—there was no vacant room. Even the available sofas were occupied. ...

How stupid he had been not to write! Yet it had been impossible, he remembered, for he had come to the decision suddenly that morning in Geneva, enticed by the brilliance of the weather after a week of rain.

They talked endlessly, this gold-braided porter and the hard-faced old woman—her face was hard, he noticed—

gesticulating all the time, and pointing all about the village with suggestions that he ill understood, for his French was limited and their patois was fearful.

"There!"—he might find a room, "or there! But we are, hélas full—more full than we care about. To-morrow, perhaps—if So-and-So give up their rooms——!" And then, with much shrugging of shoulders, the hard-faced old woman stared at the gold-braided porter, and the porter stared sleepily at the schoolmaster.

At length, however, by some process of hope he did not himself understand, and following directions given by the old woman that were utterly unintelligible, he went out into the street and walked towards a dark group of houses she had pointed out to him. He only knew that he meant to thunder at a door and ask for a room. He was too weary to think out details. The porter half made to go with him, but turned back at the last moment to speak with the old woman. The houses sketched themselves dimly in the general blackness. The air was cold. The whole valley was filled with the rush and thunder of falling water. He was thinking vaguely that the dawn could not be very far away, and that he might even spend the night wandering in the woods, when there was a sharp noise behind him and he turned to see a figure hurrying after him. It was the porter—running.

And in the little hall of the inn there began again a confused three-cornered conversation, with frequent muttered colloquy and whispered asides in patois between the woman and the porter—the net result of which was that, "If Monsieur did not object—there was a room, after all, on the first floor—only it was in a sense 'engaged.' That is to say——"

But the schoolmaster took the room without inquiring too closely into the puzzle that had somehow provided it so suddenly. The ethics of hotel-keeping had nothing to do with him. If the woman offered him quarters it was not for him to argue with her whether the said quarters were legitimately hers to offer.

But the porter, evidently a little thrilled, accompanied the guest up to the room and supplied in a mixture of French and English details omitted by the landlady—and Minturn, the schoolmaster, soon shared the thrill with him, and found himself in the atmosphere of a possible tragedy.

All who know the peculiar excitement that belongs to high mountain valleys where dangerous climbing is a chief feature of the attractions, will understand a certain faint element of high alarm that goes with the picture. One looks up at the desolate, soaring ridges and thinks involuntarily of the men who find their pleasure for days and nights together scaling perilous summits among the clouds, and conquering inch by inch the icy peaks that for ever shake their dark terror in the sky. The atmosphere of adventure, spiced with the possible horror of a very grim order of tragedy, is inseparable from any imaginative contemplation of the scene; and the idea Minturn gleaned from the half-frightened porter lost nothing by his ignorance of the language. This Englishwoman, the real occupant of the room, had insisted on going without a guide. She had left just before daybreak two days before—the porter had seen her start—and ... she had not returned! The route was difficult and dangerous, yet not impossible for a skilled climber, even a solitary one. And the Englishwoman was an experienced mountaineer. Also, she was self-willed, careless of advice, bored by warnings, self-confident to a degree. Queer, moreover; for she kept entirely to herself, and sometimes remained in her room with locked doors, admitting no one, for days together: a "crank," evidently, of the first water.

This much Minturn gathered clearly enough from the porter's talk while his luggage was brought in and the room set to rights; further, too, that the search party had gone out and might, of course, return at any moment. In which case—— Thus the room was empty, yet still hers. "If Monsieur did not object—if the risk he ran of having to turn out suddenly in the night——" It was the loquacious porter who furnished the details that made the transaction questionable; and Minturn dismissed the loquacious porter as soon as possible, and prepared to get into the hastily arranged bed and snatch all the hours of sleep he could before he was turned out.

At first, it must be admitted, he felt uncomfortable—distinctly uncomfortable. He was in some one else's room. He had really no right to be there. It was in the nature of an unwarrantable intrusion; and while he unpacked he kept looking over his shoulder as though some one were watching him from the corners. Any moment, it seemed, he would hear a step in the passage, a knock would come at the door, the door would open, and there he would see this vigorous Englishwoman looking him up and down with anger. Worse still—he would hear her voice asking him what he was doing in her room—her bedroom. Of course, he had an adequate explanation, but still——!

Then, reflecting that he was already half undressed, the humour of it flashed for a second across his mind, and he laughed—quietly. And at once, after that laughter, under his breath, came the sudden sense of tragedy he had felt before. Perhaps, even while he smiled, her body lay broken and cold upon those awful heights, the wind of snow playing over her hair, her glazed eyes staring sightless up to the stars. ... It made him shudder. The sense of this woman whom he had never seen, whose name even he did not know, became extraordinarily real. Almost he could imagine that she was somewhere in the room with him, hidden, observing all he did.

He opened the door softly to put his boots outside, and when he closed it again he turned the key. Then he finished unpacking and distributed his few things about the room. It was soon done; for, in the first place, he had only a small Gladstone and a knapsack, and secondly, the only place where he could spread his clothes was the sofa. There was no chest of drawers, and the cupboard, an unusually large and solid one, was locked. The Englishwoman's things had evidently been hastily put away in it. The only sign of her recent presence was a bunch of faded Alpenrosen standing in a glass jar upon the washhand stand. This, and a certain faint perfume, were all that remained. In spite, however, of these very slight evidences, the whole room was pervaded with a curious sense of occupancy that he found exceedingly distasteful. One moment the atmosphere seemed subtly charged with a "just left" feeling; the next it was a queer awareness of "still here" that made him turn cold and look hurriedly behind him.

Altogether, the room inspired him with a singular aversion, and the strength of this aversion seemed the only excuse for his tossing the faded flowers out of the window, and then hanging his mackintosh upon the cupboard door in such a way as to screen it as much as possible from view. For the sight of that big, ugly cupboard, filled with the clothing of a woman who might then be beyond any further need of covering—thus his imagination insisted on picturing it— touched in him a startled sense of the Incongruous that did not stop there, but crept through his mind gradually till it merged somehow into a sense of a rather grotesque horror. At any rate, the sight of that cupboard was offensive, and he covered it almost instinctively. Then, turning out the electric light, he got into bed.

But the instant the room was dark he realised that it was more than he could stand; for, with the blackness, there came a sudden rush of cold that he found it hard to explain. And the odd thing was that, when he lit the candle beside his bed, he noticed that his hand trembled.

This, of course, was too much. His imagination was taking liberties and must be called to heel. Yet the way he called it to order was significant, and its very deliberateness betrayed a mind that has already admitted fear. And fear, once in, is difficult to dislodge. He lay there upon his elbow in bed and carefully took note of all the objects in the room—with the intention, as it were, of taking an inventory of everything his senses perceived, then drawing a line, adding them up finally, and saying with decision, "That's all the room contains! I've counted every single thing. There is nothing more. Now—I may sleep in peace!"

And it was during this absurd process of enumerating the furniture of the room that the dreadful sense of distressing lassitude came over him that made it difficult even to finish counting. It came swiftly, yet with an amazing kind of violence that overwhelmed him softly and easily with a sensation of enervating weariness hard to describe. And its first effect was to banish fear. He no longer possessed enough energy to feel really afraid or nervous. The cold remained, but the alarm vanished. And into every corner of his usually vigorous personality crept the insidious poison of a muscular fatigue—at first—that in a few seconds, it seemed, translated itself into spiritual inertia. A sudden consciousness of the foolishness, the crass futility, of life, of effort, of fighting—of all that makes life worth living, shot into every fibre of his being, and left him utterly weak. A spirit of black pessimism that was not even vigorous enough to assert itself, invaded the secret chambers of his heart...

Every picture that presented itself to his mind came dressed in grey shadows: those bored and sweating horses toiling up the ascent to—nothing! that hard-faced landlady taking so much trouble to let her desire for gain conquer her sense of morality—for a few francs! That gold-braided porter, so talkative, fussy, energetic, and so anxious to tell all he knew! What was the use of them all? And for himself, what in the world was the good of all the labour and drudgery he went through in that preparatory school where he was junior master? What could it lead to? Wherein lay the value of so much uncertain toil, when the ultimate secrets of life were hidden and no one knew the final goal? How foolish was effort, discipline, work! How vain was pleasure! How trivial the noblest life! ...

With a fearful jump that nearly upset the candle Minturn pulled himself together. Such vicious thoughts were usually so remote from his normal character that the sudden vile invasion produced a swift reaction. Yet, only for a moment. Instantly, again, the black depression descended upon him like a wave. His work—it could lead to nothing but the dreary labour of a small headmastership after all—seemed as vain and foolish as his holiday in the Alps. What an idiot he had been, to be sure, to come out with a knapsack merely to work himself into a state of exhaustion climbing over toilsome mountains that led to nowhere—resulted in nothing. A dreariness of the grave possessed him. Life was a ghastly fraud! Religion childish humbug! Everything was merely a trap—a trap of death; a coloured toy that Nature used as a decoy! But a decoy for what? For nothing! There was no

meaning in anything. The only real thing was—DEATH. And the happiest people were those who found it soonest.

Then why wait for it to come?

He sprang out of bed, thoroughly frightened. This was horrible. Surely mere physical fatigue could not produce a world so black, an outlook so dismal, a cowardice that struck with such sudden hopelessness at the very roots of life? For, normally, he was cheerful and strong, full of the tides of healthy living; and this appalling lassitude swept the very basis of his personality into Nothingness and the desire for death. It was like the development of a Secondary Personality. He had read, of course, how certain persons who suffered shocks developed thereafter entirely different characteristics, memory, tastes, and so forth. It had all rather frightened him. Though scientific men vouched for it, it was hardly to be believed. Yet here was a similar thing taking place in his own consciousness. He was, beyond question, experiencing all the mental variations of—some one else! It was un-moral. It was awful. It was—well, after all, at the same time, it was uncommonly interesting.

And this interest he began to feel was the first sign of his returning normal Self. For to feel interest is to live, and to love life.

He sprang into the middle of the room—then switched on the electric light. And the first thing that struck his eye was—the big cupboard.

"Hallo! There's that—beastly cupboard!" he exclaimed to himself, involuntarily, yet aloud. It held all the clothes, the swinging skirts and coats and summer blouses of the dead woman. For he knew now—somehow or other—that she was dead. ...

At that moment, through the open windows, rushed the sound of falling water, bringing with it a vivid realisation of the desolate, snow-swept heights. He saw her—positively saw her!—lying where she had fallen, the frost upon her cheeks, the snow-dust eddying about her hair and eyes, her broken limbs pushing against the lumps of ice. For a moment the sense of spiritual lassitude—of the emptiness of life—vanished before this picture of broken effort—of a small human force battling pluckily, yet in vain, against the impersonal and pitiless Potencies of Inanimate Nature—and he found himself again, his normal self. Then, instantly, returned again that terrible sense of cold, nothingness, emptiness. ...

And he found himself standing opposite the big cupboard where her clothes were. He wanted to see those clothes—things she had used and worn. Quite close he stood, almost touching it. The next second he had touched it. His knuckles struck upon the wood.

Why he knocked is hard to say. It was an instinctive movement probably. Something in his deepest self dictated it—ordered it. He knocked at the door. And the dull sound upon the wood into the stillness of that room brought—horror. Why it should have done so he found it as hard to explain to himself as why he should have felt impelled to knock. The fact remains that when he heard the faint reverberation inside the cupboard, it brought with it so vivid a realisation of the woman's presence that he stood there shivering upon the floor with a dreadful sense of anticipation: he almost expected to hear an answering knock from within—the rustling of the hanging skirts perhaps—or, worse still, to see the locked door slowly open towards him.

And from that moment, he declares that in some way or other he must have partially lost control of himself, or at least of his better judgment; for he became possessed by such an overmastering desire to tear open that cupboard door and see the clothes within, that he tried every key in the room in the vain effort to unlock it, and then, finally, before he quite realised what he was doing—rang the bell!

But, having rung the bell for no obvious or intelligent reason at two o'clock in the morning, he then stood waiting in the middle of the floor for the servant to come, conscious for the first time that something outside his ordinary self had pushed him towards the act. It was almost like an internal voice that directed him ... and thus, when at last steps came down the passage and he faced the cross and sleepy chambermaid, amazed at being summoned at such an hour, he found no difficulty in the matter of what he should say. For

the same power that insisted he should open the cupboard door also impelled him to utter words over which he apparently had no control.

"It's not you I rang for!" he said with decision and impatience, "I want a man. Wake the porter and send him up to me at once—hurry! I tell you, hurry——!"

And when the girl had gone, frightened at his earnestness, Minturn realised that the words surprised himself as much as they surprised her. Until they were out of his mouth he had not known what exactly he was saying. But now he understood that some force foreign to his own personality was using his mind and organs. The black depression that had possessed him a few moments before was also part of it. The powerful mood of this vanished woman had somehow momentarily taken possession of him—communicated, possibly, by the atmosphere of things in the room still belonging to her. But even now, when the porter, without coat or collar, stood beside him in the room, he did not understand why he insisted, with a positive fury admitting no denial, that the key of that cupboard must be found and the door instantly opened.

The scene was a curious one. After some perplexed whispering with the chambermaid at the end of the passage, the porter managed to find and produce the key in question. Neither he nor the girl knew clearly what this excited Englishman was up to, or why he was so passionately intent upon opening the cupboard at two o'clock in the morning. They watched him with an air of wondering what was going to happen next. But something of his curious earnestness, even of his late fear, communicated itself to them, and the sound of the key grating in the lock made them both jump.

They held their breath as the creaking door swung slowly open. All heard the clatter of that other key as it fell against the wooden floor—within. The cupboard had been locked from the inside. But it was the scared housemaid, from her position in the corridor, who first saw—and with a wild scream fell crashing against the bannisters.

The porter made no attempt to save her. The schoolmaster and himself made a simultaneous rush towards the door,

now wide open. They, too, had seen.

There were no clothes, skirts or blouses on the pegs, but, all by itself, from an iron hook in the centre, they saw the body of the Englishwoman hanging by the neck, the head bent horribly forwards, the tongue protruding. Jarred by the movement of unlocking, the body swung slowly round to face them. ... Pinned upon the inside of the door was a hotel envelope with the following words pencilled in straggling writing:

"Tired—unhappy—hopelessly depressed. ... I cannot face life any longer. ... All is black. I must put an end to it. ... I meant to do it on the mountains, but was afraid. I slipped back to my room unobserved. This way is easiest and best. ..."

THE GLAMOUR OF THE SNOW

Hibbert, always conscious of two worlds, was in this mountain village conscious of three. It lay on the Italian side of the Alps, and he had taken a room in the little post office, where he could be at peace to write his book, yet at the same time enjoy the winter sports and find companionship in the hotels when he wanted it.

The three worlds that met and mingled here seemed to his imaginative temperament very obvious, though it is doubtful if another mind less intuitively equipped would have seen them so well-defined. There was the world of tourist English, civilised, quasi-educated, to which he belonged by birth, at any rate; there was the world of peasants to which he felt himself drawn by sympathy—for he loved and admired their toiling, simple life; and there was this other—which he could only call the world of Nature. To this last, however, in virtue of a vehement poetic imagination, and a tumultuous pagan instinct fed by his very blood, he felt that most of him belonged. The others borrowed from it, as it were, for visits. Here, with the soul of Nature, hid his central life.

Between all three was conflict—potential conflict. On the skating-rink each Sunday the tourists regarded the natives as intruders; in the church the peasants plainly questioned: "Why do you come? We are here to worship; you to stare and whisper!" For neither of these two worlds accepted the other. And neither did Nature accept the tourists, for it took advantage of their least mistakes, and indeed, even of the peasant-world "accepted" only those who were strong and bold enough to invade her savage domain with sufficient skill to protect themselves from several forms of—death.

Now Hibbert was keenly aware of this potential conflict and want of harmony; he felt outside, yet caught by it—torn in the three directions because he was partly of each world, but wholly in only one. There grew in him a constant, subtle effort—or, at least, desire—to unify them and decide positively to which he should belong and live in. The attempt, of course, was largely subconscious. It was the natural instinct of a richly imaginative nature seeking the point of equilibrium, so that the mind could feel at peace and his brain be free to do good work.

Among the guests no one especially claimed his interest. The men were nice but undistinguished—athletic schoolmasters, doctors snatching a holiday, good fellows all; the women, equally various and, for the most part. slightly underbred—the clever, the would-be-fast, the dare-to-be-dull, the women "who understood," and the usual pack of jolly dancing girls and "flappers." And Hibbert, with his forty odd years of thick experience behind him, got on well with the lot; he understood them all; they belonged to definite, predigested types that are the same all the world over, and that he had met all the world over long ago.

But to none of them did he belong. His nature was too "multiple" to subscribe to the set of shibboleths of any one class. And, since all liked him, and felt that somehow he seemed outside of them—spectator, looker-on—all sought to claim him.

In a sense, therefore, the three worlds fought for him: natives, tourists, Nature.

It was thus began the singular conflict for the soul of Hibbert. In his own soul, however, it took place. Neither the peasants nor the tourists were conscious that they fought for anything. And Nature, they say, is merely blind and automatic.

The assault upon him of the peasants may be left out of account, for it is obvious that they stood no chance of success. The tourist world, however, made a gallant effort to subdue him to themselves. But the evenings in the hotel, when dancing was not in order, were—English. The provincial imagination was set upon a throne and worshipped heavily through incense of the stupidest conventions possible. Hibbert used to go back early to his room in the post office to work.

"It is a mistake on my part to have realised that there is any conflict at all," he thought, as he crunched home over the snow at midnight after one of the dances. "It would have been better to have kept outside it all and done my work. Better," he added, looking back down the silent village street to the church tower, "and—safer."

The adjective had slipped from his mind before he was aware of it. He turned with an involuntary start and looked about him. He knew perfectly well what it meant—this thought that had poked its head up from the subconscious self. He understood, without being able to express it fully, the meaning that betrayed itself in the choice of the adjective. For if he had ignored the existence of this conflict he would at the same time have remained outside the arena. Whereas now he had entered the lists. Now this battle for his soul must have issue. And he knew that the spell of Nature was greater for him than all other spells in the world combined—greater than love, revelry, pleasure, greater even than study. He had always been afraid to let himself go. His pagan soul dreaded her terrific powers of witchery even while he worshipped.

The little village already slept. The world lay smothered in snow. The chalet roofs shone white beneath the moon, and pitch-black shadows gathered by the walls of the church. His eye rested a moment on the square stone tower with its frosted cross that pointed to the sky: then travelled with a leap of many thousand feet to the enormous mountains that brushed the brilliant stars. Gaunt and terrible rose the huge peaks above the slumbering village, measuring the night and heavens. They beckoned him. And something borne of the snowy desolation, borne of the midnight and the silent grandeur, borne of the great listening hollows of the night, something that lay 'twixt terror and wonder, dropped from the vast wintry spaces down into his heart—and called him. Very softly, unrecorded in any word or thought his brain could compass, it laid its spell upon him. Fingers as of snow brushed the surface of his heart. The power and quiet majesty of the winter's night appalled him.

Fumbling a moment with the big unwieldy key, he let

himself in and went upstairs to bed. Two thoughts went with him—apparently very ordinary and sensible ones:

"What fools these peasants are to sleep through such a night!" And the other:

"Those dances tire me. I'll never go again. My work only suffers in the morning." The claims of peasants and tourists upon him seemed thus in a single instant weakened.

The clash of battle troubled half his dreams. Nature had sent her Beauty of the Night and won the first assault. The others, routed and dismayed, fled far away.

II.

"Don't go back to your dreary old post office. We're going to have supper in my room—something hot. Come and join us. Hurry up!"

There had been an ice carnival, and the last party, tailing up the snow-slope to the hotel, had called him. The Chinese lanterns smoked and sputtered on the wires; the band had long since gone. The cold was bitter and the moon came only momentarily between high, driving clouds. From the shed where the people changed from skates to snow-boots he shouted something to the effect that he was "following"; but no answer came; the moving shadows of those who had called were already merged high up against the village darkness. The voices died away. Doors slammed. Hibbert found himself alone on the deserted rink.

And it was then, quite suddenly, the impulse came to—stay and skate alone. The thought of the stuffy hotel room, and of those noisy people with their obvious jokes and laughter, oppressed him. He felt a longing to be alone with the night, to taste her wonder all by himself there beneath the stars, gliding over the ice. It was not yet midnight, and he could skate for half an hour. That supper party would merely think he had changed his mind and gone to bed, if they noticed his absence at all.

It was an impulse, yes, and not an unnatural one; yet even at the time it struck him that something more than impulse lay concealed behind it. More than invitation, yet certainly less than command, there was a vague queer feeling that he

stayed because he had to, almost as though there was something he had forgotten, overlooked, left undone. Imaginative temperaments are often thus; and impulse is ever weakness. For with such ill-considered opening of the doors to hasty action may come an invasion of other forces at the same time—forces merely waiting their opportunity!

He caught the fugitive warning even while he dismissed it as absurd, and the next minute he was whirling over the smooth ice in delightful curves and loops beneath the moon. There was no fear of collision. He could take his own speed and space as he willed. The shadows of the towering mountains fell across the rink, and a wind of ice came from the forests, where the snow lay ten feet deep. The hotel lights winked and went out. The village slept. The high wire netting could not keep out the wonder of the winter night that grew about him like a presence. He skated on and on, keen exhilarating pleasure in his tingling blood, and weariness all forgotten.

And then, midway in the delight of rushing movement, he saw a figure moving behind the wire netting, watching him. With a start that almost made him lose his balance—for the abruptness of the new arrival was so unlooked for—he paused and stared. Although the light was dim he made out that it was the figure of a woman and that she was feeling her way along the netting, trying to get in. Against the white background of the snow-field he watched her rather stealthy efforts as she passed with a gliding step over the banked-up snow. She was tall and slim and graceful; he could see that even in the dark. And then, of course, he understood. It was another adventurous skater like himself, stolen down unawares from hotel or chalet, and searching for the opening. At once, making a sign and pointing with one hand, he turned swiftly and skated over to the little entrance on the other side.

But, even before he got there, a sound came on the ice behind him and, with an exclamation of amazement he could not suppress, he turned to see her swerving up to his side across the width of the rink. She had somehow found another way in.

Hibbert, as a rule, was punctilious, and in these free-and-easy places, perhaps, especially so. If only for his own protection he did not seek to make advances unless some kind of introduction paved the way. But for these two to skate together in the semi-darkness without speech, often of necessity brushing shoulders almost, was too absurd to think of. Accordingly he raised his cap and spoke. His actual words he seems unable to recall, nor what the girl said in reply, except that she answered him in accented English with some commonplace about doing figures at midnight on an empty rink. Quite natural it was, and right. She wore grey clothes of some kind, though not the customary long gloves or sweater, for indeed her hands were bare, and presently when he skated with her, he wondered with something like astonishment at their dry and icy coldness.

And she was delicious to skate with—supple, sure and light, fast as a man yet with the freedom of a child, sinuous and steady at the same time. Her flexibility made him wonder, and when he asked where she learned she murmured— he caught the breath against his ear and recalled later that it was singularly cold—that she could hardly tell, for she had been accustomed to the ice ever since she could remember.

But her face he never properly saw. A muffler of white fur buried her neck to the ears and her cap came over the eyes. He only saw that she was young. Nor could he gather her hotel or chalet, for she pointed vaguely, when he asked her, up the slopes. "Just over there——" she said, quickly taking his hand again. He did not press her; no doubt she wished to hide her escapade And the touch of her hand thrilled him more than anything he could remember; even through his thick glove he felt the softness of that cold and delicate touch.

The clouds thickened over the mountains. It grew darker. They talked very little, and did not always skate together. Often they separated, curving about in corners by themselves, but always coming together again in the centre of the rink; and when she left him thus Hibbert was conscious of—yes, of missing her. He found a peculiar satisfaction, almost a fascination, in skating by her side. It was quite an adventure—these two strangers with the ice and snow and night!

Midnight had long since sounded from the old church tower before they parted. She gave the sign, and he skated quickly to the shed, meaning to find a seat and help her take her skates off. Yet when he turned—she had already gone. He saw her slim figure gliding away across the snow … and hurrying for the last time round the rink alone he searched in vain for the opening she had twice used in this curious way.

"How very queer!" he thought, referring to the wire netting. "She must have lifted it and wriggled under. …!"

Wondering how in the world she managed it, what in the world had possessed him to be so free with her, and who in the world she was, he went up the steep slope to the post office and so to bed, her promise to come again another night still ringing delightfully in his ears. And curious were the thoughts and sensations that accompanied him. Most of all, perhaps, was the half suggestion of some dim memory that he had known this girl before, had met her somewhere, more—that she knew him. For in her voice—a low, soft, windy little voice it was, tender and soothing for all its quiet coldness—there lay some faint reminder of two others he had known, both long since gone: the voice of the woman he had loved, and—the voice of his mother.

But this time through his dreams there ran no clash of battle. He was conscious, rather, of something cold and clinging that made him think of sifting snowflakes climbing slowly with entangling touch and thickness round his feet. The snow, coming without noise, each flake so light and tiny none can mark the spot whereon it settles, yet the mass of it able to smother whole villages, wove through the very texture of his mind—cold, bewildering, deadening effort with its clinging network of ten million feathery touches.

III.

In the morning Hibbert realised he had done a foolish thing. The brilliant sunshine that drenched the valley made him see this, and the sight of his work-table with its typewriter, books, papers and the rest, brought additional conviction. To have skated with a girl alone at midnight, no matter how innocently the thing had come about, was un-wise—unfair, especially to her. Gossip in these little winter resorts was worse than in a provincial town. He hoped no one had seen them. Luckily the night had been dark. Most likely none had heard the ring of skates.

Deciding that in future he would be more careful, he plunged into work, and sought to dismiss the matter from his mind.

But in his times of leisure the memory returned persistently to haunt him. When he "ski-d," "luged," or danced in the evenings, and especially when he skated on the little rink, he was aware that the eyes of his mind forever sought this strange companion of the night. A hundred times he fancied that he saw her, but always sight deceived him. Her face he might not know, but he could hardly fail to recognise her figure. Yet nowhere among them did he catch a glimpse of that slim young creature he had skated with alone beneath the clouded stars. He searched in vain. Even his inquiries as to the occupants of the private chalets brought no results. He had lost her. But the queer thing was that he felt as though she were somewhere close; he knew she had not really gone. While people came and left with every day, it never once occurred to him that she had left. On the contrary, he felt assured that they would meet again.

This thought he never quite acknowledged. Perhaps it was the wish that fathered it only. And, even when he did meet her, it was a question how he would speak and claim acquaintance, or whether she would recognise himself. It might be awkward. He almost came to dread a meeting, though "dread," of course, is far too strong a word to describe an emotion that was half delight, half wondering anticipation.

Meanwhile the season was in full swing. Hibbert felt in perfect health, worked hard, ski-d, skated, luged, and at night danced fairly often—in spite of his decision. This dancing was, however, an act of subconscious surrender; it really meant he hoped to find her among the whirling couples. He was searching for her without quite acknowledging it to himself; and the hotel-world, meanwhile, thinking it

had won him over, teased and chaffed him, He made excuses in a similar vein; but al] the time he watched and searched and—waited.

For several days the sky held clear and bright and frosty, bitterly cold, everything crisp and sparkling in the sun; but there was no sign of fresh snow, and the ski-ers began to grumble. On the mountains was an icy crust that made "running" dangerous; they wanted the frozen, dry, and powdery snow that makes for speed, with steering easier and falling less severe. But the keen east wind showed no signs of changing for a whole ten days. Then, suddenly, there came a touch of softer air and the weather-wise began to prophesy.

Hibbert, who was delicately sensitive to the least change in earth or sky, was perhaps the first to feel it. Only he did not prophesy. He knew through every nerve in his body that moisture had crept into the air, was accumulating, and that presently a fall would come. For he responded to the moods of Nature like a fine barometer.

And the knowledge, this time, brought into his heart a strange little wayward emotion that was hard to account for—a feeling of unexplained uneasiness and disquieting joy. For behind it, woven through it rather, ran a faint exhilaration that connected remotely somewhere with that touch of delicious alarm, that tiny anticipating "dread," that so puzzled him when he thought of his next meeting with his skating companion of the night. It lay beyond all words, all telling, this queer relationship between the two; but somehow the girl and snow ran in a pair across his mind.

Perhaps for imaginative writing-men, more than for other workers, the smallest change of mood betrays itself at once. His work at any rate revealed this slight shifting of emotional values in his soul. Not that his writing suffered, but that it altered, subtly as those changes of sky or sea or landscape that come with the passing of afternoon into evening—imperceptibly. A subconscious excitement sought to push outwards and express itself. and, knowing the uneven effect such moods produced in his work, he laid his pen aside and took instead to reading that he had to do.

Meanwhile the brilliance passed from the sunshine, the

sky grew slowly overcast; by dusk the mountain tops came singularly close and sharp; the distant valley rose into absurdly near perspective. The moisture increased, rapidly approaching saturation point, when it must fall in snow. And Hibbert watched and waited.

And in the morning the world lay smothered beneath its fresh white carpet. It snowed heavily till noon, thickly, incessantly, chokingly, a foot or more; then the sky cleared, the sun came out in splendour, the wind shifted back to the east, and frost came down upon the mountains with its keenest and most biting tooth. The drop in the temperature was tremendous, but the ski-ers were jubilant. Next day the "running" would be fast and perfect. Already the mass was settling, and the surface freezing into those mosslike, powdery crystals that make the ski run almost of their own accord with the faint "sishing'" as of a bird's wings through the air.

IV.

That night there was excitement in the little hotel-world, first because there was a bal costumé, but chiefly because the new snow had come. And Hibbert went—felt drawn to go; he did not go in costume, but he wanted to talk about the slopes and ski-ing with the other men, and at the same time …

Ah, there was the truth, the deeper necessity that called. For the singular connection between the stranger and the snow again betrayed itself, utterly beyond explanation as before, but vital and insistent. Some hidden instinct in his pagan soul—heaven knows how he phrased it even to himself, if he phrased it at all!—whispered that with the snow the girl would be somewhere about, would emerge from her hiding place, would even look for him.

Absolutely unwarranted it was. He laughed while he stood before the little glass and trimmed his moustache, tried to make his black tie sit straight and shook down his dinner jacket so that it should lie upon the shoulders without a crease. His brown eyes were very bright. "I look younger than I usually do," he thought. It was unsuual, even significant, in a man who had no vanity about his appearance and certainly never questioned his age or tried to look younger than he was. Affairs of the heart, with one tumultuous exception that left no fuel for lesser subsequent fires, had never troubled him. The forces of his soul and mind not called upon for "work" and obvious duties, all went to Nature. The desolate, wild places of the earth were what he loved, night, and the beauty of the stars and snow. And this evening he felt their claims upon him mightily stirring. A rising wildness caught his blood, quickened his pulse, woke longing and passion too. But chiefly snow. The snow whirred softly through his thoughts like white, seductive dreams. … For the snow had come now; and She, it seemed, had somehow come with it—into his mind.

And yet he stood before that twisted mirror and pulled his tie and coat askew a dozen times, as though it mattered. "What in the world is up with me?" he thought. Then, laughing a little, he turned before leaving the room to put his private papers in order. The green morocco desk that held them he took down from the shelf and laid upon the table. Tied to the lid was the visiting card with his brother's London address "in case of accident." On the way down to the hotel he wondered why he had done this, for though imaginative, he was not the kind of man who dealt in presentiments. Moods with him were strong, but ever held in leash.

"It's almost like a warning," he thought, smiling. He drew his thick coat tightly round the throat as the freezing air bit at him. "Those warnings one reads of in stories sometimes. …!"

A delicious happiness was in his blood. Over the edge of the hills across the valley rose the moon. He saw her silver sheet the world of snow. Snow covered all. It smothered sound and distance It smothered houses, streets and human beings. It smothered—life.

V.

In the hall there was light and bustle; people were already arriving from the other hotels and chalets, their costumes hidden beneath many wraps. Groups of men in evening dress stood about smoking, talking "snow" and "ski-ing."

The band was tuning up. The claims of the hotel-world clashed about him faintly as of old. At the big glass windows of the verandah peasants stopped a moment on their way home from the café to peer. Hibbert thought laughingly of that conflict he used to imagine. He laughed because it suddenly seemed all unreal. He belonged so utterly to Nature and the mountains, and especially to those desolate slopes where now the snow lay thick and fresh and sweet, that there was no question of a conflict at all. The power of the newly-fallen snow had caught him, proving it without effort. Out there, up in those lonely reaches of the moonlit ridges, the snow was ready—masses and masses of it—cool, soft, inviting. He longed for it. It awaited him. He thought of the intoxicating delight of ski-ing in the moonlight.

Thus, somehow, in vivid flashing vision, he thought of it while he stood there smoking with the other men and talking all the "'shop" of ski-ing.

And, ever mysteriously blended with this power of the snow, poured also through his inner being the power of the girl. He could not disabuse his mind of the insinuating presence of the two together. He remembered that queer skating-impulse of ten days ago, the impulse that had let her in. That any mind, even an imaginative one, could pass beneath the sway of such a fancy was strange enough; and Hibbert, while fully aware of the disorder, yet found a curious joy in yielding to it. This insubordinate centre that drew him towards old pagan beliefs had assumed command. With a kind of sensuous pleasure he let himself be conquered.

And snow that night seemed in everybody's thoughts. The dancing couples talked of it; the hotel proprietors congratulated one another; it meant good sport and satisfied their guests; everyone was planning trips and expeditions, talking of slopes and telemarks, of flying speed and distance, of drifts and crust and frost. Vitality and enthusiasm pulsed in the very air; all were alert and active, positive, radiating currents of creative life even into the stuffy atmosphere of that crowded ball-room. And the snow had caused it, the snow had brought it; all this discharge of eager sparkling energy was due primarily to the—Snow.

But in the mind of Hibbert, by some swift alchemy of his pagan yearnings, this energy became transmuted. It rarified itself, gleaming in white and crystal currents of passionate anticipation, which he transferred, as by a species of electrical imagination, into the personality of the girl—the Girl of the Snow. She somewhere was waiting for him, expecting him, calling to him softly from those leagues of moonlit mountain. He remembered the touch of that cool, dry hand; the soft and icy breath against his cheek; the hush and softness of her presence in the way she came and the way she had gone again—like a flurry of snow the wind sent gliding up the slopes. She, like himself, belonged out there. He fancied that he heard her little windy voice come sifting to him through the snowy branches of the trees, calling his name that haunting little voice that dived straight to the centre of his life as once, long years ago, two other voices used to do.

...

But nowhere among the costumed dancers did he see her slender figure. He danced with one and all, distrait and absent, a stupid partner as each girl discovered, his eyes ever turning towards the door and windows, hoping to catch the luring face, the vision that did not come ... and at length, hoping even against hope. For the ball-room thinned; groups left one by one, going home to their hotels and chalets; the band tired obviously; people sat drinking lemon-squashes at the little tables, the men mopping their foreheads, everybody ready for bed.

It was close on midnight. As Hibbert passed through the hall to get his overcoat and snow-boots, he saw men in the passage by the "sport-room," greasing their ski against an early start. Knapsack luncheons were being ordered by the kitchen swing doors. He sighed. Lighting a cigarette a friend offered him, he returned a confused reply to some question as to whether he could join their party in the morning. It seemed he did not hear it. He passed through the outer vestibule between the double-glass doors, and went into the night.

The man who asked the question watched him go, an expression of anxiety momentarily in his eyes.

"Don't think he heard you," said another, laughing. "You've got to shout to Hibbert, his mind's so full of his work."

"He works too hard," suggested the first, "full of queer ideas and dreams."

But Hibbert's silence was not rudeness. He had not caught the invitation, that was all. The call of the hotel world had faded. He no longer heard it. Another wilder call was sounding in his ears.

For up the street he had seen a little figure moving. Close against the shadows of the baker's shop it glided—white, slim, enticing.

VI.

And at once into his mind passed the hush and softness of the snow—yet with it a searching, crying wildness for the heights. He knew by some incalculable, swift instinct she would not meet him in the village street. It was not there, amid crowding houses, she would speak to him. Indeed, already she had disappeared, melted from view up the white vista of the moonlit road. Yonder, he divined, she waited where the highway narrowed abruptly into the mountain path beyond the chalets.

It did not even occur to him to hesitate; mad though it seemed, and was—this sudden craving for the heights with her, at least for open spaces where the snow lay thick and fresh—it was too imperious to be denied. He does not remember going up to his room, putting the sweater over his evening clothes, and getting into the fur gauntlet gloves and the helmet cap of wool. Most certainly he has no recollection of fastening on his ski; he must have done it automatically. Some faculty of normal observation was in abeyance, as it were. His mind was out beyond the village—out with the snowy mountains and the moon.

Henri Défago, putting up the shutters over his café windows, saw him pass, and wondered mildly: "Un monsieur qui fait du ski à cette heure! Il est Anglais, donc ...!" He shrugged his shoulders, as though a man had the right to choose his own way of death; and Marthe Perotti, the hunchback wife of the shoemaker, looking by chance from her window, caught his figure moving swiftly up the road. She had other thoughts, for she knew and believed the old traditions of the witches and snow-beings that steal the souls of men. She had even heard, 'twas said, the dreaded "synagogue" pass roaring down the street at night, and now, as then, she hid her eyes. "They've called to him … and he must go," she murmured, making the sign of the cross.

But no one sought to stop him. Hibbert recalls only a single incident until he found himself beyond the houses, searching for her along the fringe of forest where the moonlight met the snow in a bewildering frieze of fantastic shadows. And the incident was simply this—that he remembered passing the church. Catching the outline of its tower against the stars, he was aware of a faint sense of hesitation that was almost malaise. A vague uneasiness came and went—jarred unpleasantly across the flow of his excited feelings, chilling exhilaration. He caught the instant's discord, dismissed it, and passed on. The seduction of the snow smothered the hint before he realised that it had touched the edge of warning.

And then he saw her. She stood there waiting in a little clear space of shining snow, dressed all in white, part of the moonlight and the glistening background, her slender figure just discernible.

"I waited, for I knew you would come," the silvery little voice of windy beauty floated down to him. "You had to come."

"I'm ready," he answered, "for I knew it too."

The world of Nature caught him to its heart in those few words—the wonder and the glory of the night and snow. Life leaped within him. The passion of his pagan soul exulted, rose in joy, flowed out to her. He neither reflected nor considered, but let himself go like the veriest schoolboy in the wildness of first love.

"Give me your hand," he cried, "I'm coming. …!"

"A little further on, a little higher," came her delicious answer. "Here it is too near the village—and the church."

And the words seemed wholly right and natural; he did not dream of questioning them; he understood that with even this little touch of civilisation in sight the familiarity he suggested was impossible. Once out upon the open mountains, 'mid the freedom of huge slopes and towering peaks, the stars and moon to witness and the wilderness of snow to watch, they could taste an innocence of happy intercourse without the dead conventions that imprison literal minds.

He urged his pace, yet did not quite overtake her. The girl kept always just a little bit ahead of his best efforts. … And soon they left the trees behind and passed upon the fringe of the enormous slopes of the sea of snow that rolled in mountainous terror and beauty to the very stars. The wonder of the white world caught him away. Under the steady moonlight it was more than haunting. It was a living, white, bewildering power that deliciously confused the senses and laid a spell of deep and wild perplexity upon the heart. It was a personality that cloaked, and yet revealed itself through all this sheeted whiteness of the snow. It rose, went with him, fled before and followed after. Slowly it dropped lithe, gleaming arms about his neck, gathering him in. …

Certainly some soft persuasion coaxed his very soul, urging him ever forwards, upwards, on towards the higher icy slopes. Judgment and reason left their throne, it seemed, completely, as in the madness of some sweet intoxication. The girl, slim and seductive, kept always just ahead, so that he never quite came up with her. He saw the white enchantment of her face and figure, something that streamed about her neck flying like a wreath of snow in the wind, and heard the alluring accents of her whispering voice that called from time to time: "A little further on, a little higher. … Then we'll run home together!"

Sometimes he saw her hand stretched out to find his own, but each time, just as he came up with her, he saw her still in front, the hand and arm withdrawn. They took a gentle angle of ascent. The toil seemed nothing. For in this crystal, wine-like air fatigue existed not. The sishing of the ski through the powdery surface of the snow was the only sound that broke the stillness; this, with his breathing and the rustle of her skirts, was all he heard. Cold moonshine, snow and silence held the world. The sky was black, and the peaks beyond cut

into it like frosted wedges of iron and steel. Far below the valley slept, the village long since hidden out of sight. He felt that he could never tire. The sound of the church clock rose from time to time faintly through the air—more and more distant.

"Give me your hand. It's time now to turn back."

"Just one more slope," she laughed. "That ridge above us. Then we'll make for home." And her low voice mingled pleasantly with the purring of their ski. His own seemed harsh and ugly by comparison.

"But I have never come so high before. it's glorious! This world of silent snow and moonlight—and you. You're a child of the snow, I swear. Let me come up—closer—to see your face—and touch your little hand."

Her laughter answered him.

"Come on! A little higher. Here we're quite alone together."

"It's magnificent," he cried. "But why did you hide away so long? I've looked and searched for you in vain ever since we skated"—he was going to say "ten days ago," but the accurate memory of time had gone from him; he was not sure whether it was days or years or minutes. His thoughts of earth were scattered and confused.

"You looked for me in the wrong places," he heard her murmur just above him. "You looked in places where I never go. Hotels and houses kill me. I avoid them." She laughed—a fine, shrill, windly little laugh.

"I loathe them, too——"

He stopped. The girl had suddenly come quite close. A breath of ice passed through his very soul. She had touched him.

"But this awful cold!" he cried out, sharply, "this freezing cold that takes me. The wind is rising; it's a wind of ice. Come, let us turn …!"

But when he plunged forward to hold her, or at least to look, the girl was gone again. And something in the way she stood there a few feet beyond, and stared down into his eyes so steadfastly in silence, made him shiver. The moonlight was behind her, but in some odd way he could not focus sight upon her face, although so close. The gleam of eyes he caught, but all the rest seemed white and snowy as though he looked beyond her to the slopes—out into space.

The sound of the church bell came up faintly from the valley far below, and he counted the strokes—five. A sudden, curious weakness seized him as he listened. Deep within it was, deadly yet somehow sweet, and hard to resist. He felt like sinking down upon the snow and lying there. … They had been climbing for five hours. It was, of course, the warning of complete exhaustion.

With a great effort he fought and overcame it. It passed away as suddenly as it came.

"We'll turn," he said with a decision he hardly felt. "It will be dawn before we reach the village again. Come at once. It's time for home."

The sense of exhilaration had utterly left him. An emotion that was akin to fear swept coldly through him. But her whispering answer turned it instantly to terror—a terror that gripped him horribly and turned him weak and unresisting.

"Our home is—here!" A burst of wildish laughter, loud and shrill, accompanied the words. It was like a whistling wind. The wind had risen, and clouds obscured the moon. "A little higher—where we cannot hear the wicked bells," she cried, and for the first time seized him deliberately by the hand.

And Hibbert tried to turn away in escape, and so trying, found for the first time that the power of the snow—that other power which does not exhilarate but deadens effort— was upon him. The suffocating weakness that it brings to exhausted men, luring them to the sleep of death in her clinging soft embrace, lulling the will and conquering all desire for life—this was awfully upon him. His feet were heavy and entangled. He could not turn, or move.

The girl was close beside him; he felt her chilly breath upon his cheeks; her hair passed blindingly across his eyes; and that icy wind came with her. He saw her whiteness close; again, it seemed, his sight passed through her into space as though she had no face. Her arms were round his neck. She drew him softly downwards to his knees. He sank; he yielded utterly; he obeyed. Her weight was upon him, smothering, delicious. The snow was to his waist. … She kissed him softly on the lips, the eyes, all over his face. And then she spoke his name in that voice of love and wonder, the voice that held the accent of two others—both taken over long ago by Death—the voice of his mother, and of the woman he had loved.

He made one more feeble effort to resist. Then, realising even while he struggled that this soft weight about his heart was sweeter than anything life could ever bring, he let his muscles relax, and sank back into the soft oblivion of the covering snow. Her kisses bore him into sleep.

VII.

They say that men who know the sleep of exhaustion in the snow find no awakening on the hither side of death. … The hours passed and the moon sank down below the white world's rim. Then, suddenly, there came a little crash upon his breast and neck, and Hibbert—woke.

He slowly turned bewildered, heavy eyes upon the desolate mountains, stared dizzily about him, tried to rise. At first his muscles would not act; a numbing, aching pain possessed him. He uttered a long, thin cry for help, and heard its faintness swallowed by the wind. And then he understood vaguely why he was only warm—not dead. For this very wind that took his cry had built up a sheltering mound of snow against his body while he slept. Like a curving wave it ran beside him. It was the breaking of its over-toppling edge that caused the crash, and the coldness of the mass against his neck that woke him.

Dawn kissed the eastern sky; pale gleams of gold shot every peak with splendour; but ice was in the air, and the dry and frozen snow blew with the wind like powder from the surface of the slopes. He saw the points of his ski projecting just below him. Then he—remembered. It seems he had just strength enough to realise that, could he but rise and stand, he might fly with terrific impetus towards the woods and village far beneath. The ski would carry him. But if he failed and fell …!

How he contrived it Hibbert never knew; this fear of death

somehow called out his whole available reserve force. He rose slowly, balanced a moment, then, taking the angle of an immense zigzag, started down the awful slopes like an arrow from a bow. And automatically the splendid muscles of the practised ski-er and athlete saved and guided him, for he was hardly conscious of controlling either speed or direction. The snow stung face and eyes like fine steel shot; ridge after ridge flew past; the summits raced across the sky; the valley leaped up as with mighty bounds to meet him. He scarcely felt the ground beneath his feet as the huge slopes and distance melted before the lightning speed of that descent from death to life.

He took it in four mile-long zigzags, and it was the turning at each corner that nearly finished him, for then the strain of balancing taxed to the verge of collapse the remnants of his strength.

Slopes that have taken hours to climb can be descended in a short half-hour on ski, but Hibbert had lost all count of time. Quite other thoughts and feelings mastered him in that wild, swift dropping through the air that was like the flight of a bird. For ever close upon his heels came following forms and voices with the whirling snow-dust. He heard that little silvery voice of death and laughter at his back. Shrill and wild, with the whistling of the wind past his ears, he caught its pursuing tones; but in anger now, no longer soft and coaxing. And it was accompanied; she did not follow alone. It seemed a host of these flying figures of the snow chased madly just behind him. He felt them smite his neck and cheeks, snatch at his hands and try to entangle his feet and ski in drifts. His eyes they blinded, and they caught his breath away.

The terror of the heights and snow and winter desolation urged him forward in the maddest race with death a human being ever knew; and so terrific was the speed that before the gold and crimson had left the summits to touch the ice-lips of the lower glaciers, he saw the friendly forest far beneath swing up and welcome him.

And it was then there came the strangest thing of all. For moving slowly along the edge of the woods he saw a light.

A man was carrying it. A procession of human figures was passing in a dark line laboriously through the snow. And—he heard the sound of chanting.

Instinctively, without a second's hesitation, he changed his course. No longer flying at an angle as before, he pointed his ski straight down the mountain side. The dreadful steepness did not frighten him. He knew full well it meant a crashing tumble at the bottom, but he also knew it meant a doubling of his speed—with safety at the end. For, though no definite thought passed through his mind, he understood that it was the village curé who carried that little gleaming lantern in the dawn, and that he was taking the Host to a chalet on the lower slopes—to some peasant in extremis. He remembered her terror of the church and bells. She feared the holy symbols.

There was one last wild cry in his ears as he started, a shriek of the wind before his face, and a rush of stinging snow against closed eyelids—and then he dropped through empty space. Speed took sight of him. It seemed he flew off the surface of the world.

•

Indistinctly he recalls the murmur of men's voices, the touch of strong arms that lifted him, and the shooting pains as the ski were unfastened from the twisted ankle ... for when he opened his eyes again to normal life he found himself lying in his bed at the post office with the doctor at his side. For years to come the story of "mad Hibbert's" ski-ing at night is recounted in that mountain village. He went, it seems, up slopes, and to a height that no man in his senses ever tried before. The tourists were agog about it for the rest of the season, and the very same day two of the bolder men went over the actual ground and photographed the slopes. Later Hibbert saw these photographs. He noticed one curious thing about them—though he did not mention it to any one:

There was only a single track.

THE MAN WHO FOUND OUT

1

Professor Mark Ebor, the scientist, led a double life, and the only persons who knew it were his assistant, Dr. Laidlaw, and his publishers. But a double life need not always be a bad one, and, as Dr. Laidlaw and the gratified publishers well knew, the parallel lives of this particular man were equally good, and indefinitely produced would certainly have ended in a heaven somewhere that can suitably contain such strangely opposite characteristics as his remarkable personality combined.

For Mark Ebor, F.R.S., etc., etc., was that unique combination hardly ever met with in actual life, a man of science and a mystic.

As the first, his name stood in the gallery of the great, and as the second—but there came the mystery! For under the pseudonym of "Pilgrim" (the author of that brilliant series of books that appealed to so many), his identity was as well concealed as that of the anonymous writer of the weather reports in a daily newspaper. Thousands read the sanguine, optimistic, stimulating little books that issued annually from the pen of "Pilgrim," and thousands bore their daily burdens better for having read; while the Press generally agreed that the author, besides being an incorrigible enthusiast and optimist, was also—a woman; but no one ever succeeded in penetrating the veil of anonymity and discovering that "Pilgrim" and the biologist were one and the same person

Mark Ebor, as Dr. Laidlaw knew him in his laboratory, was one man; but Mark Ebor, as he sometimes saw him after work was over, with rapt eyes and ecstatic face, discussing the possibilities of "union with God" and the future of the human race, was quite another.

"I have always held, as you know," he was saying one eve-

ning as he sat in the little study beyond the laboratory with his assistant and intimate, "that Vision should play a large part in the life of the awakened man—not to be regarded as infallible, of course, but to be observed and made use of as a guide-post to possibilities——"

"I am aware of your peculiar views, sir," the young doctor put in deferentially, yet with a certain impatience.

"For Visions come from a region of the consciousness where observation and experiment are out of the question," pursued the other with enthusiasm, not noticing the interruption, "and, while they should be checked by reason afterwards, they should not be laughed at or ignored. All inspiration, I hold, is of the nature of interior Vision, and all our best knowledge has come—such is my confirmed belief—as a sudden revelation to the brain prepared to receive it——"

"Prepared by hard work first, by concentration, by the closest possible study of ordinary phenomena," Dr. Laidlaw allowed himself to observe.

"Perhaps," sighed the other; "but by a process, none the less, of spiritual illumination. The best match in the world will not light a candle unless the wick be first suitably prepared."

It was Laidlaw's turn to sigh. He knew so well the impossibility of arguing with his chief when he was in the regions of the mystic, but at the same time the respect he felt for his tremendous attainments was so sincere that he always listened with attention and deference, wondering how far the great man would go and to what end this curious combination of logic and "illumination" would eventually lead him.

"Only last night," continued the elder man, a sort of light coming into his rugged features, "the vision came to me again—the one that has haunted me at intervals ever since my youth, and that will not be denied."

Dr. Laidlaw fidgeted in his chair.

"About the Tablets of the Gods, you mean—and that they lie somewhere hidden in the sands," he said patiently. A sudden gleam of interest came into his face as he turned to catch the professor's reply.

"And that I am to be the one to find them, to decipher

them, and to give the great knowledge to the world——"

"Who will not believe," laughed Laidlaw shortly, yet interested in spite of his thinly-veiled contempt.

"Because even the keenest minds, in the right sense of the word, are hopelessly—unscientific," replied the other gently, his face positively aglow with the memory of his vision. "Yet what is more likely," he continued after a moment's pause, peering into space with rapt eyes that saw things too wonderful for exact language to describe, "than that there should have been given to man in the first ages of the world some record of the purpose and problem that had been set him to solve? In a word," he cried, fixing his shining eyes upon the face of his perplexed assistant, "that God's messengers in the far-off ages should have given to His creatures some full statement of the secret of the world, of the secret of the soul, of the meaning of life and death—the explanation of our being here, and to what great end we are destined in the ultimate fullness of things?"

Dr. Laidlaw sat speechless. These outbursts of mystical enthusiasm he had witnessed before. With any other man he would not have listened to a single sentence, but to Professor Ebor, man of knowledge and profound investigator, he listened with respect, because he regarded this condition as temporary and pathological, and in some sense a reaction from the intense strain of the prolonged mental concentration of many days.

He smiled, with something between sympathy and resignation as he met the other's rapt gaze.

"But you have said, sir, at other times, that you consider the ultimate secrets to be screened from all possible——"

"The ultimate secrets, yes," came the unperturbed reply; "but that there lies buried somewhere an indestructible record of the secret meaning of life, originally known to men in the days of their pristine innocence, I am convinced. And, by this strange vision so often vouchsafed to me, I am equally sure that one day it shall be given to me to announce to a weary world this glorious and terrific message."

And he continued at great length and in glowing language to describe the species of vivid dream that had come to him at intervals since earliest childhood, showing in detail how he discovered these very Tablets of the Gods, and proclaimed their splendid contents—whose precise nature was always, however, withheld from him in the vision—to a patient and suffering humanity.

"The Scrutator, sir, well described 'Pilgrim' as the Apostle of Hope," said the young doctor gently, when he had finished; "and now, if that reviewer could hear you speak and realize from what strange depths comes your simple faith——"

The professor held up his hand, and the smile of a little child broke over his face like sunshine in the morning.

"Half the good my books do would be instantly destroyed," he said sadly; "they would say that I wrote with my tongue in my cheek. But wait," he added significantly; "wait till I find these Tablets of the Gods! Wait till I hold the solutions of the old world-problems in my hands! Wait till the light of this new revelation breaks upon confused humanity, and it wakes to find its bravest hopes justified! Ah, then, my dear Laidlaw——"

He broke off suddenly; but the doctor, cleverly guessing the thought in his mind, caught him up immediately.

"Perhaps this very summer," he said, trying hard to make the suggestion keep pace with honesty; "in your explorations in Assyria—your digging in the remote civilization of what was once Chaldea, you may find—what you dream of——"

The professor held up his hand, and the smile of a fine old face.

"Perhaps," he murmured softly, "perhaps!"

And the young doctor, thanking the gods of science that his leader's aberrations were of so harmless a character, went home strong in the certitude of his knowledge of externals, proud that he was able to refer his visions to self-suggestion, and wondering complaisantly whether in his old age he might not after all suffer himself from visitations of the very kind that afflicted his respected chief.

And as he got into bed and thought again of his master's rugged face, and finely shaped head, and the deep lines traced by years of work and self-discipline, he turned over on his pillow and fell asleep with a sigh that was half of won-

der, half of regret.

2

It was in February, nine months later, when Dr. Laidlaw made his way to Charing Cross to meet his chief after his long absence of travel and exploration. The vision about the so-called Tablets of the Gods had meanwhile passed almost entirely from his memory.

There were few people in the train, for the stream of traffic was now running the other way, and he had no difficulty in finding the man he had come to meet. The shock of white hair beneath the low-crowned felt hat was alone enough to distinguish him by easily.

"Here I am at last!" exclaimed the professor, somewhat wearily, clasping his friend's hand as he listened to the young doctor's warm greetings and questions. "Here I am—a little older, and much dirtier than when you last saw me!" He glanced down laughingly at his travel-stained garments.

"And much wiser," said Laidlaw, with a smile, as he bustled about the platform for porters and gave his chief the latest scientific news.

At last they came down to practical considerations.

"And your luggage—where is that? You must have tons of it, I suppose?" said Laidlaw.

"Hardly anything," Professor Ebor answered. "Nothing, in fact, but what you see."

"Nothing but this hand-bag?" laughed the other, thinking he was joking.

"And a small portmanteau in the van," was the quiet reply. "I have no other luggage."

"You have no other luggage?" repeated Laidlaw, turning sharply to see if he were in earnest.

"Why should I need more?" the professor added simply.

Something in the man's face, or voice, or manner—the doctor hardly knew which—suddenly struck him as strange. There was a change in him, a change so profound—so little on the surface, that is—that at first he had not become aware of it. For a moment it was as though an utterly alien personality stood before him in that noisy, bustling throng.

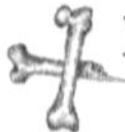

Here, in all the homely, friendly turmoil of a Charing Cross crowd, a curious feeling of cold passed over his heart, touching his life with icy finger, so that he actually trembled and felt afraid.

He looked up quickly at his friend, his mind working with startled and unwelcome thoughts.

"Only this?" he repeated, indicating the bag. "But where's all the stuff you went away with? And—have you brought nothing home—no treasures?"

"This is all I have," the other said briefly. The pale smile that went with the words caused the doctor a second indescribable sensation of uneasiness. Something was very wrong, something was very queer; he wondered now that he had not noticed it sooner.

"The rest follows, of course, by slow freight," he added tactfully, and as naturally as possible. "But come, sir, you must be tired and in want of food after your long journey. I'll get a taxi at once, and we can see about the other luggage afterwards."

It seemed to him he hardly knew quite what he was saying; the change in his friend had come upon him so suddenly and now grew upon him more and more distressingly. Yet he could not make out exactly in what it consisted. A terrible suspicion began to take shape in his mind, troubling him dreadfully.

"I am neither very tired, nor in need of food, thank you," the professor said quietly. "And this is all I have. There is no luggage to follow. I have brought home nothing—nothing but what you see."

His words conveyed finality. They got into a taxi, tipped the porter, who had been staring in amazement at the venerable figure of the scientist, and were conveyed slowly and noisily to the house in the north of London where the laboratory was, the scene of their labours of years.

And the whole way Professor Ebor uttered no word, nor did Dr. Laidlaw find the courage to ask a single question.

It was only late that night, before he took his departure, as the two men were standing before the fire in the study— that study where they had discussed so many problems of vital and absorbing interest—that Dr. Laidlaw at last found strength to come to the point with direct questions. The professor had been giving him a superficial and desultory account of his travels, of his journeys by camel, of his encampments among the mountains and in the desert, and of his explorations among the buried temples, and, deeper, into the waste of the pre-historic sands, when suddenly the doctor came to the desired point with a kind of nervous rush, almost like a frightened boy.

"And you found——" he began stammering, looking hard at the other's dreadfully altered face, from which every line of hope and cheerfulness seemed to have been obliterated as a sponge wipes markings from a slate—"you found——"

"I found," replied the other, in a solemn voice, and it was the voice of the mystic rather than the man of science—"I found what I went to seek. The vision never once failed me. It led me straight to the place like a star in the heavens. I found—the Tablets of the Gods."

Dr. Laidlaw caught his breath, and steadied himself on the back of a chair. The words fell like particles of ice upon his heart. For the first time the professor had uttered the well-known phrase without the glow of light and wonder in his face that always accompanied it.

"You have—brought them?" he faltered.

"I have brought them home," said the other, in a voice with a ring like iron; "and I have—deciphered them."

Profound despair, the bloom of outer darkness, the dead sound of a hopeless soul freezing in the utter cold of space seemed to fill in the pauses between the brief sentences. A silence followed, during which Dr. Laidlaw saw nothing but the white face before him alternately fade and return. And it was like the face of a dead man.

"They are, alas, indestructible," he heard the voice continue, with its even, metallic ring.

"Indestructible," Laidlaw repeated mechanically, hardly knowing what he was saying.

Again a silence of several minutes passed, during which, with a creeping cold about his heart, he stood and stared into the eyes of the man he had known and loved so long—

aye, and worshipped, too; the man who had first opened his own eyes when they were blind, and had led him to the gates of knowledge, and no little distance along the difficult path beyond; the man who, in another direction, had passed on the strength of his faith into the hearts of thousands by his books.

"I may see them?" he asked at last, in a low voice he hardly recognized as his own. "You will let me know—their message?"

Professor Ebor kept his eyes fixedly upon his assistant's face as he answered, with a smile that was more like the grin of death than a living human smile.

"When I am gone," he whispered; "when I have passed away. Then you shall find them and read the translation I have made. And then, too, in your turn, you must try, with the latest resources of science at your disposal to aid you, to compass their utter destruction." He paused a moment, and his face grew pale as the face of a corpse. "Until that time," he added presently, without looking up, "I must ask you not to refer to the subject again—and to keep my confidence meanwhile—ab—so—lute—ly."

3

A year passed slowly by, and at the end of it Dr. Laidlaw had found it necessary to sever his working connexion with his friend and one-time leader. Professor Ebor was no longer the same man. The light had gone out of his life; the laboratory was closed; he no longer put pen to paper or applied his mind to a single problem. In the short space of a few months he had passed from a hale and hearty man of late middle life to the condition of old age—a man collapsed and on the edge of dissolution. Death, it was plain, lay waiting for him in the shadows of any day—and he knew it.

To describe faithfully the nature of this profound alteration in his character and temperament is not easy, but Dr. Laidlaw summed it up to himself in three words: Loss of Hope. The splendid mental powers remained indeed undimmed, but the incentive to use them—to use them for the help of others—had gone. The character still held to its fine and unselfish habits of years, but the far goal to which they had been the leading strings had faded away. The desire for knowledge—knowledge for its own sake—had died, and the passionate hope which hitherto had animated with tireless energy the heart and brain of this splendidly equipped intellect had suffered total eclipse. The central fires had gone out. Nothing was worth doing, thinking, working for. There was nothing to work for any longer!

The professor's first step was to recall as many of his books as possible; his second to close his laboratory and stop all research. He gave no explanation, he invited no questions. His whole personality crumbled away, so to speak, till his daily life became a mere mechanical process of clothing the body, feeding the body, keeping it in good health so as to avoid physical discomfort, and, above all, doing nothing that could interfere with sleep. The professor did everything he could to lengthen the hours of sleep, and therefore of forgetfulness.

It was all clear enough to Dr. Laidlaw. A weaker man, he knew, would have sought to lose himself in one form or another of sensual indulgence—sleeping-draughts, drink, the first pleasures that came to hand. Self-destruction would have been the method of a little bolder type; and deliberate evil-doing, poisoning with his awful knowledge all he could, the means of still another kind of man. Mark Ebor was none of these. He held himself under fine control, facing silently and without complaint the terrible facts he honestly believed himself to have been unfortunate enough to discover. Even to his intimate friend and assistant, Dr. Laidlaw, he vouchsafed no word of true explanation or lament. He went straight forward to the end, knowing well that the end was not very far away.

And death came very quietly one day to him, as he was sitting in the arm-chair of the study, directly facing the doors of the laboratory—the doors that no longer opened. Dr. Laidlaw, by happy chance, was with him at the time, and just able to reach his side in response to the sudden painful efforts for breath; just in time, too, to catch the murmured words that fell from the pallid lips like a message from the other side of the grave.

"Read them, if you must; and, if you can—destroy. But"—his voice sank so low that Dr. Laidlaw only just caught the dying syllables—"but—never, never—give them to the world."

And like a grey bundle of dust loosely gathered up in an old garment the professor sank back into his chair and expired.

But this was only the death of the body. His spirit had died two years before.

4

The estate of the dead man was small and uncomplicated, and Dr. Laidlaw, as sole executor and residuary legatee, had no difficulty in settling it up. A month after the funeral he was sitting alone in his upstairs library, the last sad duties completed, and his mind full of poignant memories and regrets for the loss of a friend he had revered and loved, and to whom his debt was so incalculably great. The last two years, indeed, had been for him terrible. To watch the swift decay of the greatest combination of heart and brain he had ever known, and to realize he was powerless to help, was a source of profound grief to him that would remain to the end of his days.

At the same time an insatiable curiosity possessed him. The study of dementia was, of course, outside his special province as a specialist, but he knew enough of it to understand how small a matter might be the actual cause of how great an illusion, and he had been devoured from the very beginning by a ceaseless and increasing anxiety to know what the professor had found in the sands of "Chaldea," what these precious Tablets of the Gods might be, and particularly—for this was the real cause that had sapped the man's sanity and hope—what the inscription was that he had believed to have deciphered thereon.

The curious feature of it all to his own mind was, that whereas his friend had dreamed of finding a message of glorious hope and comfort, he had apparently found (so far as he had found anything intelligible at all, and not invented the whole thing in his dementia) that the secret of the world, and the meaning of life and death, was of so terrible a nature that it robbed the heart of courage and the soul of hope. What, then, could be the contents of the little brown parcel the professor had bequeathed to him with his pregnant dying sentences?

Actually his hand was trembling as he turned to the writing-table and began slowly to unfasten a small old-fashioned desk on which the small gilt initials "M.E." stood forth as a melancholy memento. He put the key into the lock and half turned it. Then, suddenly, he stopped and looked about him. Was that a sound at the back of the room? It was just as though someone had laughed and then tried to smother the laugh with a cough. A slight shiver ran over him as he stood listening.

"This is absurd," he said aloud; "too absurd for belief—that I should be so nervous! It's the effect of curiosity unduly prolonged." He smiled a little sadly and his eyes wandered to the blue summer sky and the plane trees swaying in the wind below his window. "It's the reaction," he continued. "The curiosity of two years to be quenched in a single moment! The nervous tension, of course, must be considerable."

He turned back to the brown desk and opened it without further delay. His hand was firm now, and he took out the paper parcel that lay inside without a tremor. It was heavy. A moment later there lay on the table before him a couple of weather-worn plaques of grey stone—they looked like stone, although they felt like metal—on which he saw markings of a curious character that might have been the mere tracings of natural forces through the ages, or, equally well, the half-obliterated hieroglyphics cut upon their surface in past centuries by the more or less untutored hand of a common scribe.

He lifted each stone in turn and examined it carefully. It seemed to him that a faint glow of heat passed from the substance into his skin, and he put them down again suddenly, as with a gesture of uneasiness.

"A very clever, or a very imaginative man," he said to himself, "who could squeeze the secrets of life and death from such broken lines as those!"

Then he turned to a yellow envelope lying beside them in the desk, with the single word on the outside in the writing of the professor—the word Translation.

"Now," he thought, taking it up with a sudden violence to conceal his nervousness, "now for the great solution. Now to learn the meaning of the worlds, and why mankind was made, and why discipline is worth while, and sacrifice and pain the true law of advancement."

There was the shadow of a sneer in his voice, and yet something in him shivered at the same time. He held the envelope as though weighing it in his hand, his mind pondering many things. Then curiosity won the day, and he suddenly tore it open with the gesture of an actor who tears open a letter on the stage, knowing there is no real writing inside at all.

A page of finely written script in the late scientist's hand-writing lay before him. He read it through from beginning to end, missing no word, uttering each syllable distinctly under his breath as he read.

The pallor of his face grew ghastly as he neared the end. He began to shake all over as with ague. His breath came heavily in gasps. He still gripped the sheet of paper, however, and deliberately, as by an intense effort of will, read it through a second time from beginning to end. And this time, as the last syllable dropped from his lips, the whole face of the man flamed with a sudden and terrible anger. His skin became deep, deep red, and he clenched his teeth. With all the strength of his vigorous soul he was struggling to keep control of himself.

For perhaps five minutes he stood there beside the table without stirring a muscle. He might have been carved out of stone. His eyes were shut, and only the heaving of the chest betrayed the fact that he was a living being. Then, with a strange quietness, he lit a match and applied it to the sheet of paper he held in his hand. The ashes fell slowly about him, piece by piece, and he blew them from the window-sill into the air, his eyes following them as they floated away on the summer wind that breathed so warmly over the world.

He turned back slowly into the room. Although his ac-

tions and movements were absolutely steady and controlled, it was clear that he was on the edge of violent action. A hurricane might burst upon the still room any moment. His muscles were tense and rigid. Then, suddenly, he whitened, collapsed, and sank backwards into a chair, like a tumbled bundle of inert matter. He had fainted.

In less than half an hour he recovered consciousness and sat up. As before, he made no sound. Not a syllable passed his lips. He rose quietly and looked about the room.

Then he did a curious thing.

Taking a heavy stick from the rack in the corner he approached the mantlepiece, and with a heavy shattering blow he smashed the clock to pieces. The glass fell in shivering atoms.

"Cease your lying voice for ever," he said, in a curiously still, even tone. "There is no such thing as time!"

He took the watch from his pocket, swung it round several times by the long gold chain, smashed it into smithereens against the wall with a single blow, and then walked into his laboratory next door, and hung its broken body on the bones of the skeleton in the corner of the room.

"Let one damned mockery hang upon another," he said smiling oddly. "Delusions, both of you, and cruel as false!"

He slowly moved back to the front room. He stopped opposite the bookcase where stood in a row the "Scriptures of the World," choicely bound and exquisitely printed, the late professor's most treasured possession, and next to them several books signed "Pilgrim."

One by one he took them from the shelf and hurled them through the open window.

"A devil's dreams! A devil's foolish dreams!" he cried, with a vicious laugh.

Presently he stopped from sheer exhaustion. He turned his eyes slowly to the wall opposite, where hung a weird array of Eastern swords and daggers, scimitars and spears, the collections of many journeys. He crossed the room and ran his finger along the edge. His mind seemed to waver.

"No," he muttered presently; "not that way. There are easier and better ways than that."

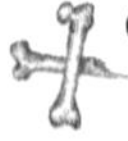

He took his hat and passed downstairs into the street.

5

It was five o'clock, and the June sun lay hot upon the pavement. He felt the metal door-knob burn the palm of his hand.

"Ah, Laidlaw, this is well met," cried a voice at his elbow; "I was in the act of coming to see you. I've a case that will interest you, and besides, I remembered that you flavoured your tea with orange leaves!—and I admit——"

It was Alexis Stephen, the great hypnotic doctor.

"I've had no tea to-day," Laidlaw said, in a dazed manner, after staring for a moment as though the other had struck him in the face. A new idea had entered his mind.

"What's the matter?" asked Dr. Stephen quickly. "Something's wrong with you. It's this sudden heat, or overwork. Come, man, let's go inside."

A sudden light broke upon the face of the younger man, the light of a heaven-sent inspiration. He looked into his friend's face, and told a direct lie.

"Odd," he said, "I myself was just coming to see you. I have something of great importance to test your confidence with. But in your house, please," as Stephen urged him towards his own door—"in your house. It's only round the corner, and I—I cannot go back there—to my rooms—till I have told you."

"I'm your patient—for the moment," he added stammeringly as soon as they were seated in the privacy of the hypnotist's sanctum, "and I want—er——"

"My dear Laidlaw," interrupted the other, in that soothing voice of command which had suggested to many a suffering soul that the cure for its pain lay in the powers of its own reawakened will, "I am always at your service, as you know. You have only to tell me what I can do for you, and I will do it." He showed every desire to help him out. His manner was indescribably tactful and direct.

Dr. Laidlaw looked up into his face.

"I surrender my will to you," he said, already calmed by the other's healing presence, "and I want you to treat me hypnotically—and at once. I want you to suggest to me"—his voice became very tense—"that I shall forget—forget till I die—everything that has occurred to me during the last two hours; till I die, mind," he added, with solemn emphasis, "till I die."

He floundered and stammered like a frightened boy. Alexis Stephen looked at him fixedly without speaking.

"And further," Laidlaw continued, "I want you to ask me no questions. I wish to forget for ever something I have recently discovered—something so terrible and yet so obvious that I can hardly understand why it is not patent to every mind in the world—for I have had a moment of absolute clear vision—of merciless clairvoyance. But I want no one else in the whole world to know what it is—least of all, old friend, yourself."

He talked in utter confusion, and hardly knew what he was saying. But the pain on his face and the anguish in his voice were an instant passport to the other's heart.

"Nothing is easier," replied Dr. Stephen, after a hesitation so slight that the other probably did not even notice it. "Come into my other room where we shall not be disturbed. I can heal you. Your memory of the last two hours shall be wiped out as though it had never been. You can trust me absolutely."

"I know I can," Laidlaw said simply, as he followed him in.

6

An hour later they passed back into the front room again. The sun was already behind the houses opposite, and the shadows began to gather.

"I went off easily?" Laidlaw asked.

"You were a little obstinate at first. But though you came in like a lion, you went out like a lamb. I let you sleep a bit afterwards."

Dr. Stephen kept his eyes rather steadily upon his friend's face.

"What were you doing by the fire before you came here?" he asked, pausing, in a casual tone, as he lit a cigarette and handed the case to his patient.

"I? Let me see. Oh, I know; I was worrying my way through poor old Ebor's papers and things. I'm his executor, you know. Then I got weary and came out for a whiff of air." He spoke lightly and with perfect naturalness. Obviously he was telling the truth. "I prefer specimens to papers," he laughed cheerily.

"I know, I know," said Dr. Stephen, holding a lighted match for the cigarette. His face wore an expression of content. The experiment had been a complete success. The memory of the last two hours was wiped out utterly. Laidlaw was already chatting gaily and easily about a dozen other things that interested him. Together they went out into the street, and at his door Dr. Stephen left him with a joke and a wry face that made his friend laugh heartily.

"Don't dine on the professor's old papers by mistake," he cried, as he vanished down the street.

Dr. Laidlaw went up to his study at the top of the house. Half way down he met his housekeeper, Mrs. Fewings. She was flustered and excited, and her face was very red and perspiring.

"There've been burglars here," she cried excitedly, "or something funny! All your things is just anyhow, sir. I found everything all about everywhere!" She was very confused. In this orderly and very precise establishment it was unusual to find a thing out of place.

"Oh, my specimens!" cried the doctor, dashing up the rest of the stairs at top speed. "Have they been touched or——"

He flew to the door of the laboratory. Mrs. Fewings panted up heavily behind him.

"The labatry ain't been touched," she explained, breathlessly, "but they smashed the libry clock and they've 'ung your gold watch, sir, on the skelinton's hands. And the books that weren't no value they flung out er the window just like so much rubbish. They must have been wild drunk, Dr. Laidlaw, sir!"

The young scientist made a hurried examination of the rooms. Nothing of value was missing. He began to wonder what kind of burglars they were. He looked up sharply at Mrs. Fewings standing in the doorway. For a moment he seemed to cast about in his mind for something.

"Odd," he said at length. "I only left here an hour ago and everything was all right then."

"Was it, sir? Yes, sir." She glanced sharply at him. Her room looked out upon the courtyard, and she must have seen the books come crashing down, and also have heard her master leave the house a few minutes later.

"And what's this rubbish the brutes have left?" he cried, taking up two slabs of worn gray stone, on the writing-table. "Bath brick, or something, I do declare."

He looked very sharply again at the confused and troubled housekeeper.

"Throw them on the dust heap, Mrs. Fewings, and—and let me know if anything is missing in the house, and I will notify the police this evening."

When she left the room he went into the laboratory and took his watch off the skeleton's fingers. His face wore a troubled expression, but after a moment's thought it cleared again. His memory was a complete blank.

"I suppose I left it on the writing-table when I went out to take the air," he said. And there was no one present to contradict him.

He crossed to the window and blew carelessly some ashes of burned paper from the sill, and stood watching them as they floated away lazily over the tops of the trees.